HIS HIGHLAND LOVE

HIS HIGHLAND HEART SERIES BOOK 2

WILLA BLAIR

OLIVER HEBER BOOKS

"This story is action-packed and full of twists and turns that will keep readers on their toes. It is fast-paced and has a sweet romance that will warm your heart. Well written and full of imagination, this story is a must read for historical romance fans!"

— THE ROMANCE REVIEWS

"...a rich, enjoyable read."

— SATIN SHEETS ROMANCE

THE HEALER'S GIFT

"A Highland romance with a truly great hero...the story is compelling..."

— IND'TALE MAGAZINE

"A story of mystery, regret, hope, danger and trust... The characters are endearing, the story is fulfilling, and the set up for the remainder of the series presents an open invitation to dive right in. THE HEALER'S GIFT is a highly recommended read."

— FRESH FICTION

HIGHLAND SEER

"...this is different enough from other Highland romances to stand out from the pack. Ms. Blair's writing style is natural and evocative..."

— ROMANTIC HISTORICAL REVIEWS

"16th-century intrigue, muscled men with claymores and a doomed romance — is it any wonder I was reluctant to leave the rich, riveting world of HIGHLAND SEER?"

— USATODAY HEA

WHEN HIGHLAND LIGHTNING STRIKES

"Ms. Blair is a consummate storyteller...Can't wait for more from this magical author."

— MY BOOK ADDICTION AND MORE

"Ms. Blair has an easy to read talent for bringing a story to life."

— LONG AND SHORT REVIEWS

HIGHLAND TROTH

"Scottish romance at its best!"

— IND'TALE MAGAZINE

"...an exciting, romantic, historical tale full of angst, action and searing hot passion...With plenty of adventure and the twist of an old murder, HIGHLAND TROTH by Willa Blair, kept me hooked from beginning to end. A wonderful Highland romance."

— FRESH FICTION

HIS HIGHLAND HEART SERIES
HIS HIGHLAND ROSE

"Masterfully and brilliantly written Scottish Romance...!"
My Book Addiction & More

HIS HIGHLAND HEART

"The plot was honestly a masterpiece. It was well thought out and orchestrated. Right out the gate I was hooked! The hero had immediate book boyfriend appeal."

— LONG AND SHORT REVIEWS

"Willa Blair knows how to make a story come to life and sweep you away on a beautiful journey into the Highlands...This is a Scottish adventure you won't want to miss!"

— BOOKS & BENCHES

HIS HIGHLAND LOVE

"Beautifully written and masterfully executed!"

— MY BOOK ADDICTION AND MORE!

"Fiery passion burns bright in HIS HIGHLAND LOVE! Readers who enjoy Highland romance should definitely try Willa Blair's books."

— BOOKS & BENCHES

"If you love romantic highland stories of warriors and danger, love and honor, you'll find this story intriguing as well as enjoyable."

— THE READING CAFE

HIS HIGHLAND BRIDE

"Ms. Blair has delivered a wonderful and captivating read in this book where the chemistry between this couple was strong; the romance hot..."

— BOOK MAGIC, UNDER A SPELL WITH
EVERY PAGE

"This is a very enjoyable and well-written book to satisfy any historical romance lover, especially one who enjoys forbidden love!"

— IND'TALEMAGAZINE

**CONTEMPORARY ROMANCE
WAITING FOR THE LAIRD**

"Willa Blair spins a beautiful romance set in the Scottish Highlands full of suspense, history and mystery... I highly suggests you pick it up and enjoy."

— NIGHT OWL ROMANCE

"About 3:00 am I finally had to force myself to stop... yes, it was that good. Give yourself a treat and grab this book..."

— THE READING CAFE

"A contemporary romantic tale with a touch of history—and ghosts...Waiting for the Laird by Willa Blair is a delightful romance and unexpected adventure set in Scotland."

— BOOKS AND BENCHES

WHEN YOU FIND LOVE

"When You Find Love is a beautiful romance filled with combative personalities, a family curse and a love that can't be quenched. Character-driven plot with supernatural undertones make this a must-read. The ending was so fantastic, I didn't want it to end. If you love fantasy romance, you'll be smitten with When You Find Love."

— N.N. LIGHT'S BOOK HEAVEN

SWEETIE PIE

"Willa Blair is known for her Scottish historical paranormal romance. She changes genres with a modern Scottish lass who escapes to the Big Island of Hawaii. SWEETIE PIE is a delicious pupu - Hawaiian word for appetizer. Blair delivers a sweet novella that captures the Aloha spirit of the island."

— K. LOWE

To my youngest brother, who swears he does not read my books, but who is still one of my biggest fans.

CHAPTER 1

ST. ANDREWS, SCOTLAND, 1411

Kenneth Brodie woke before the sun came up to the sound of someone pounding on his door. He rolled from his cot, cursing under his breath at being awakened from a particularly delicious dream of his Cat. Nay, not his…merely the lass who'd stolen his heart. The lass he'd left behind in the Highlands. He pulled on his breeks, willing his body to subside. "Come," he called, moving toward the door as he fumbled with his ties.

A junior cleric opened the door before Kenneth could reach it, letting in the damp chill of this early summer morning. It sent a shiver across Kenneth's bare upper body and finished removing all trace of the heat of his dream.

"You are summoned to fetch a shipment from the port for the bishop," the man announced without looking anywhere near him, and then immediately stepped out and closed the door.

For one wild moment, Kenneth thought the man meant he would go alone. The opportunity seemed too good to be true, then he realized it surely was. He was a hostage—one short step up from a prisoner. He would

1

not be allowed free access to the harbor and its ships. Domnhall, the Lord of the Isles, had started the latest crisis by claiming to be the rightful Earl of Ross—a title and holdings the Duke of Albany also claimed. In response, Albany had demanded a hostage from each of the Highland clans, intending to use them to keep their lairds from joining forces with Domnhall. It was an ancient tactic—and one that occasionally worked.

This visit to the harbor was probably only what it appeared to be, taking advantage of a strong Highlander hostage. Since Kenneth had been in St. Andrews, he'd been in Father Anselmo's charge. Father Anselmo had found another way to drive home the lesson that whatever status he once had in the Highlands did him no good here.

The Italian was one more curse upon Kenneth's blackened soul. Everyone suspected Anselmo was the Pope's man, here to report back on the doings of one of Scotland's most powerful bishops. By placing him in the Italian priest's care, Kenneth supposed Bishop Wardlaw hoped to keep all his troublemakers clustered together, the better to observe and control them. He couldn't blame the bishop for that. He just wished he knew how long he would have to endure being at Anselmo's beck and call.

Kenneth got himself ready in record time, knowing if Anselmo didn't see him walking out into the castle courtyard within moments, he would come to his chamber to retrieve him—then make him pay for the inconvenience on his knees during evening prayers. All of them, through the entire night.

At least the bishop hadn't assigned Father Phillippe as his keeper. He still couldn't believe God would play such a low trick on him, putting that man here, too. He'd had little contact with Phillippe for the most part, but his conscience weighed heavily at every glimpse of the Frenchman. If being here was his laird Iain Brodie's idea of penance for all he'd done wrong in the Highlands, Phillippe's presence was a constant reminder of all he'd done wrong in France. Even though he'd saved Phillippe's life, he apparently gained no favor in heaven.

As he expected, Anselmo awaited him in the courtyard when he arrived. At his gesture, Kenneth walked beside him out the castle gate and through the town toward the fisher gate that breached the town wall above the harbor and beside the wall surrounding the bishop's grand cathedral.

Once they passed through the fisher gate, the path fell quickly down the cathedral hill to the harbor below them. Two-story buildings like the ones in the upper town lined the quay. Kenneth picked out storefronts common to all ports—sailmakers, weavers, an ironmonger, and several pubs. Cheap accommodations occupied many of the upstairs spaces. Those were typically used by visiting sailors eager to sleep in a bed that rocked only with the movement of whatever doxy they'd purchased for the night. They interested him less than the ships lining the quay and visible beyond it, awaiting access to the harbor.

"If it didn't mean the ruin of your clan, you would take the first ship out of here, *sì*?"

Kenneth stopped counting the ships tied up at the quay—fifteen at least, from skiffs to larger *birlinns* to schooners in from the Low Countries—and glanced aside at his companion. The view of the port pleased him a great deal more than the severely smug expression on Father Anselmo's face.

"Ye can rest easy," he assured the dour Italian priest. "I wouldna dream of causing harm to those I left behind." In the interest of playing up to Anselmo's arrogance, he added, "I'm simply unaccustomed to the sight of such a busy port and such a prosperous town. The Highlands have naught to approach this." He waved a hand toward the merchants' stalls and the ships tied up at dock. He might be laying on naïveté a bit too thickly with that claim, especially if Anselmo had made a progress into the Highlands as part of his priestly training or duties and had seen Inverness or a western port.

But the priest failed to react to Kenneth's veiled sarcasm. "I should think not," he replied. "St. Andrews is the seat of the bishop, the true Pope's representative. A center of worship and commerce for all. Its port has few rivals." He cleared his throat and continued, "Enough, now, of sloth. We must retrieve what the bishop requires. I see the merchant he named, *avanti.*" He gestured ahead.

Kenneth let his gaze rove over the ships at dock as they walked along the quay, dodging sailors loudly intent on finding the nearest pub and merchants hurrying to buy or sell or trade goods. Several craft, from their size and the cargo being loaded, would be heading south to Flanders or France for profitable trade, carrying good Scottish wool, coal, and likely some whisky, too, and returning with wine in stout oaken barrels, delicacies, and fine crystal. Several smaller craft might be from Highland ports, but if so, the crews had chosen to forego Highland dress in favor of breeks, shirts, and waistcoats that allowed them to blend in with the crowd on the quay and up to Market Street, at least until they opened their mouths to speak.

He didn't see anyone he recognized, but that could change. He expected the mix of ships in port altered daily. And as long as he was seen by enough sailors, someone might carry word back to his laird, Iain

Brodie, that he was here. A note would be better, but Kenneth dared not be caught with one. The bishop's castle had a bottle dungeon. He had no wish to be tossed down its narrow throat. His current accommodations might be simple, but they had the advantage of fresh air, a hearth for heat, and the freedom to move about the castle grounds. Even outside its walls with an escort such as Anselmo. He supposed he owed his privileges to the difference between being a hostage for his clan's good behavior and being a prisoner. A fine distinction, perhaps, but one worth retaining.

Stirling, where Kenneth had initially been held, had been bad enough, full of royal lackeys vying for attention from Albany and each other. Then he and an escort had ridden two long days cross-country to St. Andrews. The move meant he was farther from home. His clan had no idea where he was.

He'd been closely guarded on the way to St. Andrews, but truly had given little thought to escape. He was here in the Brodie chief's stead. If he ran, the Duke of Albany would send men after Iain. Kenneth was certain Iain meant to punish him for taking off to France, like many Scotsmen who'd gone seeking their fortune as mercenary soldiers in its long war with England, without his laird's permission. The disappearing act Kenneth had pulled resulted in this banishment—for that was what this was. His adventures on the continent had strained his relationship with Iain more than he'd expected, given Iain's own history of roaming about Scotland and bedding lasses before he met and married Annie Rose, Cat's older sister. Kenneth had returned to Brodie just as Albany's demand for a hostage arrived. Ever practical, Iain endeavored to teach Kenneth another lesson, while at the same time mollifying the Duke of

Albany. Kenneth wasn't angry enough about being exiled to bring the kind of trouble to Brodie that defying Albany would cause.

However, if Kenneth was interested in absolution, the bishop's seat was the perfect place to seek it.

He wasn't.

At the merchant's stall, Anselmo quickly concluded his trade and motioned for Kenneth to carry his purchases. *Bloody hell.* Reduced from heir-apparent of a proud Highland clan to pack mule for a sour-tempered cleric. Without comment, Kenneth lifted the bundle onto his shoulder and followed Anselmo. They went back up the hill, passing the majestic cathedral on the left on their way to the castle.

Girlish laughter drifted on the breeze like birdsong, sharp, bright, and impossible to ignore. One laugh in particular brought Kenneth up short. He stopped, head cocked, listening as his blood turned to ice in his veins. Nay, it could not be.

Anselmo turned back to him and gestured at the package on his shoulder. "Come. Surely you bear little burden for a man as well endowed with strength as you appear to be. Here is no place to stop, unless you have the sudden urge to confess some sin?" He waved a benedictory hand at the cathedral.

God's bones. He could burn Anselmo's ears with tales of what he'd experienced in France. Better to keep walking and let hope bleed away from the wound that bit of laughter had sliced in his chest. It had sounded like Cat...

It didn't matter. She was in his past, the same as his allegiance to Brodie and to Iain. He was here only because honor demanded he stay, but once his presence as hostage for Brodie was no longer necessary, he'd leave. Return to France, perhaps, though not to Marilee, the woman whose arms he'd stumbled into after learning Cat was to marry. Rescuing Phillippe after Marilee betrayed both of them made doing so impossible, thank God. He would never be tempted back to her bed. Or he'd go to Italy, though a glance at Anselmo made him doubt he'd enjoy living there.

Just then, two lasses and a lad came through some trees on one of the paths from town and headed directly for the grounds of the cathedral. He only got a glimpse before they turned away, but in that brief moment, his breath caught again. One moved remarkably like Cat. But that couldn't be possible. She'd be married away by now, at Mackintosh, not here, far from the Highlands. He saw only what he wanted to see after hearing a similar laugh, nothing more.

Nay, it could not be her. But curiosity—or hope—made him try again to see her. Risking Anselmo's displeasure, he stopped and nearly dropped the package, suddenly shaking with the urge to run to the lass, grab her by the arm and spin her about. Anselmo would be scandalized, no doubt, and have him confined. He fought for control as the group passed a dozen yards uphill. He couldn't tell which lass had laughed. Since neither of them turned her face in his direction, he never got to see if one really resembled the image of Cat he held in his heart. Gazing up at him with wide eyes as he asked her to be his, her plump lips slightly parted, a bow of pleasure he longed for in the depths of the night, especially once he'd learned in France what such lips could do. The longing filling him was intense and shocking, having been brought on by a mere *glissando* of laughter. The laugh had been so like a voice he hadn't heard in a very long time, it gripped his throat and nearly stopped his heart.

If only she were here…. They were older now. They might find a way to rekindle what they had two years ago. The affection. The attraction. This time, he would finish what they'd started. She could be his in more than the dreams he woke up with at night, hard and sweating.

But nay. The trio passed on and entered a gate in the cathedral's wall, apparently never even noticing the priest and his draft-horse companion. Kenneth's jaw tightened. It seemed he ranked lower even than a draft-horse. He was invisible. If he could manage it around the lump in his chest, he'd laugh at how he'd come down in life.

But right now, missing Cat hurt too bloody much.

🙰

CATHERINE ROSE COULD NOT BELIEVE HER EYES. AS SHE, her cousin Abigail Duncan, and Abi's betrothed, Colin, approached the magnificent St. Andrews Cathedral for the early-morning mass, their path from town came near a short, swarthy priest escorting a workman with a bundle on his shoulder that hid his face. The big workman caught her eye because he reminded her of someone. Then it hit her.

Kenneth Brodie.

For one all too brief pause, she stopped and stared while Abi and Colin continued on without her.

But Abi, eager to show her newly arrived cousin the largest cathedral in Scotland, came back and pulled her away. "What are you doing? We'll be late for mass!" she remonstrated.

Catherine shook her head and didn't explain. She couldn't. She had to be imagining the resemblance. This man was bigger and more muscular than she recalled Kenneth being. Of course, she'd last seen him two years ago, and if he'd been fighting in France, as

8

she'd been told, he would have filled out and put on muscle.

If only she could have seen him better.

Well, it didn't matter. As she and Abi caught up with Colin, she decided that man could not have been Kenneth. He would never be in St. Andrews. If he'd returned from the continent, he'd be at Brodie with Iain and his wife, her sister, Annie. Annie would have mentioned his return to her in a letter. Worse, since he'd abandoned her, he might have married someone from another clan or brought a bride back from France. In an effort to protect her feelings, Annie might have kept such news from her.

For one sharp moment, Catherine missed him, missed home, missed her middle sister like a knife twisting in her gut. Annie visited Rose all too rarely since her marriage to Iain Brodie. And Catherine visited Brodie not at all. Her father, determined to keep her and Kenneth apart, had not allowed her to visit her sister, where she might come into contact with Kenneth. He had kept her away long enough for Kenneth to leave for France, and afterward, too, in case he returned without word reaching Rose.

Surely if Kenneth heard about the betrothal offer from Mackintosh, he would have also heard what followed. Rose, at first, accepted the betrothal offer. But before long, they heard rumors her intended was a brute with a history of beating women. The lad himself had ultimately revealed his true nature by beating a Rose servant. To Catherine's great relief, her father had refused the betrothal and sent the bully back to Mackintosh.

Kenneth could have written. Annie would have sent a letter to Mary, who would have given it to her. But she'd received nothing.

Catherine had only been in St. Andrews a few days,

yet her cousin was already involving her in her own elopement plans. Catherine's visit gave Abi the perfect excuse to wander around St. Andrews and the perfect cover to spend time with Colin more than she usually could. Today they were going to mass with him. Abi's situation, so like her own, didn't help ease the bile still burning its way up Catherine's throat at the thought of what her father had done, again and again. Bartering her to form an alliance with another clan, with no thought given to what she wanted.

Thank God her oldest sister, Mary, had taken pity on her and sent her to a friend of hers in Inverness. But even Inverness was too close to home. Too easy for her father to send men to retrieve her. Mary's friend had known a sailor who could bring Catherine safely here, where her aunt's family still lived. It had all gone more smoothly than she'd expected, especially since she left her father an angry note. She thought he would have immediately forced Mary to tell him where she'd gone, and then he would have sent men to Inverness to retrieve her. Either Mary's words had swayed him, or even in the face of their father's ire, she had held her tongue long enough for Catherine to leave Inverness. She owed her sister her freedom.

Catherine wanted a better look at the man she'd glimpsed. But Abi was bent on dragging her toward the cathedral. Even here, everyone seemed determined to keep her and Kenneth apart. Except that man couldn't be Kenneth. He couldn't possibly be a beast of burden for a priest.

Catherine sighed and went with her friends. Before she left home, she'd decided she would do anything to avoid an unwanted marriage—and by coming here, she had. She couldn't let her curiosity about what happened to Kenneth, and her daft notion that he might be here, drive her to do something foolish.

Nay, she had to put him out of her mind, or she'd be seeing his likeness everywhere she went.

❧

"WHAT DO YE MEAN YE CANNA FIND ANYONE TO MARRY ye?" Catherine glanced aside at her cousin and snorted. She and Abi were on their way up St. Andrews' Market Street later that morning. Abi and Colin had argued after mass and Colin had left them. "How many clerics did we see in the cathedral? Ten?" Catherine had already observed that finding a priest was—unavoidable. She gestured at the group of priests walking a little ahead of. "Look around ye. I see a dozen right now, in the street and going in and out of the shops. Surely ye canna have asked them all?"

Unlike the residential streets running parallel to the north and south, shops at ground level lined Market Street, with craftsmen and merchants living above their businesses. This morning, people, wagons, horses and livestock filled the street, all headed toward the stone mercat cross that rose nearly as tall as the two-story buildings around it. It stood in the middle of the square where market days were held. She and Abi passed the cobbler's shop and a potter, the scents of leather and wet clay mixing with the sudden odor of fish on the crowded street. She tugged Abi aside to keep her from walking right into a man who had to be the source of the smell—no doubt a fisherman. Once they got away from him, the faint scent of baking bread reached her nose. Finding a path through the crowd forced them closer to the mercat cross before she glimpsed the bakery, plump brown loaves of bread displayed on a shelf just inside its open front window. They had almost reached their destination.

"I have not asked enough of them, I guess," Abi

responded as they paused, their way blocked for a moment by the crowd on the street.

A stall-front, hung with colorful ribbons, caught Catherine's eye. The ribbons fluttered in the cool breeze sneaking between the narrow divides that separated blocks of buildings. She reminded herself she was now too old to be distracted by bright colors and tugged Abi closer to the mercat cross, hoping to find an opening they could slip through. How did anyone tolerate living among so many people all the time?

"Ye canna take two steps in any direction in this town without tripping over a priest," she told Abi. An elderly one, standing on the near side of the mercat cross, frowned at them. Likely, he'd overheard her comment. And the two lads with him, probably students, mirrored their clerical escort's disapproval, frowns drawing down their young brows. Finding priests was easy. Finding a particular priest, less so.

There were men of all ages everywhere she looked. She, Abi, and the other women out this morning were vastly outnumbered by merchants, sailors, and students —noble lads and sons of lairds, here by order of the king to be educated in Latin and law, some of whom would continue to study for the priesthood. The priests attending the Bishop of St. Andrews or teaching at the kirk's college were also charged with escorting their students and keeping them out of trouble.

According to Abi, who had lived in town most of her life and seen lots of students come and go, they didn't always meet with great success. Catherine could see the proof of that before her. Two younger students were giving her and Abi speculative looks. Feeling exposed, she got her cousin's attention, then pulled Abi away from them. "It seems a lass can get as much male attention of another sort as she wishes in this town— too much," Catherine added.

"I ken some of those lads over there," Abi said, tipping her head in the direction of a cluster of students visible through a brief opening in the milling crowd. They paused while Abi considered the lads, forcing people to move around them and earning them impatient frowns. "Perhaps one of them can suggest a cleric willing to marry two lovers—even though my stepfather disapproves. And Colin cannot seem to decide when we will do this."

"Or perhaps ye'd be better served to get yer da's agreement, aye? He may no' be yer real da, but he does love ye. He wants ye to be well cared for. He's doing what he thinks best—"

"Like yer da's delays cost yer eldest sister the man she wanted? Has she found another *beau*, then?"

Catherine bit her lip, thinking about how her father had made all three daughters miserable, refusing their choices of whom to marry. First, he'd denied and delayed her oldest sister Mary's betrothal until the lad gave up and married someone else. "Nay, Mary is still waiting." Mary's broken heart had inspired the sisters to conspire against their father to help their middle sister. They'd eventually outwitted him. "But Annie did manage to marry Iain Brodie." Regret made her sigh. "If only Kenneth and I had been brave enough to elope," she muttered. Though her father had always indulged Catherine, his youngest daughter, she'd never forgive him for denying Kenneth Brodie's request for her hand. Da had thought her too young to wed at the time. Aye, Da had also been doing what he thought best.

"What?" Abi's eyes widened. "Who is Kenneth?"

"The man I fell in love with two years ago," Catherine answered, then pressed her lips together, wondering how much to say. Had she really seen him near the cathedral? Neither Abi nor Abi's stepfather knew she'd fled here to avoid being forced to wed.

Would Abi figure out that her story about being sent by her father to renew kin ties with her mother's family was a lie, and conclude a broken heart had driven her here? Abi's mother had come to Scotland as James Rose's ward when Catherine's mother married him. He'd arranged the younger sister's marriage to a Duncan who eventually moved to St. Andrews for business. Abi's stepfather, a tailor from Flanders, had married her after Catherine's uncle died at sea. Abi and her stepfather still occupied the floor above his tailor shop, where Catherine was staying, a few blocks down the hill.

To distract Abi, Catherine told her, "In the Highlands, eloping is as easy as declaring to each other ye are married. Then consummating the vow," she added with a shrug, trying to make light of it. At the time, neither she nor Kenneth had dared take such an audacious step. Both had been young enough to think their only course was to bow to the laird's wishes and wait. Soon after, her father betrothed her to another man. Kenneth disappeared, and she'd never heard from him again.

He must be alive—her sister, Annie, would have told her if her husband, the Brodie laird, had received word Kenneth had died there. The thought made her chest hurt.

Abi wrapped her arms around her middle. "If only 'twere so easy here. But look around ye. So many priests and none Colin and I have talked to will agree to marry us against my stepfather's wishes."

Catherine stiffened, wondering why women thought they had no say in the matter of their futures. She was no longer her father's obedient youngest daughter. She'd run away—and taken charge of her own destiny. And if she ever truly encountered Kenneth again, the first thing she would do would be to box his ears for leaving her wondering what happened to him. Then she'd see if they still cared for each other as they once had. If not...? She straightened her spine. If not, she'd find another man to wed, perhaps right here in St. Andrews. Among all these instructors and older students, there must be someone from a clan that had never heard of Rose. Or perhaps a successful Highland merchant or sailor in port on business.

Her gaze skimmed over the young students. From their dress, most were Lowlander nobility. So if their youth displeased her, their origins were even more off-putting. Visiting her cousin was one thing, but to marry a Lowlander, never to see the Highlands again? Nay, she couldn't imagine a future away from the lochs and the hills of home.

Ah, but some of the lads were her age or even older. Highlanders, too, from the look of them, tall and strong. If she found one she liked from a Highland clan her da wanted to ally with, she might finally be willing to agree to a match that pleased him. But if a lad was not of the right clan, she might marry him anyway. When they found a priest to suit Abi's purposes, likely he'd do for her as well.

"Ye only need one priest to agree," she told Abi. The rebellious fantasies running through her mind made her smile. She faced the group of students Abi pointed out, and the Highlander standing with them smiled back. Tall, brown-haired, and handsome, he looked to be a few years older than his companions and had a decidedly un-priestly wicked glint in his eye. He might do.

"Let's go ask." Abi grabbed her arm and tugged her away from the enticing scents of the bakery toward the lads she said she knew.

Catherine let Abi lead her and kept her gaze on the man who'd caught her eye.

"Abi, my sweet," he greeted her cousin with a seductive grin, but without the handclasp or even kiss on the cheek that would have passed for a greeting between friends at home—such familiarity on the street here would have shocked many onlookers. "And who is this bonnie lass ye have brought us today?" He turned a provocative grin on Catherine.

Catherine liked the look of him up close even better than she had from a distance. He had to be at least four or five years older than she, which made her wonder what he was doing with students. Most young men his age would have finished their schooling by now. Unless he got a very late start, he was no student. His eyes were a cloudy blue-gray and gave away nothing. But that grin—he was a charmer, wasn't he? She had to wonder how many lasses he'd charmed into his bed up to now.

"Cameron, behave," Abi chided. "Meet my cousin, Mary Catherine Rose. Catherine, this is Cameron Sutherland. If the Highlands are missing a rogue, 'tis because our Cam is here."

Cam laid a hand over his heart. "Fair Abigail, ye wound me, ye do!" Then he swept his arm in front of him and bowed over it in the French fashion, without reaching for her hand. "How lovely to meet ye, sweet Cat. And what an intriguing name ye bear."

"I havena answered to Cat in years," she warned, not liking the demonstration that implied he'd spent time in France. Could he have met Kenneth there? She kept a polite smile in place, though it took effort. "My friends call me Catherine," she informed him. She'd left the childish nickname behind when she'd lost Kenneth, and didn't welcome hearing it from this man's lips, but she didn't dare insult a member of one of the most powerful clans in the Highlands.

She couldn't afford to get in trouble, not if she

wanted to avoid getting sent back to her father and a marriage she didn't want. The latest offer had come from clan Grant. Before that, he had tried to betroth her to a Campbell, and a Mackintosh before him. If Abi's stepfather wrote to her father, she'd be on her way home before she knew what happened, then locked away until her father could get her safely married to the Grant. She shoved the thought away and turned her gaze to the other lads. "And ye are…?"

"Bound for the priesthood and of nay use to a bonnie lass such as ye," Cam interjected.

"Cam, really. There's no need to be rude," Abi scolded. "Catherine, meet Robert, Patrick and Andrew." The lads nodded a greeting. "And aye, they are bound for the priesthood, aren't ye, lads?" Another nod. "Whereas Cam is a third son, so nay laird, nay priest, but perhaps bound to fight, or to manage one of his clan's many estates for Laird Sutherland, aye?"

"Or both, aye. I have many talents."

The gleam was back in his eye. Catherine realized the speculation in it made her uncomfortable. She decided to move things along. "Abi, ye thought one of these lads might be able to help ye?"

Abi nodded and took in the three with a glance. "I'm looking for a priest willing to marry Colin and me."

"Why, any could do so," the shortest of the lads, Patrick, spoke up in a Lowland accent. He had dark hair but a very pale complexion.

Catherine supposed he'd spent most of his life cloistered with books.

"No' when my stepfather is opposed," Abi admitted.

"Ah, that is unfortunate," he acknowledged.

"Do not let them worry you," the lad called Andrew offered with a disarming dip of his chin that made his blond curls brush his shoulders. "My Latin tutor might.

He has no parish, but he's liberal in his thinking. He could say the words and see it done."

"Or ye could wed in the Highland way," Cam added. "And say the words yerselves. 'Tis as binding, under Scottish law."

"But not in the eyes of the Kirk," Robert objected, red streaks in his pale cheeks betraying his distress. "Do you want them to be excommunicated?"

"Half the Highlands would be done so already, were yer assertion true," Andrew scoffed.

"And how would ye ken?" Cam challenged, crossing his arms.

That seemed to silence Robert's objections. The lad put his hands on his hips and turned his face away, then turned back and bowed politely to Catherine and Abi. "Milady," he said to each. "Good day to ye." With that, he moved off toward one of the many priests near the mercat cross.

With a raised eyebrow, Cam watched him go. "Awfully sanctimonious for such a young lad," he muttered.

Catherine agreed. Despite Cam's annoying personality, she thought he might share the same rebellious nature that brought her halfway across Scotland. It didn't hurt that Cam had very nice arms—well muscled from working or training with weapons. They reminded her of Kenneth's. Cam's hands were broad and strong, as well. Very like Kenneth's, too. So much so that looking at Cam made her chest tighten. She needed to stop comparing every man she met to Kenneth.

If she couldn't have Kenneth, and after all this time, she might as well admit she never would; then Cam, even with his Sutherland arrogance, might just do. She wanted to choose the man she married, get to know him and at least like him before they wed. She preferred not to wed at all rather than have her father's choice of a stranger forced on her.

"Can you arrange for us to meet?" Abi asked Andrew, pulling Catherine's attention back to the present.

"Of course. Tomorrow at the cathedral after midmorning prayer?"

"That will serve. Thank you."

"'Tis no bother. I hope he'll be able to help you."

Catherine glanced around the street. The lad who Cam had scandalized, Robert, was speaking to one of the priests and frowning in their direction.

Catherine touched Abi's sleeve. "Come, then. We're starting to attract attention."

The two remaining lads bowed and excused themselves. Cam held Catherine's gaze a beat longer, flashed his devastating grin, and tipped his head before he stepped away.

"He seems quite taken with ye," Abi remarked as they wove through the crowd and crossed the square back to the baker's.

"Something tells me Cameron Sutherland finds himself taken with any lass he meets," Catherine groused as they paused at the open doorway. The mouthwatering scent of berry pies and warm bread wafted from the bakers' shop, covering the town's less savory smells. The scent made Catherine's stomach growl. She put a hand over her belly. "Besides, I gave my heart to Kenneth Brodie nearly two years ago."

"Aye? And where is this Kenneth Brodie now?"

Catherine pursed her lips, shook her head, and stepped inside. Her appetite suddenly deserted her. She could not have seen him this morning. Fate would not be so cruel. She had lost so much when she lost Kenneth—her sister, trust in her father, even her home. It hurt to say it, but if she was ever going to move on and build a new life here with someone else, she had to accept that Kenneth had ignored her for a very long time—too long. He was out of her life forever.

"I dinna ken where he is," she answered and gestured for Abi to go ahead of her. "And it no longer matters."

WILLA BLAKE

CHAPTER 2

Kenneth wiped sweat from his eyes with his sleeve as he looked down on the group of students practicing at arms in the castle yard. The summer solstice was approaching and summers were warmer here on the coast than in the Highlands. He'd come up onto the battlements for the breeze off the water. It helped, but he would need clothing more suited to the climate here if he was to remain in St. Andrews for long.

Father Phillippe had joined him, and Kenneth judged walking away from the priest would have been rude, perhaps dangerous. Now standing at his side, Phillippe waved a pale hand indicating the lads.

"Though hardly a fit occupation for younger sons studying to become clergy, not all will qualify. In addition to their studies, we must continue the training that could mean their lives, should they return home to your intrigues and clan wars." His cultured French accent did little to soften the harshness of his words

"Our intrigues and clan wars? Have ye so quickly forgotten Burgundy and Armagnac?" He crossed his arms. "Nay, Father. Clan Brodie lives peacefully with its neighbors." More or less, and as long as he avoided thinking about the trouble he could have caused to win Cat Rose—including stealing her from her clan—rather than running to France as he had chosen to do. Given the epic feuds between some other Highland clans, Kenneth felt confident enough to weigh Brodie on the more peaceful side of the balance. "Any intrigues we suffer are those practiced by the Duke of Albany and the Lord of the Isles." He took a chance making a complaint about the nobles, but he was already a hostage for Clan Brodie's good behavior. Aye, they could throw him down the bottle dungeon Father Anselmo had taken pains to show him as soon as he'd arrived—intending to ensure his good behavior, of course. Or they could kill him outright. He counted on the niceties of the biblical commandments to prevent that. Anyway, he'd merely stated a fact no honest person could deny—not even the French priest, who, in Kenneth's experience, was far from honest.

Though he couldn't trust the man too freely, the more Kenneth thought about it, the more he counted himself lucky to meet Father Phillippe here. Phillippe had no history with the local kirk hierarchy and owed them no more than the loyalty any priest owed the kirk.

Unlike Anselmo, who was rumored to be the eyes and ears of the Pope in Rome.

But Phillippe did owe Kenneth. And from the look on Phillippe's face the first time he's seen Kenneth, soon after he arrived and went before the bishop for blessing and instruction on his stay in St. Andrews, the French priest had not forgotten. He'd just never expected to have to repay his debt.

When the time came, Kenneth would call in that debt. Phillipe would pay his due or he would find out first-hand where Highland intrigue could lead.

In the meantime, Kenneth had to cooperate—or appear to.

"The suggestion has been made for you to take yon *jeunes garçons* in hand and see to their training."

Phillippe's words hit Kenneth like a fist out of nowhere. "What? Train them? The bishop wants to put me to work for his university while I'm here?"

"Do you have some other pressing engagement planned to pass the time of your confinement in St. Andrews?"

Kenneth shook his head. Nay, he did not. It had taken only a few days for him to decide boredom was more a danger than conflict. "They are poorly skilled at arms for lads their age."

"Their master has gone to France, and the bishop does not believe in idle hands. Theirs...or yours."

"The difference is, they are here by choice. I am no'."

Phillipe chuckled. "There is less of a difference between you and yon lads than you might imagine. Many of them are here only because they, too, are forced to be here, not because they wish to be. If they had their way, they would have been the firstborn son, destined to rule after their father is gone, eh? Or perhaps they dream of being a great warrior. You can help them achieve their ambitions, *n'est-ce pas?* I saw you fight in France. *Spectaculaire.*"

"Fighting for one's life makes it appear so."

"Is not every man on the battlefield fighting for his life, or the life of his brother warrior?"

Kenneth turned from watching the lads to watching the ripples on the bay below them. The breeze blew, fresh and cool, directly into his face, wafting away the remembered stench of war. "Point taken."

"Very well, then. You are better than any of my brethren at what you do. Would you not like to give these lads the best chance to survive when the time for battle is upon them?"

He could fight, aye. Even Iain had recognized his skill, and made him his master at arms. Kenneth heaved a sigh, then pursed his lips and leveled a narrow gaze at Phillippe. "Laying the guilt on a bit thick, are ye no', Father?"

Phillippe grinned and clapped him on the back. "A favor for a favor, *oui*? Perhaps the time will come when I can do something for you."

Kenneth grimaced and spat out, *"D'accord,"* as he turned away. Exchanging favors with Phillippe had led to the trouble with Marilee in France and resulted in both of them being forced to leave in a hurry to avoid being hanged—or worse—by one or the other—or both —sides of the conflict there. Phillippe had been selling information to both sides. And Marilee found out. He headed for the steps leading to the central courtyard, wondering if history was about to repeat itself.

CATHERINE HAD YET TO SEE THE INSIDE OF THE CASTLE dominating the St. Andrews coastline, so a day later, when Abi announced she was going with her father while he made a delivery to one of the priests there, and Catherine could come if she wanted to, her curiosity got the better of her. It was a short walk. Nothing in St. Andrews was far from anything else, except perhaps the port, over the cathedral hill, through the town's fisher gate and down to the harbor. The castle hugged the cliffs to the northwest around the coastline from the port, not far from the cathedral.

They entered through a tall tower onto a cobbled courtyard. Inside, Abi and Catherine gazed around the open area while Abi's father inquired after the man his delivery went to. Straight ahead, a well sat in the middle of the courtyard. Beyond it, on the castle's seaside corners, stood towers, a curtain wall stretched between them. To the right, a large structure dominated that side. Perhaps a great hall. She caught a glimpse through an iron gate of the sea beyond the castle walls, and a breeze stirred the summer air.

Black-robed priests and students in rich clothing moved here and there, intent on their own errands. The lack of notice paid to her and Abi surprised Catherine after the way men's gazes followed them on the market street in town. They had to be on their best behavior here, she supposed.

She glanced around but saw no one looking her way. Leaving Abi seated on a bench in the shade, Catherine went toward the great hall across the courtyard and followed a loggia to steps leading up to the chapel above it and a wall walk on the sea side. As she reached the far side, two men stepped out into the courtyard from a door behind the loggia. A priest and —Kenneth?

Surely not, but she stared, studying the man's profile. Dressed in breeks and a loose shirt, his hair darker and shorter than it used to be, he looked more powerful than she recalled. Could it be?

As she opened her mouth to call his name, he looked up and saw her. His eyebrows arched and he paused, falling behind his companion. Cat would never forget how, for a moment, the corners of his mouth lifted and warmth flooded his gaze. Her heart responded, recognizing *this man* as the one she had missed. There could be no doubt. Kenneth was here, before her, seeing her, smiling at her. It could only have taken a second or two, but the glow of it seemed to last forever.

As suddenly as the smile lit his face, it disappeared.

His expression flattened and he straightened. Before she could utter a sound, he squeezed shut his eyes and shook his head. Catherine's chest tightened in reaction; a painful constriction of disbelief stole her breath and crumpled the smile on her lips. Why? For one hopeful moment, he'd seemed happy to see her. Lighter, less weighed down by whatever he was doing in this place. Then he waved her off with a stiff, sidewise swipe of one hand. Catherine's fists clenched, and she stared hard, trying to lock her gaze onto his, to reach him. He didn't want her to call out to him? To acknowledge that they knew each other? She didn't understand. He said something to his companion, then retreated the way he'd come. Before she could take another breath, he stepped into a doorway and disappeared.

Catherine stumbled to the wall and leaned into a merlon for support, painfully aware of where she was. Where Kenneth was. In the bishop's castle. He'd warned her off with that swipe of his hand. He'd been carrying a parcel for that priest near the cathedral. Her knees had gone weak in the time Kenneth took to recognize and turn his back on her, then disappear. Seconds, really. It took only seconds to change the way she saw the world. Something was wrong. If she could have made her legs carry her down the stairs, she would have followed him, demanding answers. But even his companion had disappeared through another door while she collapsed against the wall in the throes of recognition and remorse. She didn't know where the doorways led.

He was here and the gulf between them was as bad as she'd feared—maybe worse. He'd seemed glad to see her for a moment, then he'd shut down. Maybe he'd recalled he hated her for the misery her father had caused, or maybe he was in some kind of trouble. She wasn't sure which, but she was certain seeing her had been as much a shock for him as seeing him deny and refuse to acknowledge her was to her. At least he'd had the wits to speak to his companion, and then disappear inside. All she'd been able to do was collapse against the outer wall of St. Andrews castle.

She could think of no reason why Kenneth Brodie would be in this castle, or walking around the town carrying parcels for a priest. Worse, she didn't know why he would refuse to acknowledge her, unless he no longer cared for her or was in some terrible trouble he did not want to bring to her. The man who'd stolen her heart two years ago was here, and despite what they had shared in the past, he didn't even want to speak to her.

She gathered a briny breath, turned her back on the sea and the wind, and made her way down the steps to Abi just as her stepfather entered the courtyard and beckoned for them to leave. Something was very wrong. She had to go, but she would be back. She would find out why Kenneth was here, and if he needed it, she would find a way to help him.

❧

"IT WAS HIM. I'M SURE OF IT," CATHERINE INSISTED TO Abi hours later. They were in Abi's small bed chamber after the evening meal, Abi perched on her cot. Catherine paced three steps forward and back again before her. Catherine had been so depressed and silent after encountering Kenneth; Abi had finally pestered her into telling her what was wrong.

"I can't believe he disappeared like that," Abi said, reaching out and grasping her hand in sympathy, forcing Catherine to stop. "But surely he must have been as surprised as you," Abi continued, giving her hand a little shake. "Perhaps his shock explains it. He didn't know what else to do."

Catherine pulled her hand free. "He did seem shocked, but no' right away."

"Well, you said he seemed happy to see you for a moment. He must be embarrassed about not contacting you. You know how hopeless most lads are when it comes to dealing with their feelings."

"I doubt being a hopeless lad had anything to do with it. Kenneth Brodie is one of the most capable men ye'll ever meet." Catherine scrubbed her face with her hands then shook her head. "Nay, he may have been shocked, but he reacted by waving his hand as though pushing me away, then he disappeared. He didn't come out into the courtyard to meet me. He probably watched from some shadow until we were gone."

Abi snorted. "Well, we weren't there much longer. Perhaps he was delayed until after we left. Don't be sad. If he's at the castle, you will see him in town, won't you?"

"I think I already did." Catherine rested her hands on her hips, steadying herself as she recalled the memory. "Yesterday, when we went to the cathedral with Colin to see Father Phillippe. I caught a glimpse as he and another priest walked by on the path from the harbor. Ye pulled me away before I got a good look, or I might have kenned he was here that morning."

Abi dropped her gaze to her hands. "I'm sorry. I didn't know."

"Ye have naught to be sorry for. I didna ken, either."

"You said you fell in love with him two years ago. There's more to this story than you have told me, or you wouldn't be so upset about seeing him now."

Catherine studied her cousin. Could she trust Abi with the truth? "Ye canna tell yer step-da any of this."

"I won't. I would never betray your confidence."

"I mean it, Abi. It's too important. You—he—could ruin my life."

"What have you done?"

"'Tis more a matter of what I have no' done." Catherine sighed and told Abi her tale. All of it. Falling for Kenneth, her father's demand that they wait to marry, his three attempts to betroth her elsewhere. "I ran away," she finally admitted. "Mary kenned yer father had moved yer family here and that ye remained, even after yer mother remarried." She moved to the window and leaned against the wide sill, to restless to sit in a chair. "I've only ever loved Kenneth. I never expected to see him again. Certainly no' here. No' like this."

"If you return home…"

"Da will wed me to a Grant I've never met."

"Oh, Catherine, this is awful. What are you going to do now?"

She threw out her hands. "What can I do, if he doesna wish to speak to me?"

"You must find him and force him to. No matter what your da wants, you must clear the air with Kenneth, or you'll never feel free to marry anyone else…" Abi paused and grinned. "Like Cam Sutherland."

"Cameron Sutherland?" Catherine dropped back against the wall behind her, trying to recall the man's face, but she could only see Kenneth's flat expression as he waved her away. Had he been warning her about something?

"Aye." Abi wrapped her arms around herself. "If I wasn't over the moon in love with Colin, Cam would do quite nicely."

"If ye like the arrogant sort."

"He's from a very rich clan, handsome, clever with words…"

"And what is he doing here? He's too old to be a student."

Abi paused and tilted her head. "He's never said, now that you mention it. But Cam is not important if your Kenneth is here. We must find a way for you to see him. To speak to him."

"It willna matter. I dinna wish to wed," she declared.

"But you must! Life for a lass alone is hard. 'Tis no life at all!"

"Ye only think so because ye are determined to marry Colin," Catherine objected. "I will do quite well on my own. I have so far."

"Aye, with the help of yer sister and her friend, you made your way here. With my stepfather's agreement, you have a roof over your head. But Catherine, truly, if we had not been here, what would you have done? What would you do?"

Catherine shook her head and turned to peer out Abi's window. Below her, in the gloaming, the street was emptying as people returned home or made their way outside the town walls before the gates closed for the night, to return to their crofts and farms. They all had places to go. Without Abi's father's forbearance, she had nowhere to call home. Except Kenneth.

Nay, she would find a way. She would not grovel before a man who hadn't wanted her enough to convince her father to allow them to wed. Who'd never come back for her. And who had refused to acknowledge her when it was no longer possible to deny her existence. Her da would never agree to let her marry Kenneth Brodie, and after today—nay, after the last two years, but especially after today, that should be fine with her. Was it?

CHAPTER 3

He couldn't believe it. He'd been right! Catherine Rose was here, in St. Andrews. He had heard her giggle near the cathedral yesterday. And seen her on the castle's ramparts earlier today.

She'd started to call his name. He was sure of it. If he hadn't warned her off and ducked out of sight, she might have given away she knew him.

And that would not be good for her.

He shuddered at the thought of someone like Anselmo connecting her to him. Phillippe would be bad enough, but the Pope's henchman would use Cat against him, to control him. He couldn't bear the thought of her being punished for associating with him. If Anselmo ever found out how close they'd been, and how they'd wanted to marry, he wouldn't let Kenneth out of the castle. When the time came for him to escape, she'd be in even more trouble if anyone thought she aided him. Even her husband would not be able to protect her from the consequences of being associated with him.

Still, he wanted to see her, to talk to her, and to hold her in his arms. God help him, she was a married woman. That didn't stop him from wanting to kiss her senseless, but for her own good, he had to avoid her.

How?

He was a prisoner, at the whim of the priests and the guards. She could go anywhere she liked. And now that she knew for certain he was here, she'd find a way to get to him. Cat Rose never turned her back on a challenge.

"You seem distracted today, *mon ami*," Phillippe said as they made their way up the stairs to the castle's chapel for midmorning prayers, something else added to his life, courtesy of his stay here. Rather than consorting with court ladies-in-waiting in Stirling, he was attending prayers several times a day.

Today, his mind would be on Cat Rose—nothing the priests around him would approve. Phillippe might understand, but Kenneth dared tell no one. Cat's safety was too important.

His situation had gone from bad to worse over the last year and more. If he hadn't gotten involved with Father Phillippe and that whore Marilee while fighting in France, he'd have been home months sooner. On the other hand, the time spent with her had been—educational, to say the least. But his education had cost him Cat Rose.

He'd stayed away from Cat after her father refused his offer for her hand. He'd hoped some distance would quell the longing for her, or by showing restraint, he could convince her father he was mature enough to make a good husband for his youngest daughter. Then the news came—her father had betrothed her to a Mackintosh. He'd heard the clan name, but the red haze of fury—at himself and at her father, James Rose, for keeping Cat from him—had prevented him from hearing anything else. To this day, he didn't know whether she'd wed the lad or not. Instead, here he sat, in St. Andrews, the perfect place to contemplate his sins, which were many and varied.

"Distracted? Do I?" Kenneth decided feigning innocence was his best course.

"Perhaps you have heard the news and are now absorbed with thoughts of how to leave us, eh?"

Phillippe's suddenly grim tone stopped Kenneth at the top of the stairs. "News? What news?"

"Ah, something else has ye deep in thought? It must be a pretty *fille*. Nothing else would distract a man such as you from news of impending battle."

He had Kenneth's full attention now. "What battle? I've heard nothing…"

"'Tis said Albany has tasked his cousin, the Earl of Mar, to gather an army of peasants and farmers to keep your Donald of the Isles from burning Aberdeen to the ground. A *cateran*, you call it? They have a long march ahead of them, eh?"

Kenneth's pulse quickened. War was coming. The clan war Iain had foreseen and been preparing for. Brodie would fight, as would Rose and other clans along the Moray Firth, swept up with the Isle-men in the battle for control of the earldom of Ross, its territory, and more.

"I didna ken."

"And now you do. What will you do with this information?"

Kenneth paused and looked Phillippe straight in the eye. "Naught. I am a prisoner here. I canna leave, no matter what my wishes, or those of my laird, might be." True enough for now, but later? The fact that St. Andrews had a busy port could be very convenient. He was a hostage for Brodie's good behavior. His circumstances would change depending on whether Brodie joined the conflict—and on which side. If Iain fought for Albany with Mar, Kenneth might even be released. But if he joined Domnhall's forces, Kenneth could go from hostage to one of Albany's enemies. Yet how would he know he needed to gain his freedom? He dared not delay until the bishop's guards came to escort him to the bottle dungeon—or worse.

Phillippe snorted. "You must present a greater tone of conviction in your voice when you say those words to the bishop, *mon ami,* or you might become a prisoner in truth."

Kenneth nodded, taking the warning to heart. He'd found little to trust about Phillippe, but those words rang true.

CATHERINE WALKED THROUGH TOWN AND HEADED UP the hill toward the cathedral. She needed to get out of the house, away from the arguments between Abi and her stepfather. She'd never seen a more contentious pair. No wonder Abi wanted to get married—if only to get away from the unceasing tension. The tailor had found out about his stepdaughter's plans to elope. The argument that news started had not abated these last two days.

As angry as she was with her own father, hearing the two of them made Catherine appreciate Da more. He didn't make a habit of disparaging his daughters with everything he said and did. He was motivated by care and concern for them, but even so, she knew the clan came first. As much as she hated the reality, she had to acknowledge daughters were a valuable commodity.

Abi provided the only saving grace in all the shouting. To keep Catherine from being sent home, Abi had absolved her of being involved. Abi knew how important staying in St. Andrews and finding Kenneth was to her. Her stepfather, probably not wanting to spread his ire too thin, had accepted her lie. Catherine didn't feel any guilt. She'd really done nothing save walk with Abi and Colin to the cathedral. She'd waited outside while they spoke to the priest, hoping for another glimpse of the man who reminded her so strongly of Kenneth. But he had not returned, and she felt foolish for thinking it might be him.

If only she'd known then she had truly seen him, she could have saved herself some longing and found her anger instead. He'd avoided her for what seemed a lifetime. When had he returned from France? What was keeping him in St. Andrews when he'd already been gone so long from Brodie? Why had he warned her off when they recognized each other? She couldn't fathom any of it.

She took a deep breath and looked around her, forcing away the unhappy thoughts. The beautiful, sunny day promised to be warm later on. Catherine wouldn't go outside the town's wall, as far as the harbor. It wasn't safe for a lass unless she was with a group or was escorted by a man. But the precincts of the cathedral should hold no threats in broad daylight, even for a woman alone. And she might encounter Kenneth there. She was silly to hope. Chances were slim he'd be out of the castle and in that very area when she chose to go there, but priests often went back and forth between the castle and cathedral. Chance had led them to each other once before. It might do so again. And she needed some time away from Abi's house.

For now, a cool, refreshing breeze blew shoreward off the water, carrying the clean scent of salt and sea. It wasn't the same as fresh, clean Highland air, but it served to push farther inland the unpleasant smells of town life caused by too many people and animals in a small area.

The cathedral's towers loomed ahead, reaching for the heavens. On the seaward side, a group of rough-looking men climbed the hill alongside the cathedral's wall, from the town wall's fisher gate and the harbor. Catherine averted her gaze as they passed by, and then breathed a sigh of relief. She should be safe near the cathedral, but one never knew.

Just then, a man she recognized passed through the gate below her and continued up the hill toward her. He broke into an appealing grin when he saw her.

Abi's comments about him and the memory of meeting him and the students bound for the priesthood made his name pop immediately into her head. "Cameron Sutherland," she greeted him.

"Mary Catherine Rose, aye?"

"Ye have minded me well."

"A bonnie lass like ye is worth minding," he flattered her. "But what are ye doing out by yerself?"

Should she tell him Abi's plans had gone awry? Nay, it was not her place. "Just getting some air. And ye?"

"Getting the news from the port. 'Tis no' so good, I fear."

Catherine frowned. "What do ye mean?" Cam offered his arm, and to be polite, she took it.

He walked toward the cathedral, away from the busy path. "Domnhall, the Lord of the Isles, ye ken him?"

"Of him, aye. I've never met the man."

Cam nodded. "Word has come he's taken Dingwall and may march on Inverness."

"What?" Catherine stopped, forcing Cam to stop as well and turn to look at her. Rose and Brodie were not so very far past Inverness, farther east along the southern shore of the Moray Firth. "Why?" Her clan, and Kenneth's, could be caught up in the fighting.

"To stake his claim on Ross, of course."

"Then he'll stop?"

Cam shook his head. "Nay. Albany will no' stand for it. He'll gather an army under the Earl of Mar. They'll fight, somewhere between Inverness and Perth, or I miss my guess. This town is already filling up with men coming up to join Mar's *caterans*."

Catherine's stomach sank. Her home lay very near the disputed area, though up along the firth, so perhaps beyond the swath of destruction such fighting would bring.

"Why are ye in St. Andrews, lass?"

Suddenly, she felt the need to be cautious. "Why do ye ask?"

Cam Sutherland was a Highlander, but Sutherland allied with the Isles. And Rose? She wished she'd paid more attention when her father spoke of the other clans, allies and enemies. But those subjects had been too…serious…for a lass like her. Too tied to his plans to wed her to someone other than Kenneth. She'd avoided anything to do with other clans, with alliances, and with disputes over land and titles. Besides, until Kenneth, she had been more interested in ribbons and horses and other girlish things. Since then, she'd been yearning for a lad she'd thought never to see again.

She was here because her father's latest attempt to marry her off had been done with less notice and more rancor at her constant refusals. After Mary took her aside and told her their da had lost his patience with her, she'd been forced to grow up fast, and the only option she'd thought she had at the time was to flee. But she couldn't tell a Sutherland such a sorry tale. She didn't know whether Cam could be trusted, so she went with her instincts. When she'd first met him, she'd been attracted to him, but put off by his arrogance, too. Caution was warranted.

Cam frowned. "If war breaks out, 'twill no' be safe for Highlanders here, ye ken."

"Nay!" He didn't give her the kind of answer she expected at all. This was much worse. In hindsight, she would have preferred to spend the walk flirting with him than discussing the first rumblings of a war that could hurt everyone she loved.

He patted the hand she'd draped over his forearm. "Ye should go home, I'm thinking."

"To a war? Ye make it sound as if 'twill no' be safe there, either."

"At least there ye'll be with yer clan. 'Tis better than being a Highland lass alone in a Lowland town."

She could argue she wasn't alone, since she was living with her cousin, but his expression went bleak for a moment, prompting her to ask, "What about ye?"

"I will go when I must. I've work yet to do here."

"Work? Ye are no' a student then? I thought ye were…"

"Nay," he replied and laughed. "I'm a bit long in the tooth for books and examinations and such, aye?"

Catherine's mistake made her feel silly, but she had wondered at seeing him with the other lads, all of whom were students. "So why are ye here? And why were ye with those lads the day I met ye?"

Cam shook his head. "I'm a factor…a merchant's agent, if ye will. And those lads—those students go everywhere. No one pays them any notice. They see and hear more than ye might suspect, aye?"

"What does that have to do with being a factor?"

"Maybe naught, maybe everything—especially when alliances are as unsettled as they are now." He pinned her with a gaze more serious than she'd ever seen him wear. "'Tis less about being a factor and more about being a Highlander, ye ken? I must wait for a shipment from Flanders before I can sail for home. But ye should make plans to leave—and soon."

All this talk of danger and gleaning information made her look him over with a fresh eye. He didn't look much like a merchant of any sort. He looked like a warrior, broad of shoulder and well-muscled. He'd caught her eye because he reminded her of Kenneth.

She couldn't go home. Her father would marry her off. And she'd just found Kenneth—here. She had unfinished business with him. One way or the other, she was going to get answers. "Perhaps when ye leave, ye'll take the Highlanders in town with ye."

He didn't reply for long moments. He frowned and his gaze cut past the cathedral toward the fisher gate then back to her. "I canna guarantee that. The ship is no' mine to command. But I might make room for a lass such as ye." His quick grin gave her an idea of what he had in mind as payment for such a favor.

"I canna go home…just yet," she demurred, thinking frantically. She would not barter her honor to Cam Sutherland. So where in the Highlands could she go and not be returned immediately to Rose? And how would she get there?

If only she could return to Brodie as Kenneth's wife. That had been her dream these last two years. Perhaps she'd been foolish to hold on to what she'd thought they had for so long. Now that she'd seen his smile of recognition and the warmth in his gaze before he'd controlled himself, she hoped not. She'd defied her father again and again, believing Kenneth would return and claim her. But he'd frowned and waved her away. If he remained behind the bishop's castle walls—no matter the reason—the future she'd pined for would never be. Instead, she might be forced to appeal to Cam Sutherland's better nature—if he had one.

KENNETH LISTENED TO THE REPORT BEING MADE BY THE Warden's man to Bishop Wardlaw and, for self-preservation, forced himself to remain calm. Though the bishop had a kind demeanor, Kenneth's first impulse was to leave the audience chamber and get out of the castle any way he could manage. Domnhall had taken Dingwall, seat of the Earl of Ross, and was reported to be threatening to burn Aberdeen, a royal city, to the ground. Phillippe had warned him, but Phillippe could have been wrong. Hearing the news from this man's lips made it all too real. If Domnhall did move from Dingwall, would he sail from Inverness? Or march east, as Phillippe had supposed, wreaking havoc all along the way?

Phillippe raked him with a glance, then looked away. Aye, he knew. The time had come for the priest to repay his debt.

The bishop accepted the man's report with a nod, blessed and dismissed him. Then he turned his gaze to the other priests and servants in the room. "War comes again, it seems. What do any of you know of this man and his plans?"

His question was met with stony silence.

Kenneth held himself still; knowing now was not the time to attract the cleric's attention. He had no knowledge of Domnhall's plans and little information about the man himself. Certainly, he knew nothing that would illuminate the man's character or intentions for the bishop.

"This conflict may put at risk all we have built here, all we have achieved. The Holy Father, Pope Benedict, will soon receive the charter for St. Andrews University to establish a center of learning. We must pray the disagreements are quickly settled, and hope the fighting passes by us."

He paused and Kenneth remained still, his gaze on the wall behind the gathered priests while the bishop looked around the room.

"When word of this gets out," the bishop continued, "you may have students clamoring to leave to join the fray or to defend their homes. You must deny them."

As frowns drew down several brows and a low murmur arose, Kenneth hid his grim agreement. The priests had no idea, but the students he'd seen here, especially the Lowlander lads, had no business on a battlefield.

The bishop continued after another pause. "Once this latest conflagration is over, they must remain—alive—to become the keepers of their people's future. I put my trust in you to guard these lambs from the wolves of war."

The bishop's words might be comforting to those who believed they encompassed the sum of the cleric's concerns. But Kenneth was not so naive. Albany's hostages would no longer be viewed as innocent guests held in hopes of avoiding fighting. With this news, Kenneth would be seen as belonging to one of the warring factions. As the bishop dismissed the courier, Kenneth determined remaining here as hostage for Brodie no longer mattered. Domnhall was on the move and Albany was sure to send his cousin, the Earl of Mar, to answer with troops of his own. The Highlands would soon be at war with the Lowlands. St. Andrews was no longer a safe place for any Highlander.

Even a Highland lass.

A wave of urgency washed over him, tensing his muscles. He had to get free, if only to make sure Cat boarded a ship. He didn't care if she was married—it didn't matter. Once he knew she was safely away, he would worry about whether he would join the Brodie forces. Iain would likely align Brodie with the neighboring clans—Rose, Munro, Urquhart, and others. But on which side?

The bishop stood and gestured his advisors closer. Everyone else headed for the exits.

"Kenneth Brodie, you will remain." The bishop's voice rang out clearly over the muffled shuffling of soft-booted feet as others escaped the presence. As Kenneth had hoped to do. He needed to have words with Phillippe, but the French priest was in the group headed out the door.

Kenneth recalled himself to his situation. What did the bishop want with him? He stepped forward, dropped to one knee to avoid towering over the slighter man, and bowed his head over the bishop's ring. Despite their political differences, he owed this man the respect due his experience and position.

"Arise, my son," the bishop's sonorous voice rolled over Kenneth like a wave, weighty and warm.

Kenneth did as he was told, then waited, head still bowed. It was not his place to demand answers—not from this man.

"Given this news, I must ask you where your clan will stand. With the Isles or with the Crown?"

"Your Excellency, I dinna ken," Kenneth answered. It was the truth. Even though he believed he knew how Iain would act, he'd had no news from Brodie since he'd been brought here.

"You cannot say with certainty?"

"Nay, I fear I canna, Your Excellency. The question is no' so simple."

"Indeed?" The bishop opened one hand, palm up, as if reaching for the truth.

Kenneth took the gesture as permission to elaborate and looked up, not quite daring to meet the bishop's steady gaze. "Our clan's territory lies on the border of the disputed lands, between the Isles and the areas controlled by the...crown." He'd almost said *warden* and caught himself just in time. The south belonged to James I, even while he was held in England. Bishop Wardlaw, having been his teacher years before, strongly supported the young king. "The clans along the Moray firth will do what they deem best for their future. If Domnhall is strong enough, they may fight for him. If no', they will see their future lies with the king. Or they may remain out of the fray, preferring to let the Isles and Albany decide the current contest without their interference."

The bishop nodded. "A fair answer. Very well, you may go. May God's blessing be upon you."

Kenneth bowed and quit the chamber as quickly as he could without running. Rather than throwing him in the bottle dungeon, the bishop had accepted his answer and blessed him. He still had a chance to escape. But first, he had to find Phillippe.

CHAPTER 4

*H*ours later, Kenneth stood on the castle's seaside rampart, watching the clouds scud offshore. He longed for the wide vistas, open spaces and clean air of the Highlands. The offshore wind didn't help. It carried the fish rotting at the harbor and the inevitable smells created by the town's residents. Like most towns, St. Andrews stank.

He glanced to the west, where the sun was sinking into a cloud bank. The days were long now, and nights were too short to be of much use to someone who needed the cover of darkness to travel, and to put as many miles behind him as he could manage on foot.

Phillippe approached at his usual nonchalant pace, looking for all the world like he was out for an evening stroll, enjoying the breeze. But Kenneth planned to take advantage of the breeze to carry anything he or Phillippe said out to sea and keep their conversation private from anyone inside the castle.

"A lovely evening," Phillippe greeted him. "Though I'm certain you did not ask to speak to me here so we could enjoy the view."

Kenneth leaned against the balustrade. To anyone below, they would appear to be having a casual conversation. "Ye ken me too well. 'Tis time to settle things between us."

"Ah, the matter of my debt to you—"

"Can be paid in kind—by helping me leave here as I once helped ye escape."

"Are you so eager to join in the coming battle?"

"To fight? Nay. What sane man is? But nay matter who wins or loses, Albany will have nay reason to release me—or to keep me alive. If he wins, he has nay need for hostages. If he loses, I go from guest to prisoner of war and liability."

Phillippe turned to gaze out over the dark water. "I see. But what you ask is very dangerous— for you and for me—if I help you and am discovered."

"I risked as much to save ye from the hangman's noose in France, ye ken." Kenneth joined him in facing outward, but turned his head to regard Phillippe and the mud flats beyond him. Past them, a wide sandy beach stretched up the coast for miles at low tide. "I must go before it is too late. Ye are the only one in this castle I can trust to help me."

"A fighter such as ye—"

"I will no' damn my immortal soul by harming or— God forfend—killing a priest to escape. No' if I can leave here by any other means."

"Your nobility is one of the qualities I most prefer about you, *mon ami*."

Kenneth snorted. "Nobility does me no good if it gets me killed. Ye have been here long enough to learn the weak points of this structure and its guards." He forced his arm to his side to keep from waving at the castle walls and attracting attention. If anyone guessed what such a gesture meant, coming from him, he'd never get away. "Surely by now ye have learned the best way to leave this castle unnoticed and used it? Or have ye reformed after Marilee betrayed ye?" Betrayed Kenneth, too.

"She was a viper, to betray a priest."

"She was also a good lay, and ye were dabbling in the resistance and selling information to both sides," Kenneth growled, but kept his voice low. "If ye had picked a side, she might no' have been able to condemn ye as she did, but she found out and made certain both Armagnacs and Burgundy's followers distrusted ye. 'Twas all I could do to keep ye from them both and get ye away."

"An effort I applaud most heartily, *mon ami*."

"I was happy there, ye ken, until we both learned what a bitch Marilee truly was. Since I've returned to Scotland, nothing has gone right. Iain wasted no time sending me to Sterling. So here I am. And, to my good fortune, here ye are as well, Phillippe."

"Where will you go, if, as you say, you need to leave Scotland?"

Kenneth shook his head. "One problem at a time, eh? Get me out of the castle unseen. I'll worry about the rest. The nights are short, so I must be out one of the city gates as soon as they open and use every hour to put distance between me and this place."

"I must think on this. Let us speak again tomorrow..."

Frustration mounting, Kenneth clenched a fist, then remembered they might not be heard, but they were in full view of anyone on the other ramparts or in the castle yard. He forced himself to relax and smile. "Dinna think too long, *mon ami*. I ask only the help I once gave ye. Without me, yer head would adorn a French castle gate."

Phillippe gave him a tight smile. "Of that I am most aware."

"I dinna wish to suffer a similar fate, Phillippe. 'Tis time to make good on yer promise."

Voices sounded, down on the cobbled courtyard, but close by. Someone had come out from the cloister below them.

Phillippe nodded and walked away.

With a sigh, Kenneth turned back to regard the sea—and his prospects for freedom. Phillippe sounded sympathetic, but his request for a delay was telling. Kenneth knew him well enough to be certain the man would not lift a finger if doing so put himself in danger. Though Kenneth had saved Phillippe's life in France, he'd also learned he could not trust him there. He was no more trustworthy here.

He would have to find another way out.

&

CATHERINE NEARLY DROPPED THE LENGTH OF WOOLEN fabric she held when Kenneth and two escorts walked into Abi's stepfather's place of business. They stood blinking at the transition from daylight to the shop's relative dimness. None of them had noticed her yet, so she faded behind the curtain hiding the stairway to the upper level where Abi and her stepfather lived—and where Catherine was staying.

Abi's stepfather's voice rang out in greeting. "What can I do for you this fine day?"

She peeked through a narrow gap between the curtain panels as one of the priests cleared his throat and gestured at Kenneth, who remained still and silent.

"This man needs suitable clothing." The priest's gaze raked Kenneth from head to foot, and his upper lip curled. "He looks too much the Highland ruffian."

Catherine stifled a gasp. Highland ruffian? They

should see him in the Highlands. Her proud warrior. Almost her lover. Her thoughts drifted back to a day she'd spent teasing him on a walk to a nearby loch. When they reached it, he'd kicked off his boots and dropped his kilt. She'd never seen a man's body so near—and so eager—for her. She'd been mesmerized, taking in the strength—and the length—of him. Then he'd dared her to strip and dive in the loch with him. His gaze had held her captive until the cry of a hunting eagle broke the spell his gaze and his will had created. She'd turned and run from his laughter. If he had chased her, he could have easily caught her and dropped her, fully clothed, into the loch. Instead, he'd respected her choice and her strength of will, even then, and let her go. That day, she'd sworn never to run from him again.

Now, taller, stronger, more experienced in war, he would be much more formidable than those priests imagined. They had no idea who he was or what he could do—even to them—if sufficiently provoked.

And why were priests speaking about him that way? What kind of escorts spoke so disrespectfully of their charge? The thought hit her so suddenly she had to put a hand over her mouth to keep from gasping. Not his escort. His guards.

"The bishop requires he be attired in a more civilized manner by tomorrow's St. John's Eve feast."

"That's tomorrow? I'd forgotten. Why, that is not nearly enough time..."

"If you cannot do it, the kirk will be forced to find another to complete this task, as well as to assume the rest of the kirk's trade."

Catherine winced as Abi's stepfather, his face in profile, blanched and cleared his throat. "Of course I can. With your permission, I must measure..."

The priest gestured for Kenneth to do as the tailor directed.

"I happen to have a set of garments nearly completed—with minor alterations, they might do very well," Abi's father muttered as he wielded a string across Kenneth's shoulder, then down one arm. He muttered as he marked lengths on it with a wedge of chalk. "Ye will ruin my trade with an important gentleman, but what choice do I have?"

"We'll wait outside," one of the priests finally said as the tailor knelt to measure Kenneth's inseam. "You're not likely to go anywhere," he added with a smirk at Kenneth, "so long as he's got his hands on ye there."

Abi bit her lip to stifle an exclamation at such rude talk from a priest. She could not believe what she was hearing, but it confirmed to her that Kenneth was a prisoner of some sort.

Kenneth took it stoically, not responding to the jibe until the priests turned away. Then he shifted his weight.

Was he deciding whether to follow them and pay them back for their insolence?

Apparently unaware of the mayhem Kenneth was capable of, Abi's father frowned at the priests' backs as they quit his shop. He then went back to attempting his measurements, fussing about the tape being too short for the length of Kenneth's legs. Finally, he grimaced and stood. He tipped his head and said, "I'll return in a moment."

Kenneth sighed and dropped his shoulders, his gaze lifting over his head to the beams supporting the floor above as he frowned and muttered something she could not hear well enough to understand.

Catherine could just imagine he was asking heaven when this indignity would end. He'd be twice as mortified if he knew she watched. But she would risk his displeasure. If only Abi's stepfather would finish and leave the shop, too, so she and Kenneth might have a chance to talk before the priests returned.

*

KENNETH'S TENSION EASED WHEN HIS ESCORTS DECIDED to wait outside. They thought he had nowhere to go? The curtain at the back wall led somewhere. Even if it was only a window, he could be through it quickly. Or upstairs and away across rooftops. The news he'd heard needed to reach Iain and Cat's father, James Rose, before they got drawn into a fight no one could win. Instead, he was stuck here while the old tailor poked and prodded and muttered and made markings on a length of thin rope.

"I'll return in a moment," the man said after a sigh.

Once the tailor disappeared into a back room, Kenneth moved to the small front window to check on his escorts. He could hear them talking in low tones near the door, but they were out of his line of sight. No matter. As long as they remained out front, he would find a way out through the back. Since he couldn't rely on Phillippe, this might be his best chance to escape. He strode to the curtain, but the tailor came back before his fingers could connect with the fabric, the man's gaze on the breeks in his hands.

"I fear these will not do. They are not long enough," the man said, "but if ye would indulge me and put them on, I will have a better measure of the alterations I must make to a pair for ye."

Kenneth tightened his jaw, but forced a nod. He would not harm the man to get away. Not yet. Surely, he'd go after something else, giving Kenneth the opportunity he needed.

As he pulled his shirt out of perfectly serviceable woolen trews he wore, he heard something rustle behind the curtain. He paused and studied the way the fabric shifted as a tingle of alertness spread through his belly. Someone was there and watching. But who?

Soft footsteps ascended the hidden stairway, the footsteps light and quick. A woman watched. But who, indeed? It seemed the watcher suddenly suffered from shyness and didn't want to see what he had to offer a lass. He grinned, stripped, and in case she turned back, he took his time donning the breeks the tailor handed him.

CHAPTER 5

Since he made many of the students' attire as well as clothing for priests, Abi's stepfather was regularly included at castle feasts as a guest of the bishop or someone else in the kirk hierarchy. Tonight, the St. John's Eve celebration feast would be held in the castle's great hall. It was the reason Kenneth and his guards, for guards they surely were, had arrived at the shop yesterday demanding new clothes by tonight. Hearing he would be at the feast had tempered some of Catherine's disappointment in not being able to speak to Kenneth yesterday in the shop. She was overjoyed to be able to attend as a member of Abi's family, and knew she had Abi to thank for that.

She dressed with care in her best silky cream-colored *léine*, then slipped over it the deep blue brocade kirtle her sister Mary had insisted she pack. The brocaded fabric had a luster and sheen similar to the *léine's* and was much fancier than her warm wool kirtles. "I feel overdressed," she complained to Abi, fearing she'd be conspicuous, and attract more than Kenneth's attention. "I don't want to be glared at by priests as we were by the mercat cross the day we met Cam Sutherland."

"This is an important event for you," her cousin insisted. "If you get a chance to talk to your man, or even to be seen by him, you must look your best."

Catherine couldn't argue with her logic and liked hearing Kenneth called *her man*. She wanted to make a good impression, nay, a memorable impression on him. Good enough he would not turn away from her again. Good enough he would be willing to speak to her. To tell her why he'd spent the last two years away from her while she fended off her father's attempts to wed her to other clans, other men.

"It will be perfect for the bishop's feast," Abi insisted when Catherine failed to answer her earlier assertion. "You'll see. Everyone will be dressed in their finest—even the clerics."

Abi fussed with her hair until she had arranged it to both their satisfactions, upswept and trailing down Catherine's back. Then Abi draped a ribbon of pearls around her neck and knotted it before Catherine could open her mouth to object. "These belonged to my mother," Abi told her. "So do try not to lose them. If the dress doesn't get Kenneth's attention, surely these will."

Catherine hugged Abi. "Thank ye. If I canna find a time to speak to him at the dinner, I will find another way." Yesterday's glimpses through the curtains had only whetted Catherine's appetite and made her anger toward Kenneth fade into hunger again. She'd been about to whisk the curtain aside and speak to him when the tailor returned. She missed Kenneth. Tonight, she would change that.

"There will be a bonfire on the beach below the town, after the feast, to celebrate the summer solstice," Abi told her. "Perhaps he would be there."

Even if he attended with guards. The noise and confusion of the celebration might allow him to escape his escort for a few minutes and provide a perfect opportunity to speak to him. "I hope so."

The walk to the castle took only minutes, but a freshening breeze kept blowing back the hood of her cloak. Catherine was glad Abi had braided and secured her hair as she had, or it would have flown away by the time they reached the bishop's hall.

When they entered, the steward mentioned to Abi's stepfather that the feast would start a few minutes late. "Some kirk business," he announced with a touch of a Roman accent. "Please not to trouble yourselves on its behalf." They were given to understand the bishop would join them as soon as it was concluded.

While they waited, Catherine studied the grand space. Heavy arched beams supported the ceiling. Beautiful carved plasterwork decorated every corner of the room. Gorgeous stained glass accented high windows, the lower parts of which were open to the cool sea breeze. Tapestries depicting sacred scenes graced the walls.

Townspeople were dressed as Abi had predicted—in silks and embellished with more lace and jewels than Catherine was used to seeing at home. Abi caught her gaze and Catherine nodded, acknowledging her cousin's assurances.

After another brief interlude, priests and their attendants finally started filtering in. Catherine held her breath, eager to see Kenneth and hoping he would be included in the feast. When he appeared, he came in quietly, wearing the breeks and tunic Abi's father had altered in such a hurry, following a shorter, dark-haired priest she thought she recognized from the day near the cathedral. When Kenneth took up a position standing behind the man's chair, Catherine looked away, appalled. He was being forced to act as a servant. Seeing him in a subservient role confirmed in her mind the man she'd seen carrying a bundle outside the cathedral, along with this same priest, had indeed been Kenneth. It hurt to see him so subdued. Two years ago, he'd been cheerful, even playful, with her. Full of optimism and good spirits. But the smile she missed had been absent each time she'd seen him here. Then again, what did he have to smile about? She didn't understand why he was no longer at Iain Brodie's side —his friend and laird—why he was here and why he was being treated as a prisoner, worse, as a servant. None of this made any sense.

When the bishop arrived, he appeared as subdued as Kenneth, though his benediction was appropriate to a celebration feast. Perhaps the kirk business had been something unpleasant, now concluded.

Despite the rich feast, Catherine could barely eat. Abi noticed and leaned over to her. "Is he here?"

"Aye, he is." Catherine nodded in Kenneth's general direction and left it to Abi to decide which of the men on that side of the hall might be Kenneth.

"Then what's amiss? Look around you at all the fine fabrics and jewels. Did I not tell you your dress would be perfect for the feast? Oh, he has not noticed you?"

Catherine didn't want to start a long conversation in the midst of the town's gentry about why Kenneth was serving a priest and not seated at table as an honored guest. She simply nodded and chewed on a bit of bread.

"Then you must do something to make sure he sees you," Abi encouraged, then went back to enjoying the repast.

Abi's stepfather, on her other side, was deep in conversation with someone Catherine didn't know. He'd used the delay before the bishop arrived as an opportunity to speak to most of the gentlemen present. Catherine wondered if he knew them all or was simply taking advantage of the opportunity to make them aware of his business.

Catherine watched all through the evening to see where Kenneth went. Which entry he used when the priest he served sent him to fetch something. Which hallway. He never met her gaze. Finally, he left yet again at a time when all of the other attendants remained by their patrons, and she saw her chance. She whispered to Abi that she would return soon, then made her way to an archway giving out to the same hall as the doorway Kenneth just used.

He was there! Moving away, too far for her to call out his name without being heard by the serving staff, or even worse, the dignitaries in the great hall. Instead, she counted on him returning as he had twice already and positioned herself behind a column, in hopes of escaping the servants' notice. The hallway was dimly lit, and she stepped into the shadowy depths against the wall.

Kenneth paused at the far end and spoke briefly to someone she couldn't see, then started back.

Her heart leapt. He couldn't avoid her here. As he drew within a pace of her hiding place, she stepped out into his path.

"Who…!" His soft exclamation was accompanied by the movement of his hand clutching at his side, as if reaching for the sword or dirk he had worn there his entire adult life.

But of course, as he was not an honored guest of the bishop of St. Andrews at the feast, he was not permitted a weapon. How naked he must feel! "Kenneth, 'tis I," Catherine whispered.

"Ach, Cat," he breathed her name, then took her arm and dragged her roughly behind the column. "I can see that, ye daft lass." He stood for a moment, his gaze fierce as he searched her face. Then he released her as if touching her hurt him.

No more than it hurt her. She was sure his grip would leave marks.

"What are ye doing here, Cat?" He lifted a finger toward her cheek, then dropped it, his expression wistful. Then it hardened. "Ye canna be seen with me!"

"Why no'?" Cat glanced at the finger he'd nearly used to stroke her cheek. He wanted to touch her, and she wanted his touch. She breathed in his scent. He was as potent a temptation as he'd ever been, despite their time apart. She put a hand on his arm, hoping to encourage him. "What happened to ye? Why are ye here, and what kind of trouble are ye in?" Her arm no longer hurt, but she burned with the heat of his hand where he'd touched her. She wanted more. His hands holding her face. His arms around her. His lips on hers.

"I'm no' in trouble…"

"Ye canna deny it, Kenneth. Let me help."

He shook his head and cast wary glances past her, then quickly behind him. He picked her hand from his arm, but held it, warm in his callused grip. "Get ye back inside. I mean it—ye canna be seen with me, or even to be gone from the feast at the same time." Then he released her hand and ran his through his hair. "God's teeth, lass, ye dinna ken what ye risk." He took her arm again and turned her around, then gave her a gentle shove. "Go. Tell Iain I am here."

She spun back, not willing to give up so easily. His last words lodged her heart in her throat. His clan did not know where he was? He was in trouble and alone. She had to know. Had to do something. "Kenneth!" She reached out to him again, but he stepped back. "When can we talk? If no' now, when?"

He shook his head, a grimace tensing the muscles of

his face. "Perhaps never….nay, lass, dinna cry out." With a groan, he pulled her into his arms.

Catherine's knees went weak. Here is where she belonged. With her cheek resting on Kenneth's shoulder, his heartbeat under her palm. All too soon, he let her go. Catherine wanted to step back into his embrace, to breathe in the scent of him, and press her lips to his mouth.

But he read the intention in her eyes and shook his head. "If I can, I will find ye. I hope someday to be able to explain. But no' if ye are seen with me. It will mean yer freedom." Footsteps echoed in the far cross-corridor. "Now go!"

Kenneth faded into the hiding place Catherine had recently left. She spun and hurried back to the doorway she'd left from, heart pounding. What did he mean, it would mean her freedom? Had he said that to frighten her? Pausing on the threshold, she glanced back, but saw only a servant coming up the hall. Kenneth had disappeared as completely as if he was made of the shadows where he hid.

She gulped a deep breath, smoothed her skirts, and forced her expression into one of nonchalance before she reentered the room. A full ten minutes later, out of the corner of her eye, she saw him finally reappear, lean forward to whisper something in the priest's ear, and then take his place standing behind the man, never glancing her way. As much as she wanted to drink in the sight of him, she kept her gaze averted and her attention on the conversations taking place near her. She still wanted him, even more than she had two years ago. And his words proved he still cared for her.

Kenneth had promised he would explain someday—if he could. And the Kenneth Brodie she knew, or at least the lad she used to know, kept his promises.

The next morning, Catherine woke early to Abi knocking on her door, then entering.

"Get dressed. I'm going to the harbor, and you're coming with me."

Catherine waved her away. She had slept poorly, her dreams filled with the sensation of Kenneth's hand on her arm, his palms pressing into her shoulders as he pushed her away from the cage that held him. Then in her dream, she'd freed him somehow, and Kenneth caught her arms and pulled her back against the hard, hot length of his body. Vowing he would never let her go, his hands traced her neck and smoothed over her breasts to wrap around her waist, imprisoning her against the evidence of his desire for her. In her dream, he was even longer and thicker than he'd been as a lad, branding the small of her back with his need. While his lips burned a path from her shoulder along her throat, she turned her head and her lips met his kiss.

She'd rather stay in bed, reliving her dreams, but Abi was insistent, opening the shutters so early sunlight spilled across her face. She winced and sat up. Abi would not leave her in peace. She might as well give in and go with her. Perhaps at the harbor she could find a way to get word to Iain.

She missed the Kenneth she once loved, younger and infatuated with her. Not the Kenneth she'd met in the castle's hallway, pulling her to him one minute and gruffly determined to push her away from him the next. If she could only bring the lad she'd loved back to life. But that looked less likely in the harsh light of morning than ever it had while she waited and longed for Kenneth's return. He was in some kind of trouble, and determined to keep her out of it. A future with him was an old dream. A hopeless one, too. She should forget him—if she could—which was not likely, not especially if he needed help.

Soon thereafter, dressed and still yawning, she made her way with Abi past the cathedral and down the hill to the St. Andrews harbor.

Catherine was always amazed at the activity there. Nothing she was used to in the Highlands compared to it. Even Abi seemed surprised at just how busy and crowded the quay was this morning. They passed knots of sailors at work preparing to go out or just coming in from fishing overnight. Other men appeared to loiter, their hands on the hilts of their weapons, more blades visible tucked into boots or belts. What business did they pursue that required them to be so heavily armed?

She kept an eye on the men as she and Abi made their way along the quay. They were here on a simple errand, to buy fish for the evening meal, not to get into trouble. Abi had one boat in mind, a sailor she'd dealt with before whose catch was always fresh.

"He doesn't hold over..." Abi said, then paused long enough for them to dodge a wagon loaded with casks of ale, "to the next day fish he couldn't sell, as some fishmongers do. Ye must have a care when buying from some of these boats, or up in the market square, but Henke is trustworthy and his price is fair."

How much simpler at home in the Highlands to catch whatever they needed, from a burn or from the firth. Here, one had to go to the port to buy many things, including fish for supper.

As Abi haggled with Henke, Catherine let her gaze rove over the boats tied up nearby. One interested her —a *birlinn* belonging to a clan she knew—Murray. Could Kenneth find a way to get to the port before that ship sailed? If he knew it was here, he might find a way. But how could she get the word to him? She'd hoped to find him at the port today, with or without an escort, but there was no sign of him.

She left Abi to her negotiation and wandered closer to the *birlinn*. She didn't see any movement on board, so she went closer and finally stopped at the plank used to board it. At first, she thought no one was about. How could she ask when they planned to sail if they'd left no one aboard? Just as she was about to give up and turn back to Abi, she heard a loud snort followed by a grumble and then soft snoring. The sound gave away the man sleeping on a pile of nets on the side away from the dock. He'd sunk into them far enough to make him difficult to see.

"Good morrow," she called to him, but got no response. "I said, good morrow to ye," she repeated, louder this time. "Can ye no' hear me?"

Another snort and grumble gave her hope.

She put one foot on the plank. It rocked a bit, side to side, as it flexed under her weight. Dare she try to go aboard? What if she fell into the water? Or what if the man objected to her presence on board and threw her into the harbor?

Oh, for God's sake, she could swim. And she needed to know how long they would be here.

For Kenneth's sake.

"Are ye awake, then?" she continued. Just as she took the first hesitant step onto the plank, the man snorted and sat up, rubbing his face with more vigor than she thought he'd possess.

"I am now, damn ye, lass." He turned and saw her on the plank. "What do ye think ye are doing? Get ye back on the dock."

"I'm trying to discover how long ye will be here. When do ye sail?"

"What does it matter to a lass such as ye? Ye canna travel alone..."

"I ask for a friend," she interjected. "One who desires to return home to the Highlands. There's trouble..."

"Here? Aye. There, too. No sense going anywhere to avoid it—trouble will follow." He put his hands on his knees and pushed to his feet, then crossed the deck to stand by the plank. "What did yer friend do?"

"Do? Why, naught."

"Naught, eh? What clan?"

"Brodie."

"I ken it. Murray has no feud with Brodie."

"Exactly. So ye could take him. He kens his way around a craft such as this so he could work for his passage. When do ye sail?"

"'Tis up to Malcolm, no' me, whether to take on more crew—and when to sail."

Catherine clenched a fist and glanced aside. Abi was still talking to the man, Henke, so she turned back to the Murray sailor. "Where do I find Malcolm?"

"Nowhere a lass like ye should be found, and that's a fact."

Catherine huffed out a breath, fighting the sudden urge to stomp a foot. "Will he be back soon?" She could give the captain Kenneth's message to Iain. She didn't trust this rough sailor would recall it. He was either half asleep or still drunk enough to be unreliable in her eyes.

The Murray glanced at the sun, then around the dock. "As early as ye roused me, I misdoubt it. Likely he and a lass will be busy for hours yet."

"I'll come back."

"Or ye could stay. Since ye woke me. 'Twould be the...friendly...thing to do."

"Ach, nay...I have to go."

"I'd be more inclined to argue for Malcolm to help yer Brodie..."

Catherine shook her head and stepped away. "I'll come back and ask him myself."

The man's laughter followed her back to Abi, who finished her transaction and turned to Catherine with an expectant smile—and a fish.

"Ready to go?"

Catherine glanced over her shoulder at the Murray *birlinn*. The man stood at the plank, hands on his hips, grinning. She was a fool to think about returning, but for Kenneth's sake, she must. "Aye, let's go." For now.

THE NEXT MORNING, CATHERINE STARED AT THE EMPTY spot on the quay, bitter disappointment filling her. The Murray birlinn was gone. Abi's father had been ill, so she hadn't been able to recruit Abi to leave him and go back to the harbor with her the previous afternoon. She had even searched the market square for a familiar face, such as Cameron Sutherland, who might accompany her, but to no avail. She had considered but hadn't been foolish enough to go on her own. Except for early in the morning when the fresh catch came in and other vendors opened their stalls, the harbor was no place for a respectable woman alone.

If only she'd been able to talk to Malcolm Murray, they might have delayed until she could get word to Kenneth and he could find his way to them. Or at least they could have carried Kenneth's message to Iain. She consoled herself with the expectation there would soon be more Highland ships in port, and more chances to sail for home.

She'd been brave enough to speak to the crewman on the Murray *birlinn*. She could do it again. Another boat. Another crew. Another chance.

Abi finished the errand that had brought them to

the harbor, and they walked back up the hill toward the cathedral.

"Colin is speaking to Father Phillippe today. We want to elope tomorrow," Abi confided leaning close to Catherine and lowering her voice. "No' in there," she added with a nod at the massive cathedral, "but in the small chapel, I think."

"You've made the arrangements at last? Where ye will live? What ye will do?"

"Aye. We cannot wait any longer," Abi answered, with no response for the practicalities.

She giggled and Catherine understood what they could not wait for. The marriage bed. "Ye havena yet…"

"Nay!" Abi laid a hand on her chest and shook her head. "'Twould be a sin."

"Ah…but ye have…"

"Done much else, aye. I have seen…all of him. And touched him. As he has touched me. Oh, Catherine, ye canna imagine how good lying in a man's arms can make ye feel."

Catherine swallowed, unable to speak past the lump in her throat. In the throes of their infatuation, she and Kenneth had dared much the same, but left so much undone. And unsaid.

"Ah, but it can no' be any man," Abi continued, apparently oblivious to Catherine's reaction. "It must be the right man. And Colin is the right man for me." She paused, her wistful expression turning to a frown. "But my stepfather refuses to care how I feel. Why do fathers always think they ken better than their daughters? 'Tis my heart, after all. My body. My future."

"Abi, *wheesht*," Catherine interrupted her cousin's growing tirade. If Abi raised her voice any further, her words would echo across the town. "It will work out. Just be patient." Not that patience had worked out for her, or her sister Mary. She couldn't believe she'd uttered those words to Abi.

Abi put a hand on her arm and stopped. "Will you stand with me?"

Catherine swallowed again and nodded. "Of course, I will," she promised, though the thought of being part of a wedding made her ache for Kenneth.

CHAPTER 6

$\mathcal{I}$n the weeks since he'd arrived in St. Andrews, Kenneth had developed the habit of retreating to the castle's library when he wasn't training the college's students in weaponry, or with Phillippe at a local pub. Heavenly rewards being somewhat in doubt for both of them, Phillippe saw their pub visits as an earthly reward for Kenneth's efforts for the bishop. Kenneth avoided asking the obvious question—what had Phillippe done to earn the same earthly reward?

Kenneth kept his eyes and ears open. Pubs were full of news—and speculation. So far, he'd learned nothing useful. Nothing that told him which clans had aligned with Domnhall, or whether it was time to leave St. Andrews. Nothing that eased his conscience about putting Iain in a difficult position when he did go. Apparently Domnhall lingered at Dingwall, consolidating his hold on the castle and town. An implied threat, but not yet an active one.

At the moment, Kenneth was confined to this castle, so besides relieving his boredom, being in the library had the added benefit of allowing him to stay out of Father Anselmo's sight. Kenneth was in no way afraid of hard work, but the Roman seemed to take unholy delight in assigning him the most mundane or onerous tasks. To Kenneth's chagrin, other than his priestly responsibilities to the kirk and the bishop, most of Anselmo's dutiful attention fell on him. And according to this priestly pain in his arse, Anselmo intended to ensure Kenneth would carry a newfound humility back to his clan when—or if—the time ever came for Kenneth to return to the Highlands. Anselmo was determined to school him well in his own brand of wisdom.

Humility. *Bollocks.*

When the library door opened, Kenneth groaned, expecting Anselmo or one of the junior priests Anselmo would have sent to look for him. Instead, the swish of skirts reached his ears and he looked up in surprise.

Cat!

She held a finger to her lips, signaling for silence while she closed the heavy oaken door behind her and looked for a way to lock it.

It had no lock, or Kenneth would have locked it against Anselmo weeks ago. At the moment, he was ridiculously glad it had none.

Cat gave up and turned to face him, her back against the door. "I canna believe 'tis ye."

Kenneth shook off the stupor that had seized him when the woman of his dreams came through the door. He laid aside the book he'd been reading. "What are ye doing here, Cat?"

"Right now? I made a delivery for my cousin Abi's stepfather. The tailor. Then I came looking for ye. And I found ye."

Her words propelled him to his feet, aghast. "Ye asked for me? After I warned ye no' to be seen with me?"

She shook her head. "I'm no' a dafty. I merely wandered about then recalled your fascination with Da's library. Every castle should have one, aye? So I asked after it." She crossed her arms. "Where have ye been, Kenneth?" She pushed away from the door and approached.

Kenneth fought the urge to meet her halfway, and lost. He'd been desperate to take her in his arms since holding her briefly in the hallway outside the St. John's feast. As her scent reached him, warm and spicy, all Cat, he gave in, despite knowing that showing any sign of affection was the worst thing he could do to her—or himself. She was married. He let her get right up to him, where she had to lean her head back to gaze into his eyes, then sanity prevailed. He sat down and pulled the book close. "Reading, of course." He waved a hand. "This is a library."

Her crestfallen expression nearly swayed him from his purpose, but her safety was more important than how much he wanted her. "What are ye doing here? Is yer husband with ye?" He kept his tone neutral, as though his question was only meant to be polite conversation, not to give voice to the desires of a man who hadn't seen her in much too long.

She colored.

He fought down his protective instincts. She deserved some time spent feeling uncomfortable. She'd made him miserable enough. "Ye are the one who agreed to be betrothed," he challenged, recalling the pain the news had caused. How it stayed with him— and how furious he'd been after hearing it, driving him, foolishly, to leave for France.

"I did no such thing. I was forced..."

"So ye are married now." The confirmation stung. He took her hand and ran his thumb over her finger where a wedding ring should be. Her hand was ice cold in his, betraying…what? "Why no ring? Where is yer husband?" He let it go.

"My…? Nay, I am no' wed. Though Da has tried often enough. I came here to avoid his latest attempt."

The upwelling of joy in Kenneth's chest nearly overwhelmed him into reaching for her, pulling her into his lap and kissing her senseless. But he couldn't do that to her. He had to know.

"I heard ye were betrothed to a Mackintosh."

"The first time."

She still stood before him, one arm crossed over her chest, protecting herself; the hand he'd released crumpling, then smoothing the front of her skirt. "I convinced Da to break it off. Then again, and again." She took a step closer to his chair.

"What do ye mean?" He suddenly needed to stay seated while she explained herself. He wasn't sure his legs would support him, now he'd found out Cat was a free woman.

"Da has tried his best to find an alliance—and a husband—I would accept," she continued. She fisted her hands and glanced around the room as if making sure they were alone. "The only husband I want…the only man I ever wanted…is ye." She took a breath. "I wanted ye, but ye never came. So why have ye no' come for me? We had an agree…"

"Childish fancy," he said, cutting her off before her words could wound him any worse. She'd waited for him, fought her father to honor her promise to him and his to her. Kept herself pure. All the while he'd been fighting in France, and whoring with Marilee and others he could barely recall. He was not worthy to have her regard, much less her love.

She blinked at his curt remark and took a step back.

It hurt him to say what needed to be said nearly as much as it probably hurt her to hear it, but Kenneth could not let her get involved with him again. Not while he languished in Albany's care, and given his past, not ever. So he twisted the knife. "Ye were a wee lassie, and I no' much more grown."

Her lips thinned.

Kenneth expected her chin to wobble as she fought back tears, but instead, a muscle in her jaw jumped.

"And we are so much older now, aye?" she retorted. "Or ye are so much more experienced, a lass like me can no longer satisfy ye..."

Ach, Cat. Still spitting and hissing and going after what she wanted. She made him proud, and terrified him.

She should not be here. What if someone came in and found them together? He glanced toward the door.

"So 'tis true." The hunger was gone from her gaze now, replaced by cold and damp despair.

He rubbed the bridge of his nose long enough to close his eyes and shut away the sight of the pain he caused her for one blessed moment. "What is true?"

"Ye never meant to offer for me. Iain forced ye to say the words, thinking we'd...done more than we had. Ye never wanted me. Only what we did..."

"Nay, lass." This was too much. He could not lie about those days "I did care. Iain had nothing to do with it, save agreeing. My offer was sincere..."

"Then. But ye wouldna make it again now."

He waved a hand around the room. "I'm not exactly in a position to."

"Are ye truly a prisoner? Ye said ye are no' here by choice."

"Of a sort."

"Ach, Kenneth..." This time, she reached for him.

He ignored her hand. "If ye want to help me, do what I asked the other night Send a note to Iain, telling him where I am."

She blinked.

He'd surprised her with the sudden change of subject. Yet, she might be the only person in St. Andrews he could trust, no matter how his words hurt her. Hell, she might not even believe what he'd said. He pulled a sheet of vellum from the drawer in the table next to him and dipped a quill in ink. "Will ye do it?"

He'd thought to have her write it. A woman's hand might escape notice, but if she got caught with the information he wanted to give Iain, it would be better if she could claim ignorance of its contents.

She nodded, still wordless, but still willing to help him, despite his hurtful claims.

He bent to work writing a brief note Iain would understand, but would not get a courier in trouble if caught with it.

While he wrote, Cat found her voice and told him about the Highland ships she'd been seeing at the harbor. "I dinna ken when the next will arrive or when they'll leave. But ye could sail for home with them," she added.

She was so strong. After what he'd said, how could she even form words meant to offer hope to him? She should have stormed out, cursing his name. He finished the note with a trembling hand, folded and sealed it with wax from a candle while Cat waited silently. He was tempted by the picture she painted. If only he could escape without putting Brodie—and Cat—in jeopardy. He cleared his throat, and then spoke. "I canna do it, lass. But ye can. Go with them. Take this to yer father. He'll see it gets to Brodie." He handed her the note, and she slipped it into the pocket of her skirt, yet her gaze remained on him.

He couldn't hide his longing for her. He was sure it filled his gaze and, even when he managed not to reach for her, revealed how his heart swelled at her nearness.

He tried to force it back, to turn his thoughts to how daring for a lass to make her way about the castle alone. His Cat had always had more courage than was good for her. *His Cat.*

"We both could go."

She must have seen something in his face, in his body, that gave him away. "I canna," he insisted, fighting the urge to cross himself for speaking the lie under the bishop's own roof. Possibly, he could escape the castle and the town walls, but there would be consequences he did not want to be responsible for. "And ye must no' be seen with me. I'm no' here because I wish to be. So flee, Cat. Go home."

"Catherine...I'm called Catherine now."

He ignored her attempt to take on the mantle of maturity and dignity. What he had to tell her was too important. "And dinna speak to me, or of me, again. Yer da will do what is best for ye." He waved a hand as if pushing her away. "I canna."

Tears glimmered even though the fierce frown never left her face.

"Ye were always what was best for me." She shook her head and held up a hand when he opened his mouth to object. "Why do ye think that has changed?"

Damn it, he was going to have to tell her. She would never give up if he did not. "My feelings for ye changed when I lay with a lass in France."

Cat's hand flew to her throat, and she gasped as if he'd punched her in the belly.

"She taught me everything a wee country lass like ye never could," he continued, fury at having to hurt her this way making his voice gruff and sharp. "Now any lass I bed must..."

"Teach me."

Kenneth's throat closed on an icy knot of shock. It quickly melted into burning—unquenchable—desire.

He heaved a breath. He should have known better than to trade challenges with Cat. She'd always taken any dare of his and thrown it back in his face. She'd just done it again and by God, if they were anywhere else, if there were any chance at real privacy, he'd do just what she asked, and make her his—forever. But they weren't.

He'd always enjoyed their battles of wits, but not this time. This time, there was too much at stake. "Nay. I willna. Ye are too good for the likes of me. I'm no longer the lad ye kenned." He stood, forcing her back a step while she shook her head, denying his words. "Ye deserve a man who has no' done what I have done. Who has no' seen what I have seen."

She moved in, giving him no quarter. Instead, she lifted her arms and pulled his head down for a kiss, her body pressed fully and firmly against his. "Teach me," she demanded again, but softer this time, then her lips found his.

They moved over his like velvet over steel, Cat's determination evident even in her probing kiss. His hands roamed over her back of their own will, stroking, pulling her closer, delving under her hair to cradle her nape with one while the other cupped her bottom. He hadn't realized how keenly, how acutely he had missed her until her kiss brought it all slamming back; the longing, the heat, the intoxicating taste of her. It took all of his willpower to release her, to turn his head aside instead of plundering her mouth. Even that simple kiss brought back everything they'd shared two years ago; her taste, her touch, all the ways they'd helped each other learn what the other liked. Her brief kiss fired his blood and left his heart pounding. He recalled the geography of her body, the hills and valleys and secret places he'd delighted in exploring, the heat in her kiss and, most of all, the hunger in her eyes he had refused to satisfy. His cock hardened at the memories and the scent and taste and heat of that woman standing before him now, panting, with desire and hurt warring in her gaze. If only he had taken her then. They might be married now, and he would not have gone to France. "I willna teach ye," he choked out. "I canna do that to ye, Cat. No' when I will never be able to do what's right by ye. To marry ye. I'm hostage here for Iain. I dinna ken how long I'll be held here. The letter for Iain—he thinks I'm in Sterling." He expected that would make her flee, or at least, make her cry in earnest, but she simply regarded him, studied him, and waited for him to capitulate. If he had no honor, he could hate her, teach her, take her, and leave her. Seeing her was torture. Her offer, shocking. Her kiss...devastating. He wanted more.

"I hear what ye didna say. I ken ye well enough to believe ye are trying to protect me."

Nay! Her understanding would unravel the knots of his resolve. He clenched his fists. "I am," he admitted. *From myself.*

She backed up a step, her expression grim. "Then I will go now. But we will..."

"Nay, lass, we will no'. Ye will return home and obey yer da. 'Twill be the best for ye." Now the knife was twisting in his own gut.

Cat shook her head, tears again glinting in her eyes, as though she found everything that had just passed between them impossible to believe. Then she turned, her back straight, and walked to the door.

"Ye havena seen the last of me, Kenneth Brodie," she said without turning her head. She spoke to the oaken door, sounding for all the world like a seer making a vow to a sacred tree. Before he could reply, she slipped out.

At that moment, he realized this was the second time he had failed to ask her why she was here. He'd been so determined to keep Cat safe when she accosted him in the hallway during the feast, he'd failed to ask her why she was in St. Andrews. She mentioned a cousin and the tailor. Could that be where she was staying? Surely her father had not sent her as hostage for Rose. He shuddered to think what might happen to a lass put in that position. Nay, Cat was here for another reason. She'd said she came here to avoid her father's latest attempt to betroth her. But why St. Andrews? Because it was as far from James Rose as she could run and have kin to live with? His heart broke for her. For the desperation that drove her here. For the lad and the lass they used to be—when being in love was simple. Nay, her presence in the bishop's town had nothing to do with him, or she would not have been so surprised to encounter him.

Was she even free to leave St. Andrews?

He realized her last words were as prophetic as he'd imagined. He would have to find a way to talk to her again after all. Finding her here was a complication he didn't need, yet she could be in as much danger as any Highlander. How could he think of escape if in doing so, he left her behind?

To Catherine, passing under the portcullis and through the castle gates felt like breaching a wall between her past and her future. Tears had threatened since she closed the library door behind her, but she'd forced them back, refusing to flee the castle distraught and embarrass herself in front of all those priests and guards and servants. If only she could look forward and forget the past. Forget Kenneth and all he'd meant to her, all they'd shared. The dream of a life with him that had kept her stubbornly defying her father. Forget all the heartache of not knowing where he was, and when, or if, he would return for her. Forget the embarrassment, no—mortification—of begging him to teach her what he'd learned from whores in France.

One taste of him, one simple kiss, and her body had melted with desire. Dear God, what had she become, to stoop so low? Would her sisters recognize her? She barely recognized herself. No man was worth surrendering her dignity in that way. Not even Kenneth. Most certainly not Kenneth, the man who'd failed to fight her father's hidebound notions of what was best for the clan and convince him to let them wed when he had the chance. The man who had disappeared and left her to be bartered away by her father, not once, not twice, but three times. Were all men so heartless?

By the time she reached the North street, she'd worked herself into a state of indignation to match the storm clouds amassing on the horizon. She dared not return to Abi's place. Instead, she turned downhill and made her way through town, away from the harbor, toward the long beach bordering the coastline. Without meeting a soul, she could walk for miles along the wide stretch of sand while the northerly wind tore at her hair and dress. She could walk into the sea and let the waves claim her life. It wasn't worth much to her right now, not if it didn't include Kenneth. The one man she'd thought she wanted, the one man she'd thought she loved, didn't want her.

Or she could stiffen her spine, turn around, and do what she'd planned when she first contemplated leaving Rose—make something of herself. Without her father, without Kenneth, without any man. Women could earn a living at many honorable pursuits in a town such as this. She had no special skills, but she was intelligent and a fast learner. She would adopt a common practice of the students at the university. She would find a mentor. She would find a way.

Her boots were coated with sand and the hem of her dress soaked with sea spray by the time she'd calmed enough to start back up the hill into town. There was still the matter of the letter in her pocket. She might be angry with Kenneth, but she would do what she could to help him. She'd send it in her own letter to Annie. No one in St. Andrews would think to care about a letter from one sister to another. Then Annie could safely give it to Iain. Catherine would not send it to Mary. Her father might intercept it and discover where she'd gone.

Resolved, she continued on her way. Her hair had come loose from its braid while she walked and now streamed around her head, so she turned to face the wind and gathered it in both hands as it blew out behind her, and then twisted it into a coil at her neck. That would hold long enough for her to get indoors.

"Good day, sweet Catherine."

The voice sounded just behind her. Surprised, she whirled, swinging a fist, intent on defending herself, before she registered the voice—and the words she should have also recognized—belonged to Cam Sutherland. He easily blocked her with an open palm, the sound of her fist smacking his warm flesh making her cringe. "Cam! I'm so sorry. Ye startled me."

"I can see that." He grinned and shook his hand as though she'd hurt him, then put his hands on his hips and leveled a stare at her. "What has ye so *fashed*, lass, ye are ready to do battle? Ye're out here by yerself, windblown and—have ye been crying?"

"What? Nay. The wind made my eyes water."

"Indeed."

Well, it had. She was sure it must have at some point.

He gestured toward a nearby pub. "Let's get an ale—or some stew," Cam amended when the clouds finally let loose a torrent of rain. "Stew it is. Then ye can tell me what has happened."

The nearest pub was of a respectable sort frequented by town ladies and university scholars rather than the rough crowd inhabiting the pubs near the harbor. Cam claimed seats at a small table near the window. Catherine appreciated his regard for her reputation. Anyone passing by would see nothing amiss. Two acquaintances come in out of the rain, sharing a meal on a chilly afternoon, nothing more. Still, she could hope word would get back to Kenneth she'd been seen with another man. A large, handsome Highlander, too. She found herself studying him as he gave their order to a serving girl. Charming, when he wasn't being arrogant. A merchant's factor—or something more.

"What's amiss, lass?"

Cam's question interrupted her musing. She hoped she hadn't been staring at him while she pictured Kenneth's reaction to the imaginary gossip. "'Tis nothing—and everything," she amended. "A painful lesson hard learned and an uncomfortable truth—best forgotten."

Cam eased back in his seat. "That sounds intriguing."

"Aye, well, 'tis naught I wish to share. But I appreciate yer concern for my well-being."

Cam eyed her, seeming to consider her words. "Have ye thought about what we last discussed? About leaving St. Andrews and returning home? Even now, ye should never be on the street without Abi. She's a Lowlander. Yer speech marks ye as a Highlander—as does mine."

Once again, he'd changed subjects with lightning

speed. Catherine wondered if that was an indication of his intelligence—rapid and wide-ranging—or an impatient nature. She wasn't ready yet to give up her fantasy of skewering Kenneth by her association with Cam. Nor had she seriously considered leaving this town, despite his warning. She knew of no danger to her here, save as Kenneth kept insisting existed if she was found with him. She'd rather wonder if she could make Kenneth jealous. Then again, after today, why would she want to? Especially with Cam sitting right here. He could be pleasant company when he wished to be. Solicitous, even.

"I have had no' thought about leaving, nay. Such news seems…unreal…given nothing seems to have changed." She gestured at the window and the people passing by, hoods pulled over their heads to keep off the cold rain.

"A Highlander was arrested this morning at the harbor. Someone didna like his speech and claimed he stole from them. I'm told they fought, and the Highlander was badly beaten by his attacker—and friends." He gestured out the window. "Look again, lass. There are more men on the street than a fortnight ago. They might be built like fishermen used to hauling in nets, but these are nay sailors. I've seen them coming green and sweating off of boats from Edinburgh and further south."

"Where are their arms?"

"They carry dirks and such on their persons. Anything bigger is likely stowed where they sleep while they await the next ship to take them north."

"A ship such as ye want me to take—alone—back to Rose?"

"*Ach*, aye, now that ye mention it, not my best idea." He drummed blunt fingers on the tabletop. "Unless ye have a man…or a husband…with ye."

"Why, Cameron Sutherland, are ye proposing to me?" After her conversation with Kenneth, she might be inclined to accept.

He leaned back even further, prompting Catherine to soften her question with a grin at his obvious discomfort.

"Nay, though a husband might solve several of yer problems."

The spoonful of stew she'd taken suddenly tasted bitter. "And there ye have landed squarely on the source of my upset today."

"Ye have a husband? Lady Catherine, I apologize." He glanced at her hand.

She dropped it into her lap. He was the second man today to remark on her lack of a ring.

"I didna ken ye were wed. If I've said or done anything improper..."

"*Dinna fash*, Cam." She held up a hand. "*Pax*. This is a meal only. And conversation out of the rain. Naught to cause objection." She carefully neither confirmed nor denied his leap to a conclusion. Letting him think she was wed might be just enough to keep Cam Sutherland at arm's length, until and unless she decided she needed—or wanted—him closer. Though not today. The pain of her confrontation with Kenneth was too fresh. She needed time. She might be better able to accept Kenneth belonged in her past once she was sure her future was in her own hands to decide.

✦

KENNETH STORMED OUT TO THE PRACTICE YARD AND signaled to a guard to join him. The man nodded and came forward. "Care to spar a while?" he asked. He needed to work off the frustration of Cat's visit and her revelations, or he would go mad and chase after her. He dared not do that—for her sake more than his.

The man grinned. "I've seen ye with the lads. I'd be pleased to have a go at ye." He fetched another sword and handed it to Kenneth.

"I'll try no' to damage ye too severely," Kenneth warned him as he settled into a fighting stance.

The man did the same and nodded. "Same to ye." Then he swung.

Their blades crashed together. Kenneth felt the force all the way into his chest. Aye, he'd picked the right partner.

The fight went on until both were sweating, and Kenneth's arms felt weighted with lead. Both had acquired new bruises, but neither had drawn blood. Even when it started to pour, cold rain sluicing down the back of his neck, he kept on. He needed oblivion, and he hadn't quite reached it yet.

The other man finally cried off. "'Tis coming down so hard, I can hardly see ye. One of us will get hurt in truth."

Kenneth had to agree. "Ye speak rightly. Thank ye. Ye are a good partner. I'll spar with ye any time ye wish, as long as I remain here."

"And I canna guess how long that will be, but I appreciate the offer. Another time, then." The man dropped his sword onto his shoulder, took Kenneth's, and walked off. Kenneth saw him last heading inside, out of the rain.

He should go in, too, before he caught his death. But he wasn't ready. He'd worked out most of the anger and dismay left from his conversation with Cat, but as he climbed the stairs to overlook the angry sea below the castle walls, he realized what was left was his love for her. And he had no idea what to do to root that from his soul.

CHAPTER 7

A fortnight later, after the evening meal, Kenneth settled down in his chamber with the same book he'd been reading when Cat appeared in the library. He hadn't touched it since that day, when he'd carried it to his chamber. Even the sight of it inevitably led to the memory of seeing her standing just inside the library door—and what followed. As he read, he thought about the promises she'd made when they argued, and tried to get his mind off hoping to see her with every visit to town. Today, he'd glimpsed her on the street laughing with another man, ruining what should have been a pleasant afternoon in a pub with Phillippe. The trip hadn't been wasted, though. He'd met yet another Highlander who lived on a farm outside of town. The man had sold his crop in the morning's market and was in the pub before returning home. When Phillippe briefly left them alone, the man had admitted to being aligned with the Lord of the Isles and offered his place if Kenneth wanted to get away from town, saying he could use a man of Kenneth's size to help on the farm. Kenneth had thanked him and Phillippe had returned, ending their discussion. But he would remember what the man told him.

Cat had to be staying away because of the fight they'd had and the lies he'd told. Though at the time he'd wanted to dissuade her from the feelings she seemed to have for him, his words still weighed heavily on his conscience.

Eventually, the words on the page ran together, his worries mixed in until he didn't know what he was reading, and he dozed. He came awake suddenly, not sure what had pulled him from the first rest he'd gotten in days. Then he heard men shouting just as someone pounded on his door.

"A moment," he grumbled and stood. He expected no one and wondered if this was trouble coming his way. His conversations with Phillippe had convinced him he'd get no help there unless and until Phillippe saw some advantage for himself. So far, he'd done nothing. But now the news had come that Domnhall had left Dingwall for Inverness with a large army. Given the trouble such a move portended, Kenneth's wanted to add pressure to his demand for Phillippe's assistance. But he realized doing so might convince Phillippe he would be better served to relate Kenneth's intentions to Father Anselmo. If he did, Kenneth would be thrown in the bottle dungeon and never see daylight again. Unless he could fight his way free. Weaponless, against the castle guards, he had little chance of success.

Someone pounded on his door again. He took a breath and opened it.

"Ah, *bien*, you are here," Phillippe announced and shoved his way inside.

Before he shut the door, Kenneth got a sense of the direction the shouting came from and smelled smoke.

"Why have ye come?"

Phillippe started tossing his paltry belongings onto the cot. "To fulfill my promise to you, *mon ami*. Why else would I come to you at this time? The guards have been drawn to the kitchen side of the castle. Smoke billows from every opening. Buckets of water are being passed hand-to-hand and tossed into the cook's domain." He paused, hands on hips, looking around. "Something has caught fire. "

"Ye came to my chamber to avoid having to help fight the fire?"

"Gather your things and let us go. I have the key to your freedom." He pulled a large brass key on a chain from under his robes and waved it in front of Kenneth's nose. "There is no time to lose. Did you once tell me you wished to take advantage of every moment of darkness? To those guards, staring into the fire, the rest of the castle is as dark as a moonless night. *Alors, tout de suite.* We must go."

Kenneth surveyed what Phillippe had tossed on the bed. "Ye didna bring a weapon with ye, by chance?" He added a few more things, and then tied the lot into one bundle.

"*Non.* Where would I get one of your claymores?"

"A dirk? An eating knife? A rusty blade of any sort?"

"*Pardon,* it slipped my mind in my haste to get here *to help you escape.*"

The opportunity was too good to miss. Kenneth nodded and grabbed an extra plaid off the bed, then gestured for Phillippe to lead the way. The priest opened the door a crack and peered out, then slipped out and down the stairs. On the ground floor, he paused at the door, then stepped out into the courtyard. Kenneth followed and closed the door firmly behind him. Phillippe led him quietly to the nearby postern gate. Kenneth thanked all the saints it lay on the opposite side of the castle from the commotion. Thanks to the fire, it was unguarded.

Phillippe inserted the key into the lock and swore. "It does not turn."

"Let me try." Kenneth pushed him aside and twisted the key. It turned easily. He cut a glance at Phillippe, who watched him with a grin. "Trying to scare me to death, are ye?"

"I thought you might need a little jolt since this escape I am doing for you is going so smoothly."

"Dinna say such a thing!" Kenneth hissed. "'Tis bad fortune. Ye'll bring the guards down on us, for certain. Come on." He pulled open the small servants' doorway and slipped out into the night. Phillippe did not follow.

"Are ye coming?"

Phillippe shook his head. "This is your peril to escape. This time, I am content to remain."

"Do ye think that wise? If someone finds out…"

"They will not. Dark as a moonless night, eh? Go now. Find a place to hide until the Angelus bell. The town gates will open then. Do not come back. We are even. My debt is paid."

Kenneth took a deep breath of the chill night air, redolent with the scent of sea and smoke, then nodded. "Be well, my friend. God be with ye."

Phillippe made the sign of the cross. "And with ye."

Kenneth nodded and turned away, not waiting for Phillippe to lock the gate. He had to find somewhere safe to bide until he could decide where to go and make a plan to get there. Not back to Brodie. Kenneth figured he had an hour, perhaps two, before anyone thought to check on the Highlander hostage. He didn't have long before his absence would be discovered.

❧

AT THE EDGE OF TOWN, KENNETH PAUSED, LISTENING, but heard nothing except the commotion in the castle and the surf rolling below the cliff where the bishop's castle perched, masking any sounds following footsteps might add and making his neck itch. He hated going anywhere in this town in the dark. Not that St. Andrews was truly dark this night. Between the shop fronts and homes in the town, the cathedral, and now the castle, candles glowed in many windows, probably thanks to the fire at the castle. Normally, most of the town's inhabitants would be asleep soon after the sun set. But even after a year in France, being in a town made him uncomfortable. It wasn't just the close quarters and numbers of people. Cutpurses and drunk sailors made walking the street after dark an exercise in caution and alertness.

He'd been on his own before, and Iain had done a thorough job of making sure he could take care of himself since one day when they were wee lads in training. A bigger lad had been intent on bashing in his skull. Iain pulled off the bully, and then made sure Kenneth learned to protect himself. They'd been fast friends until recently. But Kenneth told himself he no longer missed Brodie or the Highlands. *Or Cat.* He would make a future for himself somewhere else.

He hadn't gone far toward the cathedral and the port beyond it, though, before more guards approached on the run for the castle gate. Someone had sent for help.

If the ship Cat had seen was still in port, and if the crew would keep him out of sight on board until it sailed, he would make it. He could blend in with townsfolk and, at first light, get through the fisher gate to the harbor. But if the Highlanders had already left, he'd be stuck roaming the harbor for another ship or a place to hide in the first place any guard would search for him.

Should he strike out across country? With no money, no weapon, and little more than the clothes on his back, it would be a long and dangerous trip. He cursed himself. He'd thought about this eventuality often enough. He should have been better prepared. But seeing Cat Rose had stolen his reason until all he could think about was their last argument, seeing her again, being with her, despite seeing her in the company of another man.

She was still in danger—and he'd added to it by giving her a note for Iain, making her an accessory to an escaped prisoner if they caught her with it.

Instead of continuing toward the harbor, he turned around and went back through town. He ducked into the only place he might find her this time of night and get help—the tailor's shop. Surely among all those bolts of fabric, or behind the curtain where he'd heard a woman's footsteps—Cat's or her cousin's—there would be a place he could go to avoid searchers through the rest of the night.

He'd barely gotten in the door and paused to let his eyes adjust to the deeper darkness when the curtain parted and Cat stepped through, a small lantern in hand.

She stopped short and gasped, then hissed, "What are ye doing here?" She winced as an oath echoed down the stairs behind her. "Abi and her stepfather dinna get along…"

A lass shouted and was answered by man's deep roar in an accent that sounded more Flemish than French.

"Indeed." Kenneth managed to force out one word while he drank in the sight of Cat in her night-rail and robe. Her hair hung loose around her shoulders and down her back. Her feet were bare. He fought back the urge to gather her into his arms and strip the nightclothes from her body. This was not the time to think about all the things he wanted to do to her—and with her.

Cat set the lantern on a table and wrapped her arms around her middle. "What are ye doing here this time of night? And I thought ye had to have an escort when ye left the castle."

"No' this time." He shook his head and let his gaze roam around the shop he'd only seen in daylight. The weak lamplight did little to improve it, not that he cared. He simply meant to keep from devouring Cat with his gaze. "They dinna ken I'm gone. There's a fire in the castle kitchens...I need a place to hide for a few hours until the gates open and I can get out of town unseen." He cut his gaze back to her with a frown. "Ye need to burn that letter I wrote to Iain."

Cat nodded. "Did ye set the fire?"

He wished he'd thought of doing it weeks ago, but such destruction for no reason was not in his nature. "Nay, of course no'."

"Won't ye get Iain in trouble by leaving?"

"Ye havena heard then?"

"Heard what?"

He filled her in on Domnhall of the Isles's latest movements while the argument raged upstairs. "It makes holding me...unnecessary. But that letter links ye to Iain and to me and adds to the danger ye are in here. So ye must destroy it."

Finally silence descended and Cat cocked her head. "I think they're finally worn down."

"Do they argue like that often?" Kenneth moved around the room, seeking someplace he could remain unseen should searchers start to comb the town. He knew Cat watched him when she hesitated before answering his question.

"Every day. Abi wants to marry a lad named Colin. Her stepfather is against it. I dinna ken why Abi is arguing with him. She keeps talking about eloping. First it's tomorrow, then next week. It never happens, though she and Colin might eventually do it, if her da doesna lock her away before then."

He must be making her nervous. Cat rarely spoke so quickly or for so long, He turned back to her and shrugged, dismissing any thought of her cousin's problems. He had plenty of his own. "Is there a place I can stay out of sight for a few hours?" He had to trust her. He knew no one else.

Cat nodded and gestured for him to follow. "The back room. Only Abi's father, the tailor, goes there, and he won't come down here at night. When ye are ready to leave, there's a doorway from there into the alley."

"Convenient."

She paused at the threshold and looked over her shoulder at him, her expression unreadable. "Take me with ye."

Kenneth shook his head, surprised. "I've seen ye with another man. Won't he worry if ye are suddenly gone?"

She frowned. "He's an acquaintance, only." She frowned. "How were ye in town? I didna see ye."

"I earned some favors—never mind. Take the boat ye told me about."

"By myself? Ye keep saying I'm in danger here. I would be safer traveling with ye than on my own."

Her comment made too much sense. But did it because it was true, or because it gave him a chance to spend time alone with Cat? If he couldn't be sure of his own motives, Cat would not be safe with him. He tried an argument he knew she would believe. "If I return to the Highlands, it's because I'm goin' to fight, lass. 'Twill be no place for such as ye."

"There will be no women to help the army? To tend the wounded? Or cook the food?"

He should have known she'd have an answer for

that. "Few of the sort ye should ever be associated with. 'Twill be too dangerous."

"I see. Ye dinna want me."

"Catherine..." A lass's voice rang down the stair. "Where are you?"

Cat glanced up. "I must go," she whispered, then opened the lantern and lit a candle on the tailor's workbench from its candle. "I'll come back if I can."

"Dinna do that. I'll be gone in a few hours."

Suddenly stiff, she reached for him. "I still dinna ken why ye abandoned me. Why ye gave up on us..."

Her fingertips warmed more than his arm. He fought down the need for her surging through him. "And I still dinna ken how ye came to be here, instead of at home. Both tales are too long for this night. Go, or she'll come down here looking for ye." He forced himself not to reach for her in return, though he was dying to pull her into his arms. But that kiss in the library was too fresh in his mind. If he kissed her now, he wouldn't let her go, and they'd be caught. "Go, lass. If I'm found with ye, 'twill no' go well for ye either. I willna have ye harmed on my account."

Cat opened her mouth to speak, then closed it without uttering a sound, turned and moved toward the stairs, picking up a spindle of thread and a needle as she went. "I'm coming, Abi."

Kenneth watched her go with a heavy heart, knowing he might never see her again, and that he was leaving her wounded.

Even after she disappeared, he could hear her telling her cousin she'd gone down for the things she needed to repair a rent in the sleeve of a gown. She would not give him away.

He took the candle and stepped into the back room. It was filled with skeins of wool, trays of buttons, spindles of threads, and more. There was a door, as

Cat had promised. He moved to it and opened it a crack. It led to an alley as she'd described. He closed the door and put his back against it, studying the area around him. If he had to hide, there was barely enough space below a worktable for a man his size, but little else. If someone approached, his best option would be to go out the door to the alley and continue on his way.

Without seeing Cat again.

He need wait only a few hours, until the castle settled down, the town went to sleep, and the guards became less vigilant. He lowered himself to the floor in the corner by the door, blew out the candle, and willed himself to rest as he'd learned to do in France before a battle. The coming journey would be hard.

When he woke, he checked outside. Judging by the predawn stillness, he deemed enough time had passed. The town would stir in another hour at most. The port was too risky. The only other option meant going across country. South, not north toward the firth of Forth as they would expect. South, he might be able to catch a ship. He didn't care where it was bound, even the Highlands. Or back to France. For the near term, travel both north and west were out of the question.

Then he heard someone coming down the stairs, the tread light and careful. Cat? Or Abi? Or someone else who knew he was here.

"'Tis Catherine," she softly said. "Are ye still here?"

He breathed a sigh of relief as he moved quietly to the doorway into the shopfront and met her. She wore a day dress this time, and carried the same lantern. "I told ye no' to come back down here."

"I have news." She walked toward the back of the shop and set down the lantern. "I overheard two men talking as they walked by outside my window. They said they've put out the fire at the castle and declared all's well. They made no mention of a missing man. There's been nay alarm to say ye are gone."

"Are Abi and her stepfather still abed?"

"Aye, he and Abi both are sleeping. I burned yer letter."

She stepped closer. Close enough to fold in his arms, if he dared. He did. She stepped into his embrace without hesitation, and lay her head on his shoulder.

"I couldna rest without telling ye. Ye are safe, at least until the castle rouses. But I wish ye dinna have to go. Or that I could go with ye."

AS SOON AS SHE SPOKE, CATHERINE WISHED HER WORDS away, fearful they would reinforce Kenneth's earlier refusal to take her with him. She did want to go with him, but not home. She had seen enough longing in his gaze, enough hesitation when he tried to convince her he didn't care for her, to make her hope he still did. She had dreamed about returning to Brodie as his wife. His expression didn't give her any encouragement. His brows drew down and his lips compressed as though he was holding back telling her how foolish she was being. How little he desired her—or her company.

"Ye said there was someone else." The words left her lips almost before the thought crossed her mind. "Did ye marry her?"

"Why would ye think that?"

The sudden hint of a grin playing on his lips reminded her of the Kenneth she fell in love with—and it made her angry. He thought her broken heart amusing? "Ye ken what I mean. Ye lay with her. Ye might have married her." She stepped back and crossed her arms. Kenneth's expression smoothed, then he frowned, and the crease between his brows grew fiercer as she put some distance between them.

"Nay, I didna marry, though I could have."

Catherine's heart dropped into her belly. "Ye loved her?"

"I thought I did. I was wrong."

Relief flooded her and made her reach for support to the nearest cabinet. The wood was dented and battered under her fingertips, much like her emotions at the moment.

"That's why ye were gone so long, aye?"

He frowned and nodded.

"Did ye ever love me?" She forced out the words, needing the answer though she didn't want it, not really. Not if his answer was nay.

"Did I ever love ye? Why are ye no' asking what ye really wish to ken?"

She swallowed hard. "What is that?"

"Whether I love ye still."

Catherine clung to the cabinet top, the knuckles of her hand as pale as bleached muslin. "Apparently ye dinna, or ye would have sought me out before now. And ye would no' have avoided me when ye found me here."

Kenneth scrubbed a hand over his face. "Ye are wrong, lass. When I heard ye were to be married, I loved ye enough to do what was best for ye and stay away."

"Best for me?" Catherine's pulse raced. How dare he assume he'd sacrificed what they'd shared—sacrificed her—for her own good? "Ye had nay idea what was best for me then. Ye still dinna ken."

"Wrong again." He reached out and smoothed a lock of hair from her shoulder.

His touch made Catherine want to crumple at his feet and beg him to keep her with him always. Perhaps she was being as foolish now as he had been then. Yet she vowed she could love him enough for both of them. He could grow to love her again as he had then, not just care for her or want her or want to protect her. "Am I wrong? Why did ye no' come to me once ye kenned I was here?"

"And put ye at risk?" His mouth softened. "I couldna let ye come to harm." He crossed his arms. "And now I have refused the bishop's hospitality, I'm even more of a danger to ye. Yet, ye could be in peril on yer own, if ye are known here as a Highlander."

"What if I am?" Ice slid down Catherine's spine. Despite Cam's warnings, she'd never seriously considered she, too, might be in danger. She'd made the journey here safely. She had a safe place to stay. Or did she? Both Cam and Kenneth thought St. Andrews would not remain safe for long.

"Trouble is coming. If it goes badly for Highlanders, ye could be made a prisoner, too."

"A prisoner!"

He glanced around the shop as if seeking answers on the shelves, then took her hands in his.

"Damn it, I dinna want to do this, but ye must come with me."

Catherine's heart soared, then crashed again. His touch felt so familiar, so good, she knew she had not imagined that the bond between them still existed. Yet he didn't want her with him. He only felt obligated to see to her safety. And what would Abi and her father think if she suddenly disappeared? There was the excuse she needed to stay right here if Kenneth did not want her enough to marry her. "I canna go with ye. My cousin will worry."

"She will worry more when Albany's men come for ye."

The image that formed in her mind froze her breath

in her chest as she recalled what Cam had told her about a Highlander being arrested at the harbor. "Ye canna be serious." Yet his gaze had hardened, drawing his brows down into a forbidding line.

"I am, Cat. I've never been more serious."

Cat, she thought drily. She was still a wee lass to him. Hence his fierce expression, so like her father's when he chastised her. "Catherine," she reminded him with force, determined to make him see her as a woman grown.

He ignored her warning. "I willna leave ye to be harmed, no' if there's a chance I can keep ye safe."

"Ye left me before."

"Ye were in nay danger."

"That's what ye think. Da wouldha married me off to—"

He tugged on her hands, stopping her complaint. "We've nay time for this, lass. We need to be ready to go through the town gate with the Angelus bell."

Still reluctant, she offered another excuse. "I should leave Abi a note."

"Nay, ye canna." Kenneth went to the back door and glanced outside, then closed it softly. "Nary a soul is stirring. Is there a woman's cloak in the shop? Ye need more than yer shift and a thin dress." He glanced at the soft slippers peeking out below the hem of her dress. "And ye need yer boots."

"Mine are upstairs."

Kenneth clenched his fists, then nodded. "Get them. Be silent. If ye wake yer kin, ye'll no' be able to explain what ye are about."

Catherine hesitated. This was not the way she'd imagined her dream of being with Kenneth coming true. Somehow, it didn't feel dreamlike at all.

"Go on with ye," he growled, gesturing with the

candle toward the front of the shop. "We canna delay much longer."

Catherine nodded and moved silently away. She couldn't believe they were about to go on the run. She grumbled to herself as she dug through the belongings she had with her for the sturdy travel dress she'd worn on the way here. This was not the sort of reunion she'd spent the last two years imagining. Kenneth was practically kidnapping her—with her reluctant cooperation. She found the dress she sought and decided it would be wise to wear it over the one she had on. The heavy fabric slid over her head and settled on her shoulders along with the weight of her decision to go with Kenneth. She'd come here alone, running from her father. By chance, she'd found the man she loved, but they were going to run from the crown, possibly back to her father. Could her life get any worse?

It could, she supposed, if something happened to Kenneth before they got back to Brodie. But somehow she knew this new Kenneth, so different from the easy-going lad of two years ago, could handle any challenge they faced. He would protect her. Yet, she missed the light-hearted lad he'd been. Where was the Kenneth she had fallen in love with?

She belted the dress and bent to retrieve her boots. She dared not don them until she made her way—silently—downstairs. She slung her cloak around her shoulders and grabbed the bundle of belongings she didn't want to leave behind, then minced in her stocking feet to the pantry and added dried fish, bread and cheese. Certainly, they would need something to eat.

Would they sail home? Since no one seemed to be looking for Kenneth yet, surely making their way to the harbor would be the quickest way to leave St. Andrews.

In which case, they wouldn't need the provisions. She almost put them back, hating to steal food from Abi and her father, but practicality won. She didn't know what Kenneth planned. She didn't want to starve.

Should she leave a note? Kenneth seemed to think doing so would be dangerous, but she knew how Abi would fret, and with her marriage to Colin in shambles, Abi would be upset enough already without adding Catherine's disappearance to her worries. She was running out of time. Abi's stepfather would be up before the sun to open his shop to early customers. Abi would sleep later and only take her stepfather something to break his fast after he'd been at work for hours.

Sentiment won over practicality. She found a scrap of parchment, then wrote only that she was well and not to worry. She'd contact Abi when she could. The note would be safe anywhere in the kitchen, since Abi and she were the only ones who came in here. Abi had once remarked, without her, her father would starve unless someone took him in. Catherine counted on his habit to keep her safe for enough hours to get away. She hoped it would not cause problems.

She wanted Kenneth to see her as an adult. She, too, had to put away her childish notions—all of them. Kenneth might not want to take her with him, but he loved her enough to take the risks he felt required to keep her safe. Love was not something made out of pretty flowers and ribbons and poems. True love was made of this kind of devotion. Of sacrifice. Protection. He did love her. He just didn't know it yet.

WHILE CAT WAS UPSTAIRS, KENNETH SEARCHED THE shop, looking for a weapon. A broadsword would be too much to hope for, but even a dirk would do. The tailor had a pair of good, sharp shears hanging on a peg above his worktable, but only one. Kenneth would not stoop to taking them, stealing the man's livelihood in the process. Finally, he found a dirk in a dark leather sheath on a shelf in the shop's back corner. Judging by the other things there, this was where the tailor saved items his customers accidentally left behind. Kenneth tucked the dirk through his belt and felt better for being at least minimally armed.

He turned back to the stairway, anticipating Cat coming down at any moment. At least Cat seemed to understand her peril and was cooperating. Yet, what if she wasn't? What if she was sitting upstairs, knowing he could not call out her name, or risk going up there. If he woke the tailor—nay, she was smarter than that. She had to go with him.

He had dreamed of having her back in his life and wanted her with him, but not like this. Not on the road, and not in danger. Still, he had no choice. They had no choice, not since Domnhall decided to march on Inverness. Damn the man. Clan Ross had already caused trouble for Brodie. Now Domnhall had made things many times worse; igniting all of the northwestern Highlands.

After hearing Cat had been betrothed, Kenneth never intended to go back to Rose to face Cat's father. But he'd never expected to see her again, either. He'd thought she'd married and, by now, had children to care for. He expected she'd forgotten him and settled into a new life with another man. Fate played cruel tricks on mortal men—and women. He didn't yet know if bringing them back together counted as such.

Nor had he planned on returning to Brodie. He'd intended to go anywhere but there. Yet, because Cat was also in danger, he would do his duty to her and get her home. At the moment, he had no idea what he'd do after he returned her to her father. He could only deal with one problem of such magnitude at a time.

Kenneth knew he was the last person Cat should trust, and that truth tore at him. Yet, she did. Her trust warmed him, a feeling he could scarce afford. He had to keep his emotions out of this and get them both to safety. Maybe then, he and Cat could find a way back to the love they'd once thought they shared. The love he'd thought her father had forced her to betray—only to find out she hadn't. The love he *had* betrayed with a woman who could not measure up to Cat in any way. With the advantage of hindsight, he couldn't understand why he'd fallen for Marilee. He'd been lonely, he supposed. And angry with Cat's father, even with Iain. But none of what he'd felt excused the way he'd hurt Cat.

He'd owe her even more if they escaped. The castle guards would be looking for him, but alone. With Cat on his arm, he'd appear to be a townsman, leaving with his wife. He spotted a folded cloak he'd missed before, the same color as the pile of fabric on which it lay. When he shook it out, a hood fell down its back. Perfect. It would cover his head. If he stooped, he'd appear shorter, perhaps older. The gatekeeper would not know his face, and if a castle guard loitered at the gate, looking for him, they'd never suspect a man and woman leaving together.

CHAPTER 8

When they finally left Cat's uncle's shop, Kenneth was displeased to find guards searching the town, for him or someone else, he didn't know, and he wasn't about to inquire. Pairs of armed men patrolled the main streets, a few even walked the side streets and narrow closes. His head covered and his posture slumped, he herded Cat carefully from garden to alley, from one possible place of concealment to another, holding his breath as each patrol passed them by without comment. Cat stayed quiet, her face hidden by her hood and kept walking as if nothing were amiss.

"Why are we going away from the port?" she whispered during one pause. "If a Highland ship is docked there, they can take us home."

"And if there are none, we'll be caught in the port. We're better off to make our way cross-country out of one of the south gates."

"Why?" She grabbed his arm as he started to move, stopping him. "We can go to the harbor. Then I can come back and tell a patrol I saw a lone man headed to the south. I can delay them long enough, ye should have time to get away on any ship in the harbor." She paused, then added, softly, "Without me."

Tempting as a chance to sail home was, he knew she was wrong. He recognized her sacrifice for what it was, too—she was giving up yet again on the two of them. Risking the future she'd hoped for, with the two of them, together. And walking about town, a woman alone out on the street this time of early morning? No way would he allow her to take that risk. He rubbed a hand over his aching chest, sadness making each breath feel heavy and bitter. If she let him leave her, she could not know if she would ever see him again. He couldn't take the chance. And he wouldn't let Cat sacrifice herself for him. Just the opposite—it was his place to sacrifice for her.

The guards would keep looking. Even if they had her in irons, they'd still look for him. Anselmo would not willingly let a man in his charge go free. And who knew what the crew of any of those boats would do? Protect him? Or turn him in, hoping for some reward of coin or favorable future treatment from the town's constable?

"Nay, lass. They willna stop, and they will search the ships in the harbor. We must go another way, and I have an idea, but it means we have a long walk ahead of us."

"Have ye forgotten? I'm a Highland lass. I'll keep up with ye."

At least she'd accepted they would keep moving. As long as she didn't try to head off on her own, he'd get them away.

Though they reached the gate later than Kenneth had anticipated, their exit went as smoothly as he'd hoped. No one blocked their way out of the gate, though they had to thread through a line of farmers and craftsmen with loaded wagons and carts, each waiting to pay a small share of their goods as a toll to enter within the town walls. Once inside, they would make their way to the mercat cross in the square, where Kenneth had seen their like before.

Hours later, after walking all day, exhausted by moving carefully out of town, hiding when they heard anyone approach, and making a final dash across an open farm field, they reached the tiny croft the owner, Craig Grant, had described to him briefly during one foray to a pub in town with Phillippe. He'd claimed to be loyal to the Isles, though living on the opposite side of Scotland, and had gone on to give Kenneth his home's location while Phillippe was out of earshot. Kenneth could think of many reasons not to trust the man, but Cat needed rest and he needed to know if word was spreading about his escape, or if anyone yet knew Cat was missing.

"There's another Highlander here," Craig told him as he ushered them into his cottage, Cat in the lead.

"Cam! What are ye doing here?"

Cat's exclamation startled Kenneth into stiffening and putting a hand on the hilt of his stolen dirk.

"Ah, Lady Mary Catherine, fortune is smiling upon me indeed." A man rose from his seat by the fire and sketched a bow to her. "I quit town as soon as the gates opened this morn."

"Ye ken this man?" Kenneth demanded, then looked again. Catherine had been with this man the day he'd spotted her in town. Kenneth's hackles rose.

Cat nodded. "Kenneth Brodie, this is Cameron Sutherland, a friend of my cousin Abi's."

"Yers as well, sweet Cat," Sutherland interjected. "After the confidences we've shared?" He cast a glance in Kenneth's direction.

Cat narrowed her eyes.

Kenneth stiffened at the man's familiarity with Cat. He held his posture as Sutherland turned to him.

Sutherland nodded. "Brodie, eh? Ye are a long way from home."

"Sutherland lies even farther away," Kenneth answered smoothly.

Sutherland laughed and inclined his head.

Cat's frowning gaze traveled from him to Kenneth and back again. Surely she was aware they were taking each other's measure.

"And St. Andrews is no longer hospitable to men—or women—like us." Sutherland continued. "'Tis a shame."

"It seems to be so, aye," Kenneth replied.

"How do ye plan to get home, then? Surely ye dinna mean to make Lady Catherine walk the entire way."

Kenneth waved a hand back toward town, now probably eight miles behind them. They would have arrived here sooner if not for needing to hide and wait. "St. Andrews' harbor is out of the question."

Sutherland nodded. "Prudent. But 'tis no' the only port along the coast."

Kenneth leaned against the door. "Chancy at best. Any ship we encounter might be against us. Better to stay out of sight cross-country."

"Or to walk a short distance, then sail the rest of the way. Albany doesna control the seas. Highlanders sail there. As do ships from France and Flanders, and others..."

Others, indeed. Could Sutherland know of a smuggler's cove nearby? "What do ye have in mind?"

Craig interrupted long enough to get them seated and drinking a mug of ale. "Ye canna plan with naught between yer ribs. The stew will be ready soon."

"Thank ye for your hospitality," Cat offered as she

settled back into a wooden chair by a small table and sipped her ale. "Ye canna ken how welcome it is."

Kenneth hid a grin when the man colored at Cat's praise.

"'Tis little enough," Craig answered. "Now make yer plans while I see to supper."

"Eager to see us gone, are ye?" Sutherland taunted.

Craig snorted and moved to the hearth where a cast iron pot hung on a hook. "We may be in the Lowlands, but I have no' forgotten what true Highland hospitality means."

When they first entered, in the surprise of Cat greeting a strange man, Kenneth hadn't noticed the appetizing aroma filling the croft. But he did now, and his stomach grumbled its impatience. "So, Sutherland, what *do* ye have in mind?"

"The shipment I've awaited in St. Andrews is late," he began, cradling his cup between his hands and frowning at the liquid in it. "Likely, we could catch it up the coast at Montrose." He raised his head and looked Kenneth in the eye. "Failing that, there's always shipping headed for the Highlands from Aberdeen. Sailing will be a damn sight easier—and closer—than making our way through the mountains. If an army is marching east, we'd have a hard time avoiding it going overland."

Kenneth raised a hand. "Except for having to cross the Tay and pass near Dundee. The port there will be crawling with Lowlander troops. Only a few trails run through the mountains an army might take. Many more can be used by a handful of men—or women."

"Can we ride?" Cat's voice broke into the tension growing between the two men. "'Twould be faster."

"Aye, but we have little coin and a long way to travel," Kenneth told her. He had none and doubted Cat had much. Sutherland might—or might not.

"So we'll go up the coast and hope for a friendly ship to pass by," Sutherland said.

His grin made the trip sound like a lark instead of a deadly serious flight from danger.

"Have ye forgotten the difficulty of getting by the Warden's *cateran* army that's probably gathering at Perth?" Kenneth reminded him. "Unless ye mean to take a boat built only to cross the Tay and row it out into the northern sea."

"Nay." Sutherland shook his head. "I am no' addled enough to tempt fate so much."

Kenneth nodded. "Glad to hear it."

CATHERINE SHIVERED AS SHE CROSSED THE SMALL YARD from Craig's croft to the barn. They were still close to the coast, so the day's warmth had given way to a damp chill. Their host gave each of them a blanket so they could bed down for the night in the empty barn. The livestock was out to pasture for the summer. Craig offered to allow Catherine to sleep in the croft, but Kenneth refused to let her be separated from him.

She suspected he didn't trust their host far enough to leave her alone with him.

In the barn, Cam gave her a wink and a tilt of his head, whether in invitation or merely a silent good night, Catherine didn't know, but given he must think Kenneth was her husband, it had to be the latter. The thought of an invitation made her uncomfortable. In the few times she'd met Cam and spoken with him, she'd come to revise her initial opinion of him. She liked him well enough. But, she stayed by Kenneth, making it clear she would pass the night near him, if not with him. When Cam took himself off toward an opposite stall without further comment, Catherine sighed in relief. Not an invitation.

She gave Kenneth a sidelong glance. He was busy watching Cam walk away, his expression unreadable. Catherine pursed her lips, suddenly glad they'd run into Cam. If his presence made Kenneth jealous, so much the better.

She stepped into the nearest stall to decide how to array their blankets. Would Kenneth insist on sleeping separately in the hay, or agree to use one blanket underneath them and sleep together with their other on top? Though the idea made her nervous, Catherine could see the sense. If only Kenneth would cooperate. They'd be warmer and have a layer between them and the hay, which was none too clean and smelled faintly of mold.

He laid his blanket over a railing and went outside, so she didn't wait for him. She grabbed his and spread the lighter of the two on the cleanest area she could find, then stretched out and covered herself with the heavier blanket. She lay there, heart pounding, waiting for his return.

What would he do? The lad she'd known was gone. In his place was a man who had seen and done things she could not imagine and probably did not want to know. So how would he treat a lass he once felt affection for when given the chance to share blankets? Should she worry for her virtue? Did she care?

Nay, this was Kenneth. No matter what changes the years had wrought in him, she couldn't fear him. Besides, Cam lay only a few stalls away.

She could dream of getting back what they'd shared, aye, but she could also do something about it. What they'd once had was worth trying for again. She would be his shadow, always next to him, always visible, never out of his mind, until, perhaps, he recalled what he once felt for her, and perhaps started to feel it again.

Kenneth came in then and paused at the stall door. He laid a hand on the railing at his side. As a man waiting for a lass to invite him to her bed, he looked more patient than she expected he felt.

She spoke softly to keep Cam from hearing her. "Is this acceptable to ye?" She lifted up onto her elbows. "We'll be warmer together than apart." She reached for the far corner of the blanket and pulled it back. "'Tis roomy enough for both of us."

He didn't move for a long moment, then shrugged, pulled aside the blanket and stretched out on his back, all without uttering a word.

Lying next to the edge, he couldn't be farther away unless he moved off the blanket and slept in the straw. Catherine wanted to groan. After a moment, he rested his head on his hands, elbows out, and crossed one ankle over the other. What would he do if she laid her head in the crook of his shoulder and used his arm for a pillow? Such simple closeness was innocent enough, but where would it lead?

At long last, they were together. For the moment, at least. She should be satisfied, but knew being with him was only temporary. Only for as long as they traveled together, and until he found somewhere he deemed safe enough to leave her. She didn't yet have the answers she craved, but if they stayed together long enough, those words would come. Eventually, he would tell her what he truly felt for her, and why he'd gone to France even after her betrothal had been cancelled.

Would she scare him off if she moved closer?

He took the decision away by turning his back to her and pulling the blanket he'd pushed aside to cover him. His intent couldn't be more clear.

"Go to sleep, Cat."

His words left no room for doubt, but his voice, as soft and intimate as their surroundings, tempted her to snuggle closer and drape her arm across his narrow waist. She imagined her bent arm would put her hand just over his beating heart. If she pressed her cheek to his back, she'd hear it as well as feel it under her hand. Would it be strong and low, a slow and measured beat? Or fast, betraying feelings he hid from her? She wanted to know. Anger at him still made her want to cry, but the urge to touch him was strong. Yet, if she did, he might leave her, thinking to protect her from himself. She didn't want to lose him, not when he lay so close. She wanted him near. Needed him near, his scent in her nose, his heat warming her, even if from inches away. And after two years, she wouldn't let him go.

KENNETH WAS GOING TO LOSE HIS MIND BEFORE HE GOT Cat somewhere safe—safe from marauding armies and safe from him. Sleeping with her for only one night had tried him beyond his limits. Waking with her lush, round bottom snuggled against his thighs had hardened him in an instant. He'd rolled away to keep from prodding her awake with the evidence of his need for her. He didn't want her to know how much he still wanted her. How being with her was sweet torture. How sleeping next to her, even in their rough camp, was heaven on earth. And how feeling her body pressed to his nearly made him come.

If he was a less honorable man, he would conclude if she wanted to play at being married, he should be able to play, too—and claim a husband's rights. Did she insist on sharing their blankets because she wanted him to?

He had to leave her someplace safe. She was too

much of a temptation. Many more days—and nights—like this one and he'd be as much of a danger to her virtue as any army they might encounter would be to her life.

Arguing with her got his blood up. Sleeping with her aroused him even more—nearly past his control. What he wanted would be natural and right if they married and stayed together, but he intended to leave, or to join the fight. What if something happened to him? He would not leave her with a child to raise without him. Nay, he had to find a safe haven for her.

He got up and slipped away, leaving her to rest while he talked to Craig and got some food to break their fast. Their host was already up and headed for the barn when Kenneth stepped outside.

"I was on the way to tell ye to get moving," he announced without preamble. "A ghillie just brought word they're rounding up Highlanders in town. It's getting ugly. A priest believed to be a Highland sympathizer was hanged."

Kenneth tensed. "Do ye ken who it was?"

"A Frenchman, I believe."

Kenneth's heart sank. Phillippe was the only French priest he knew within the walls of the St. Andrews castle. Someone must have seen him let Kenneth out of the servants door, and reported him. In the end, he'd done the right thing and paid his debt to Kenneth—and been killed for it.

Kenneth eyed Cat through the open door. She still slept the sleep of the innocent, wrapped in a borrowed blanket. He was loathe to wake her—or Cameron Sutherland—but this news demanded action. Now, after this tale of horror, would she believe him?

"'Twill no' be long before they search beyond the town's borders," Craig continued, then nodded to

Sutherland who came out yawning and rubbing the rough stubble darkening his face. "What news?"

"None good," Kenneth told him.

Craig handed Kenneth a cloth-wrapped bundle. "Here's food for the road. Ye'd best wake yer wife and go now."

Sutherland cut a wide-eyed glance at Kenneth, then took a similar parcel from Craig.

Cat, still blinking sleep from her eyes, came out before Kenneth had a chance to correct Craig.

"Good morrow to ye, Lady Catherine" Craig greeted her. "I just told yer husband the unhappy news about events in town. I hope ye are ready to travel."

Kenneth winced at the look of confusion on her face, but decided the fiction of their marriage might be one more layer of protection for Cat.

"I…we are no'…"

"Quite ready to go," Kenneth interjected. If Craig thought she was his wife, anyone he told about their visit would accept the fiction and assume they were after the wrong man. If Sutherland believed the same, it might serve to curb the flirting he favored Cat with. "But we thank ye for the food. We'll leave in moments."

"Good enough, then," Craig said and turned away.

With narrowed eyes, Kenneth watched him walk back to his cottage. Why hadn't he heard this runner? Even a man on foot should have awakened him. A horse definitely would have.

"Do what ye must, but quickly," Kenneth warned Cat.

Cat nodded and returned to the barn.

Then he turned a frown on Sutherland. "Something's amiss." At Sutherland's quizzical expression, he continued, "Did ye hear a runner arrive in the last hour?"

"Nay, but I only awoke a little while ago."

"I heard naught, and I should have." Kenneth clenched a fist.

Sutherland shrugged. "Mayhap ye slept too deeply after a night next to yer wife…" He trailed off at Kenneth's frown. "Or mayhap now the sun is up, our friend only wants to be rid of us quickly in fear of searchers coming this way."

"Then the sooner we leave, the better. Gather yer things."

Sutherland nodded and returned to the barn.

Cat and Sutherland came out together moments later.

Cat had her small parcel of food and keepsakes. The blankets they'd used draped over her arm. "What should we do with these?"

"Leave them. If we're caught, they could connect us to Craig. I dinna wish to repay his hospitality in so dangerous a fashion." He glanced at Sutherland, whose gaze scanned the countryside around them. Kenneth presumed he was watching for trouble. Then he looked back to Cat. "Are ye ready to go?"

"Aye, if we must." She laid the blankets on a pile of hay just inside the barn, then glanced around. "'Tis quiet. What…"

"I dinna ken." Kenneth took her arm. The sooner they put some distance behind them, the sooner the back of his neck would stop prickling. They left. Cat moved beside him across Craig's open field into the adjacent forest as quickly and as quietly as he'd ever known a lass to move. She must feel the same sense of disquiet. They dodged thorny bushes and ducked tree limbs, the forest loam beneath their feet muffling the sound of their footfalls. Sutherland kept pace just behind them. Kenneth glanced back. Aye, watching their back trail. Having him along could be useful.

A low rumble sounded far behind them, startling Cat into a run.

Kenneth caught up with her and grabbed her arm, halting her. "*Wheesht*," he cautioned, then stood still for a moment, listening. "Riders, arriving at Craig's croft. Despite my misgivings, he did us a great service, getting us gone so quickly."

Sutherland rose from his crouch behind some bracken and gestured onward. "We're deep enough in these woods, they willna see us from the croft. I suggest we dinna delay any longer."

Kenneth took Cat's arm and kept moving, quickly, but carefully. They'd hear horses long before riders could spot them in these woods.

"He'll no' send them after us, will he, after warning us away?"

Cat's fearful tone and widened eyes prompted him to reassure her. "I dinna think so, but we'd best no' tarry."

Cat nodded and picked up the pace.

Kenneth kept them moving quickly southwest for another hour. Sutherland made no comment, though that direction took them away from the coast and the ship he hoped to meet. They heard no more horses. Craig must have seen the direction they took when they left and sent the riders another way. Finally, Kenneth called a halt at a burn to let them rest and catch their breath.

CHAPTER 9

By the time they stopped for a brief rest, Catherine was already tired of traveling. They'd been on the run for only a day, a night in Craig's barn, and half of another day—not so very long. Sailing would certainly have been easier than walking, but the harbor at St. Andrews was now only a fond memory—out of reach.

Her feet hurt, and to distract herself, she thought about how she'd sailed into St. Andrews in the company and care of a friend of Mary's on his ship. Catherine would forever be grateful her sister had taken pity on her and arranged passage without their father's knowledge.

Without Mary's help, she wouldn't be sharing a fallen log seat with the only man she'd ever loved. She tossed a stick she found on the ground by her feet. As mad as she was with Kenneth over his pig-headed idea of what was best for her, her horror at the thought of him dangling at the end of a rope like the priest they'd heard about showed her she still loved him. She wanted to do whatever it took to get him to safety, even if it meant walking all the way to Brodie. Or even home to Rose, though that was the last place she wanted to go.

All too soon, they moved on. The hours dragged by in silence, the trees they passed between seeming to swallow any sound their boots made. Near dark, Kenneth again called a halt. They set up a rough camp around a small fire built in a hollow that would hide the fire's glow. Kenneth and Catherine gathered deadfall to feed the flames through the night while Cam hunted something for their supper. They still had the provisions she'd taken from Abi's kitchen and most of what Craig had provided. But they would live off the land as much as they could and hoard those supplies in case they found no friendly stopping places along the way.

Cam returned with two rabbits. He cleaned them quickly and skewered them on sticks to roast. While their supper cooked, they debated which way to go to return to the Highlands.

"Turning north to take the ferry at Portincragge across the Tay to Dundee makes the most sense," Cam argued. "Wool merchants there have a thriving export trade. Failing that, we could blend in with other pilgrims going to the wee harbor at Arbroath, bound for the abbey, where we might also find a friendly ship. Or south to Crail. We'd easily blend in with their market day and find a ship in the harbor there."

Kenneth pulled out his dirk and started drawing a map in the dark soil next to their fire. "Going quietly overland is best," he insisted, pointing to towns he marked with X's. "So long as we avoid coming too close to Perth and the Earl's army."

They argued routes for a while, then Kenneth added a complication. "I think 'tis best to leave ye somewhere," he said to Catherine. "The convent said to be located at Crail would do if we couldn't find another place we considered safe. Another lies farther south near Kilconquhar, if we have no luck in Crail."

Catherine gasped in outrage. "Ye—we—will do nay such thing! I am no' chattel to be abandoned…"

"I am no' talking about abandoning ye, lass. I'm trying to keep ye safe."

"And forgotten in some abbey," she snarled and clenched her fists. "Though I suppose 'tis better than being married to a stranger my da chooses for me. What is it about men that makes ye think ye can do what ye like with a woman?"

Cam grinned, but wisely remained silent.

Catherine narrowed her eyes at him anyway.

"The sooner ye are settled, the happier I'll be," Kenneth continued. "I should try to return to Brodie, and Sutherland to his clan. If—when—we encounter one of the armies, ye'll be out of harm's way."

Cam nodded. "I fear we canna get across country and avoid Domnhall's forces. 'Tis why I think it best to remain near the coast."

Cat chafed as their discussion dragged on into the night. After one argument about their destination that went on for much too long, Catherine made the mistake of wondering aloud if they'd be safer traveling with an army rather than avoiding one.

"I canna protect ye from so many men at once," Kenneth spat, then glanced at Cam and quickly away.

Catherine held her breath and kept her gaze away from Cam. Would he take offense at the implication Kenneth also had to protect her from him? But while Kenneth fumed, Cam wisely refrained from commenting, and Kenneth didn't do anything to make the implied insult more direct.

Catherine was beginning to think their years of separation had been a good thing. If she and Kenneth had married when they were so young, they would not have discovered until too late they would fight like this. Yet she couldn't think of anyone she wanted protecting her—from Domnhall's army or the Duke's—than Kenneth Brodie.

"How many days and nights are we going to go on like this?" she finally asked, risking another explosion. They all knew the farther they went overland into the Highland mountains, the more difficult their journey would become.

After a tense pause, he told her, "Ye should be grateful 'tis summer," and narrowed his eyes as if daring her to say more.

Catherine supposed he'd delayed while he wrestled with how to answer. His mood had darkened with every step they took.

"We could be up to our arses in snow," he added with a sigh, tossing a bone into the fire.

"Instead of being eaten alive by these damn midges, ye mean?" she complained, then immediately felt guilty. Kenneth was doing what he thought best for both of them—for all of them. It wasn't his fault they were in this mess. Or was it? If only they'd gone straight to the port. They could have been sailing home in comfort and arriving so much sooner.

Yet Catherine was horrified by what Craig told them had happened to the priest. Kenneth refused to discuss whether he'd met the man in the bishop's castle, except to remind her she was well served to be away from St. Andrews. She could only hope Abi and her father were unmolested by the violence breaking out there. Violence could spread out of control, and when it did, it affected the innocent. The only safety she could imagine lay behind Rose's walls. Or if all went well, in Kenneth's arms. She sucked in a breath, then forced herself to relax. Nay, she had to stop imagining a future like that, especially if they kept arguing as they done since before they left St. Andrews.

"Where are we?" Catherine asked as she leaned her back against a broad oak tree and thought about removing her boots and soaking her feet in a tub of warm water. The fantasy provided little comfort from her aches and pains.

"Away from St. Andrews in a direction they won't expect, I hope," Kenneth said. "We'll keep going 'till midday tomorrow. By then we may have enough distance from town to safely turn northward. 'Tis no' so far for a man on horseback, but if fortune is with us, 'twill be enough for us to go on in safety."

Sutherland leaned into the elbow he'd placed on a raised knee and nodded. "If we turn northward, the Tay narrows well east of Perth. We should be able to cross and stay away from Perth to avoid Mar's men. Or, as ye suggested, we could turn south to Crail."

"Perhaps once across, we can find some horses," Catherine added, ignoring the comment about Crail. If Kenneth thought he could leave her there with nuns, she would go north by herself instead.

He and Cam hadn't complained about how far they'd walked, but Catherine suspected their feet were no happier about their hurried journey than hers. Yet she knew they had no coin for mounts. Unless Sutherland did. Kenneth had the clothes on his back and the blade he'd taken from Abi's stepfather's shop, the one he'd used to sketch a map near the fire. She was no better off.

"I have…an associate…above the Tay who might be persuaded to lend mounts," Cam suddenly offered. "And coin enough to pay for passage, no matter the ship."

Cat perked up. They would be better off riding than marching across country, even if their journey eventually brought them to a port and a ship as

Sutherland expected. She could hope for such good fortune.

"But we must be prepared to walk as far as Aberdeen," Kenneth advised, his bad mood evident yet again, "living off the land and sleeping on the cold ground if we dinna find a crofter or an isolated bothy to shelter us."

Catherine slanted Kenneth a frown, though to be fair, he was only being realistic. She regretted leaving Craig's blankets behind, but she understood why Kenneth would not endanger a man who'd helped them.

THE NEXT DAY, BY CHANCE, THEY FELL IN WITH A GROUP of pilgrims headed for the ferry at Portincragge that would take them north across the Tay.

"I've enough coin for our passage," Cam admitted in a low voice.

Kenneth shrugged and agreed.

The opportunity to travel with others pleased Catherine. It took them north, away from the abbeys Kenneth had mentioned, though the pilgrims' path meant they'd double back toward St. Andrews for a few miles. Cam seemed cheered to be headed for the coast. There was a chance they might catch another ship at Arbroath where the ferry stopped. She hoped they'd find a way to sail from there to Inverness and avoid the trip through the mountains Kenneth favored. If they didn't find another ship, at least from Arbroath, they'd start their trek above the Tay.

The pilgrims avoided towns, which suited her because it lessened the chance they would be seen and recognized as they circled around and passed within a few miles of St. Andrews. Their greatest peril would be at the ferry. If it was guarded and they were recognized, they'd stand little chance.

They reached it more quickly than Catherine thought possible, and thankfully, boarded without incident. She was sad to leave St. Andrews behind, and hoped Abi had found her note and was reassured. She'd write to her cousin again once she reached home.

Taking the ferry north allowed them to avoid Dundee and any royalist soldiers who might be billeted there. After arriving, they discovered no ships were due in at Arbroath over the next few days.

"Even the smugglers are hanging off the coast, waiting for the outcome of the impending battle," Cam complained as they walked away. "The nearby countryside is in too much of an uproar to risk their cargoes. We'll keep heading north. No' far from here, I ken a man who may help us."

While Cam's gaze was on their path, Kenneth glanced at him and frowned. "How do ye ken what smugglers are likely to be doing?"

Cam eyed him and grinned. "There's more to being a merchant's factor than dealing with ships sailing under royal seal, ye ken. Sometimes the best merchandise and the best prices can be had from...others."

"Merchant's factor, aye? Why do I doubt that's what ye are?"

Cam shrugged. "I canna help what ye believe or no'. Just believe me when I tell ye we've more walking to do before we get to where I hope to borrow horses."

"Borrow?"

"Aye. A man up the coast there," Cam said, pointing ahead of them, "owes me a favor. And *dinna fash*, I'll return his mounts—eventually."

True to his word, Cam took them to someone he'd dealt with in the past. To Catherine, the man looked like any other farmer or fisherman living along the coast, but his stable was big enough to hold a dozen horses, maybe more. She wondered what Cam could have done for him that he would loan them three good mounts. There was much more to Cam Sutherland than he'd told her or Kenneth. Yet, the farther they traveled with him, the more glimpses of his secrets they got. The man took Cam inside the stable. Kenneth took up a position leaning against the doorway. Catherine stayed outside. Kenneth appeared to be listening with great interest to Cam's conversation with the man. He could tell her later what they said.

Leaving the men to their talk, she walked away and went to the cliff overlooking the ocean. The wind in her face carried the tang of brine. Below her lay a perfect semi-circle of pebbles and sand. A lovely hidden cove, guarded on both sides by high bluffs, with a nicely slanted path down to the beach that started not far from where she stood. A pirate cove, indeed. She stood for a few minutes, enjoying the wind and imagining men jumping into the surf, pulling long boats above the tide line and offloading kegs and barrels, all under the cover of night. She glanced back at the stable, suddenly aware of another use for all those mounts. Cam's acquaintance could be running a way station for smugglers and pirates. How did Cam know this man?

She turned and walked back toward the stable, wondering what else it hid. Very likely more than horses. Kenneth now stood outside, holding the reins to two sturdy steeds. She gave Cam a bright smile as he led out a third. By the end of the trip, perhaps she would know exactly who and what Cam Sutherland was.

For now, Catherine could have hugged him for arranging for their mounts and sparing her feet many more miles, but Kenneth would not have reacted well if she did. She simply smiled her thanks and let Kenneth help her onto the horse that would be hers. Then the men mounted up, and with a final farewell from Cam's acquaintance, they rode north.

Catherine enjoyed the chance to ride. They made better time, aiming for yet another cove where Cam expected to meet one of several ships he knew.

"Bloody pirates," Kenneth muttered when they reached the empty cove. "Canna count on them."

Cam laughed and pulled a pouch from his shirt. The clink as he bounced it in his hand told her it was full of coins. "'Tis good when they owe ye," Cam boasted and tossed the pouch to Kenneth.

Kenneth opened it and his eyes widened at what he saw inside. "What did ye do to be owed all this?" He frowned as he gestured at the horses, then retied the pouch. He held it out to Cam.

Cam waved it away. "Keep it. I've another."

The frown that followed told Catherine he was still worried about something. Kenneth was frowning, too, as he tucked the pouch into his shirt. "Let's go then," she urged. "Unless ye want to camp here and see if they come ashore soon."

Cam looked out over the water and scanned the empty horizon. "Nay. They'll no' risk it."

By late afternoon, they also started to see signs of where Mar's army had passed through. There were too many churned up fields and broken tools for the cause to be anything else. A few braver souls stared at them with empty eyes from darkened doorways. Catherine hated to think what might have happened here. As they crossed some low hills, they passed through several glens, all empty until the last. Broader than the others they'd just traversed, it had been farmed and someone lived there. Or had. Catherine surveyed the destruction before her with dismay. Burned-out crofts and blackened fields filled the glen. "Who did this? And why?"

Kenneth glanced her way, then returned his gaze to the wreckage before them. "Mar's men, most likely, to keep Highlanders from making use of it if they manage to come this far. Of course, if Mar prevails, his men won't be able to make use of it, either."

On her other side, Cam laughed, a choking, brittle sound carrying no mirth. "A wee shortsighted, that."

Kenneth's gaze fastened on her. She knew he must be thinking he had no good options. He couldn't leave her, and he couldn't take her with him.

She turned from him to look at Cam. "Do ye think we can reach yer port, still?"

Cam shrugged. "What choice do we have but to press on? If we turn west, we'll follow the army that did this. I dinna care to run into them. Do ye?"

"Nay, but we're safer behind them, aye?"

"If we follow them, we'll ken where they are and be able to avoid them," Kenneth agreed. "But eventually, they'll turn around, and then we'll be square in their path. Let's keep going north and find that smuggler's cove ye claim is well used," he added, glancing aside at Cam. "The sooner, the better. We've risked Cat's safety too long as it is."

Dismay filled Catherine at Kenneth's words. He was still determined to be rid of her so he could join the fight. He might still hold some affection for her, but it paled in comparison to his urge to find the Brodies and join the battle. She clenched her jaw, determined not to give voice to her disappointment. She would not embarrass him in front of Cam, who still thought they were wed.

They rode on and near sunset found an inn north of the town of Stonehaven outside the path of the army's destruction. They stopped for the night, hoping for news. Catherine also hoped some sense of normalcy might reduce the tension between her and Kenneth. She'd argued again and again that she was safer staying with him than being left somewhere with strangers. What they'd seen on the way proved no settlement was safe from Mar's men—even this far east, in a part of Scotland that did not border the Highlands.

Given Cam's behavior when she first met him, she might not be safe alone with him, either, if the fiction of her marriage to Kenneth fell apart. She still caught Cam studying her every now and again. He'd look quickly away, which made her nervous enough to stick close to Kenneth's side. Since they'd decided on their route, the two men had maintained a cooperative demeanor with each other, but Cat wasn't certain how deep it ran—on either side. The times she'd caught Cam studying Kenneth made her wonder whether Kenneth would be safe with him, either, though Cam had been a helpful traveling companion so far. Kenneth had to sleep sometime. Her only solace was knowing Kenneth was a blooded fighter who'd seen the worst men could do to each other and had certainly developed instincts that kept him alive. If she wondered about Cam's intentions, certainly Kenneth did, too—and kept a careful, if unobtrusive, eye on the northerner.

Kenneth arranged for a room for her before they sat down to eat. The inn's downstairs common room was full of rough-looking men. Before Cam joined them, Kenneth said, "Ye'll enjoy sleeping in a bed for one night, aye?"

"What about ye?" Catherine asked softly. She didn't want to have this discussion in front of Cam, who'd offered to sleep in the barn to keep an eye on the horses. "Cam still thinks we're wed. Ye must stay with me."

"I will, if only to make sure none of the other guests disturb ye."

After they ate, Cam returned to the stable, and Catherine followed the innkeeper up the stairs with Kenneth on her heels. The room boasted a wide cot, a washbasin, chair, hearth and window for the guest's comfort. Simple enough, but it appeared clean. Catherine nodded, so Kenneth gave the man a coin and he left them, promising to send up hot water for the basin. She wouldn't get a bath, but she'd be able to wash off some of the travel grime.

"I'll sleep in front of the door," Kenneth announced.

Catherine gestured at the bed. "There's room for both of us." She took Kenneth's hand. "I'd feel safer with ye near me."

He squeezed her hand, then released it. "I will be near ye. The cot is only a few feet from the door."

Determined, Catherine tried again. "Then at least help me out of this dress," she requested. She had no doubt she could lift it over her head, but once it was off, she'd ask Kenneth to unlace the day dress underneath it, which would leave her in her shift. After days in the same clothes, she looked forward to getting out of them. And if Kenneth could not resist what he found when they were off, well, she looked forward to what he'd do then, too.

"Raise yer arms, lass."

His voice fell over her shoulders, like warm honey over bread hot from the oven, and teased her nipples to peaks. She lifted her arms and leaned back as he pulled the heavy travel dress's skirt upward then over her head.

As he laid it aside on the bed, his gaze fell to her chest. He swallowed.

She pushed her advantage, stepping close enough to brush her breasts against his chest. "Could ye unlace this one, too, please? I canna reach it." She turned, making certain her hip brushed his groin as she did so.

The heat and pressure of his fingers as he fumbled with the laces at the top of her dress made her long for more. If he wanted to, he could easily turn her around, slip the rest of her clothes from her body and bind himself to her as she longed for him to do. She reached up and pulled her hair aside, exposing her nape. Would he touch her there, trailing warm, blunt fingers down her neck to spread her dress and help it fall from her shoulders? Would he even kiss her there?

Someone knocked on the door. Kenneth's fingers stilled, tangled in the laces at her waist. He pulled them free and went to the door. Catherine turned to face it, disappointed. She'd forgotten about the innkeeper's promised hot water. At least, she was still dressed. A lad came in with towels slung over his shoulders, lugging a steaming bucket. He poured its contents into the wash basin, dropped the towels on the chamber's one chair, then turned and left, all without a word or making eye contact with either her or Kenneth.

Kenneth caught the door before it closed completely. "I'll step outside and let ye bathe," he said, his voice deeper and more gruff than usual. "Use it all. I dinna need to."

"Stay, Kenneth." She wanted him to. She wanted *him*.

"I'll be right outside. Call for me when ye are finished."

He didn't give her a chance to reply. He slipped out and closed the door behind him. Just as well, Catherine thought. She would have begged him to stay, and for a lass determined to preserve some remnant of her dignity, doing so would have been foolish.

She stripped to her skin and took care of her needs. The hot water was bliss as was the rough towel she used to dry off. If she could have moved the basin to the floor, she would have soaked her tired feet in it. Instead, she soaked the towel she'd dampened drying off and wrapped it around her feet, enjoying the moist heat until it cooled. Then she moved the chair nearer the fire, washed her shift in the basin's remaining hot water, and hung the garment over the chair to dry. Come morning, she would have something clean next to her skin.

And when Kenneth came in and found her naked in the bed, perhaps what he saw would entice him to join her. She considered for a moment calling him in while she stood unclothed before the fire, but her nerve failed her before she could call out his name. She would be bold, but not quite that bold. Not yet. She wanted more from him than seduction. She wanted him to want to be with her. To stay with her, not just for the night. She got into bed and pulled the covers up to her shoulders, leaving the dry towel at the foot of the bed.

If that meant he slept on the floor, so be it.

He opened the door and came in moments after she called. He barely glanced around the room. Surely he saw her bare shoulders peeking out above the blanket? Her shift on the chair. But he didn't react, and something in Catherine gave up. Perhaps she should have stood naked before the fire.

He closed the door and stretched out across the entryway, then closed his eyes. His determination to avoid her reminded her so strongly of how he'd lain on the very edge of the blanket in Craig's barn, she sat up and threw the dry towel at him. Let him use it for a pillow, or a cover, she didn't care. She turned her back to him and pulled the covers up to her neck.

THE NEXT MORNING, HE LEFT THE ROOM TO LET HER dress, then they rode onward along a good track used by drovers that ran from Stonehaven up to Aberdeen. When they reached the bluff above the smugglers' bay, no ship waited. Catherine's heart sank.

"By my reckoning, it would have left two days ago," Cam admitted, still yawning after his night in the barn. "Though I hoped I was wrong."

"What next, then?" Catherine asked. She expected Cam had passed a more peaceful night than she had. Knowing Kenneth lay mere feet from her, refusing to come to her, kept her tossing and turning. Kenneth had remained silent as she struggled to find sleep, and he did so now, apparently content for the moment to survey the pebbled beach below them.

"We might catch it at Aberdeen," Cam replied with a frown, "or miss it entirely and have to hope a ship bound for the Highlands is in port."

"Let's go, then." Kenneth turned his mount. Catherine followed and Cam brought up the rear. Their path took them inland, away from the coast for several miles, and the farther north they went, the worse the countryside looked.

"Can Domnhall have already gotten this far and burned Aberdeen to the ground as he threatened?" Kenneth wondered aloud. "Or will Mar's men do it for him? They are doing more damage the farther they go."

Catherine had to agree.

"As much as sailing home would be easier and safer, getting to a ship looks to be harder and not safe at all,"

Kenneth complained. "Especially no' for Cat. Too much destruction."

"'Tis safer than cutting across war-torn countryside full of desperate people and two armies," Cam argued.

Kenneth shook his head. "In the mountains, we can stay out of sight."

When they found burned bodies at the next croft, Catherine had seen more than enough. Belly churning, she covered her mouth and choked out, "This is no' good. We're too exposed near the coast. I'm for turning inland right now."

"With luck, we could be sailing by sunset," Cam argued, his expression pinched. The smell must bother even him.

"Or wind up like them," Catherine responded, hoping what she was feeling was prudence, and not that she was losing her nerve. They were still a long way from home. "We've had nay luck at finding a ship." She made eye contact with each man, daring them to argue, then added, "Kenneth was right. We can take the narrower tracks through the mountains an army can no' use. We can hide in the trees. That is how we should go." She turned her mount and took off, forcing the men to follow.

Near sunset, they encountered men headed west, some injured, some hale, all glad to be alive. Kenneth's mouth settled into a grim line when they learned from them the battle had already happened two days before, northeast of their present location, on the way to Aberdeen. Kenneth traded a look with Cam that said they might never have made Aberdeen at all. Though horrified by the tales the men told of the ferocity of the battle and the astounding number of the dead, Catherine was relieved. Kenneth had missed the fighting. He was safe and with her. Now if they could get to Brodie, they'd have a chance at the future she wanted. At the future Kenneth had once wanted. She had time to change his mind and make him imagine a life with her again.

Kenneth questioned the men they met. Since they were not pursued, everyone supposed Mar's remaining forces had turned east for Aberdeen. Eventually one man told them when he'd last seen Brodies and how they'd passed him by while he searched for a lost comrade. Kenneth thanked the man, then rode off.

Catherine exchanged a glance with Cam, who gestured for her to follow. She frowned and complied, though suddenly reluctant. The men of Kenneth's clan couldn't be very far ahead. Brodie fighters meant the end of her relative privacy with Kenneth. Kenneth's obligations to his clan would suddenly be impossible to ignore. It meant facing Iain, too, if he'd survived the battle. She wouldn't have to go as far as Brodie or Rose to be in trouble. She was certain she'd hear about all of her shortcomings from Iain first.

They caught up to Kenneth, and soon found the Brodie contingent following a burn through a grassy glen. Iain was not with them. A man Catherine didn't know explained, "He's arranging a way to get more wounded men home. Do ye ken about Calum?"

Kenneth dismounted and spoke quietly to the man, whose voice carried to Catherine.

"Hours ago, we managed to claim an abandoned wagon," the man said. "Iain sent Calum on ahead with three men, to get him to the healer."

"Is Iain still at the battlefield?" Kenneth demanded in a louder tone.

"Nay. He's coming behind," the man explained, pointing at a more northerly angle from their back trail. "He should be along soon."

Catherine's heart sank at the news. Brodie would

not be the only clan with dead and injured men. She dismounted and approached them. "What about Rose?"

The man shook his head. "Sorry, lass. I dinna ken what happened to the Rose fighters. We got separated in the battle..."

Catherine shook her head as ice slid down her spine. Guilt suddenly weighed on her for running away, replacing the righteous indignation she had carried these past weeks. She had refused three betrothals that would have led to alliances good for clan Rose. Had her absence made her da think he had no choice, and driven him into joining The Lord of the Isle's army to secure what he saw as an even more advantageous alliance? As angry as she was with her father, she didn't want him dead on some battlefield to the east. Where was he, and where were her clansmen?

❧

KENNETH TURNED THEM IN THE DIRECTION THE MAN had indicated, looking for the main group of Brodie warriors—and Iain. His laird would have news of neighboring clans, including whether the Rose had joined the fight himself or just sent men to Domnhall. For Cat's sake, he hoped her father was well. With only daughters to inherit, clan Rose territory would be easy pickings for Domnhall, should he care to add Rose's land and people to the Ross and other western holdings he already claimed.

Cat rode beside him, looking pensive and worn out. She'd shown great fortitude during the trip, but he could see the miles and her worries taking a toll on her. Sutherland looked little better.

Kenneth was tired after staring all night at the ceiling of the chamber he'd shared with Cat, listening to her toss and turn and knowing she wore nothing under the bedcovers. He'd had plenty of time to contemplate his sins, past and prospective. They alone had kept him in place, on the floor, instead of naked and in bed with Cat, enjoying all the delights she so gently offered. If he'd come in and found her naked before the fire, he would have taken her. Such behavior suited the whores in France, but he'd refused to teach Cat what they knew. Though he regretted his sins, he regretted the missed opportunity, too. Cat wanted him. He had no doubt she'd thrown that towel at him in frustration. And he wanted her. But undressing and hiding from him under the covers proved to him she was still innocent. He was glad her bold challenge to him in the library had been far from her mind last night. What they both wanted had consequences he wasn't ready to accept.

When he noticed Iain approaching up the glen, Kenneth's elation at finding a group of Brodie warriors headed home turned to anxiety. He'd been gone from Brodie for weeks and had thought about never returning. Yet one glimpse of his friend and laird set his heart to racing as though preparing for battle, and the sense of homesickness he'd felt when he encountered the familiar faces of those men swamped him anew. All this time, he'd been more angry at himself, he realized, than at Iain. He had a lot to atone for—to Cat and to Iain.

He knew the moment Iain spotted him.

Iain pulled up on the reins, slowing his mount, then kicked it into motion again and rode up. "What the hell are ye doing here? Ye are supposed to be in Stirling." Then he leaned over and grabbed Kenneth around the neck before he could reply and gave him a fierce hug. "I am glad to see ye," he said as he released him. "I am. Now explain."

Kenneth didn't waste a breath. Iain wanted answers

and in typical Iain fashion, he wanted them now. "I've come from St. Andrews, where I was taken from Stirling. I heard what Domnhall was up to and escaped. Once hostilities broke out, there was no point in continuing to claim the bishop's hospitality. I hoped to join ye before the battle."

"So ye are late as usual, aye?" Iain reached over again, but this time to slap him on the back. Then he laughed. "Ye are a sight for sore eyes, and aye, we couldha used ye...days ago." He paused, then added, "Though, without weapons, ye wouldna have been able to do much." He nodded. "We picked up plenty of steel on the battlefield. Ye can have yer choice of blades of any size."

Kenneth shrugged, fighting the urge to grip the handle of his stolen dirk. "How did Brodie fare?"

Iain's mouth pinched, and he gave a little shudder. "Better than most, worse than some." He gestured at the Brodie riders still gathered nearby. "Did that lot tell ye about Calum?"

"Aye." Kenneth put as much regret as he could into the tone, then sighed. If he'd fought with Brodie, perhaps their losses would have been fewer.

"I pray our healer can save his sight, but I'm no' hopeful." He turned his horse and slapped the reins on its neck to get it moving—homeward.

Kenneth, perforce, did the same. He glanced over his shoulder where Cat and Cameron Sutherland waited. Iain had yet to notice them, which surprised him. Iain usually saw everything. But perhaps he was still distracted by the battle and its aftermath.

Iain's gaze roved the countryside around them, searching, Kenneth supposed, for more wounded, or for ambush. That thought brought him up short and he scanned the surrounding tree-covered hills. "What are ye looking for?"

"Brodies I've yet to find. Domnhall demanded such a hasty retreat overnight, we had nay chance to search the battlefield for our dead and wounded. We were slowed by the injured we did manage to find, so some of my men may have gotten ahead of us."

"Domnnhall lost?" That surprised Kenneth. The Lord of the Isles surely commanded an overwhelming force.

"He claims we won. But in truth, both sides lost." Iain frowned. "Both had such heavy casualties, the ground ran red with blood." He stayed silent for a long time, then added, "I think Domnhall realized carrying on the fight would have been pointless." He ran a hand roughly through his hair. "All those Scots died, and they didn't solve anything."

Kenneth reached over and briefly clasped a hand on Iain's shoulder.

Iain nodded. "Well, let's speak of other things. How did ye get from Sterling to St. Andrews? And from there to here?" He swept a hand aside, taking in the glen they rode through.

Kenneth shrugged and tried for a bit of his old humor, thinking if anyone needed a chuckle, Iain surely did. "The usual way. On foot and on horseback."

Iain cut him a glance, but didn't smile.

Kenneth shifted his weight in the saddle. So much for trying to lighten Iain's mood. "Someone put the idea into Albany's head that moving the hostages would keep their clans from rescuing them," Kenneth continued. "Those of us at Stirling got sent in different directions. In St. Andrews, I was the only hostage—the bishop treated me well enough. But when the news arrived that Domnhall had taken Dingwall, then headed for Inverness, I knew my status would change, and no' in a good way. 'Twas time to get outside the castle—and the city walls. Highlanders were no' safe on the streets."

"And ye came all this way alone?"

Kenneth winced and glanced aside. Cat and Sutherland were well behind him and Iain. "Nay, I had...companions."

"Where are they?"

Kenneth hooked a thumb over his shoulder. "With the lads, behind us."

Iain pulled up. "I want to meet them," he demanded.

Kenneth stiffened and reined in his mount, too, knowing what was coming. Iain would not be pleased to see his wife's sister in Kenneth's company in any case. Even less so to find her here. But he couldn't avoid the confrontation. He nodded and turned his mount. Sutherland's larger form was easy to spot, but for a bad moment, he couldn't see Cat among the ragtag remains of the Brodie fighters. Then he located her, trailing behind the northerner, in conversation with someone he couldn't see. He kicked his mount and headed their way.

Iain kept pace, then slowed. "*Ach, nay.* Ye canna be serious."

Cat's gaze met Kenneth's and went wide-eyed. After a moment's hesitation, she pulled her mount around Sutherland's and approached. "Iain," she greeted him. "'Tis good to see ye alive—and hale."

Kenneth noted the set of her shoulders and the lift of her chin as she regarded his laird. Aye, she was daring Iain to chastise her. He was certain that was a very bad idea, but her courage made him proud, nonetheless.

"Sister. I'm surprised to find ye here." Iain's tone was deceptively mild.

Kenneth expected sparks to fly at any moment, most of them in his direction. He could take them. He didn't want Cat singed. "'Twas my decision. I judged St. Andrews no safe place for any Highlander, even a lass, once the news reached us…"

Sutherland rode up in time to hear Kenneth's comment. "And a sound judgment it was," he added, "given what we heard only a day later, was done to a Highland sympathizer. A priest, no less. I'm Cameron Sutherland," he added. "Or Cam. And ye are?"

"Iain, Laird Brodie," Kenneth, Iain, and Cat chorused in unison.

"Ah…." Sutherland cleared his throat. "Well then, 'tis good to meet ye, Laird Brodie. I'll be glad of a larger escort, at least as far as the firth, on my way home. We all might get more sleep."

That comment startled Iain into uncharacteristic silence.

"Kenneth and Cam have been very good escorts," Cat put in with a narrow-eyed glance toward each. "Most of the time."

Iain found his voice at the same time Kenneth and Sutherland objected, "Most?"

Cat snickered at the sound of three male voices raised in outrage, but Kenneth wondered what Iain must think. Cam's phrasing could be interpreted as provocative, or simply a statement about the difficulty of posting a night guard with only two men available to take the duty. Cam could be flippant. Kenneth hoped he had not just put Cat's reputation at risk.

"Well, there has been a fair amount of arguing about which way to go," Cat told Iain, as though she'd missed, or was ignoring, Cam's possible slur. "Cam favored finding a port and a friendly ship. Kenneth judged heading toward Aberdeen too risky, given what we were seeing of the countryside. He hoped to avoid the armies by going farther inland." She shrugged. "So here we are."

"Almost in the middle of the conflict," Iain growled and cut a glare at Kenneth.

"But no' quite," Kenneth reminded him. "Cat is safe…"

"Catherine, if ye please," she said with a frown.

He ignored her. "I mean to get Cat home to Rose. Sutherland can continue north from there. It should be simple enough to find a ship in Inverness—"

"Perhaps no'," Iain interrupted him. "Once Domnhall's army goes through there again, I dinna ken what will be left. He brought gallowglass men with him."

"Irish warriors?" Cat frowned. "Why?"

"Irish and Scots," Kenneth supplied, recalling their shrill battle cries and merciless skill with any weapon. "They were among the fiercest men I fought beside in France."

"Fierce drinkers, too," Sutherland added with a wink at Cat.

"I'm aware," Kenneth replied dryly. Painfully aware, as it happened. He turned back to Iain. "And still, with their help, Domnhall did no' win the day?"

Iain pursed his lips. "He tried to bring the English in to support him, but they refused. And nay, no' even with the gallowglass. Our force was larger, but the Earl of Mar brought more than *caterans*. His mounted knights took a heavy toll on our infantry."

"Ye dinna seem in a hurry to be away. Are they no' chasing Domnhall's forces?" Kenneth asked.

"Oddly, nay. Likely Mar has retreated to Aberdeen in case Domnhall changed his mind and decided to make good on his threat to torch the town. I'm uneasy lagging behind, but I owe it to our men." He paused and studied Cat with narrowed eyes. "What I canna decide is whether ye would be safer remaining with the larger group of Brodies, or to continue on as ye have done."

His gaze shifted to the men with her. "Ye can cover ground more quickly than the men on foot can travel, to get my wife's sister home to Rose."

Kenneth thought back on the nights they'd already spent on their journey. To keep her safe and away from Sutherland, he'd endured the sweet pain of sleeping with Cat nearby, even in his arms. She'd be safer with the Brodies. Safer from him. He nodded. "It would be good to have some company for a few days. Once we near Brodie, we'll leave ye and go on to Rose. I promised to return her home."

Out of the corner of his eye, he saw Cat open her mouth—to object, most likely—but then she closed it again and kept her gaze on the burn burbling alongside them. He glanced at Sutherland, who shrugged.

"What's another few days? I'll get home soon enough, either way. In the meantime, I'll be able to continue to enjoy the company of this lovely lass."

"Stop it, Cam," Cat interjected. "Iain does no' ken yer sense of humor like I do."

"I would never jest about a beautiful Highland Rose."

Kenneth could see Iain and Cat thought Sutherland was teasing, but he wasn't. Sutherland appeared to be one of those men who took his pleasure anywhere he found it, which is why Kenneth kept Cat close each night. He'd seen the type before and knew Cat would be defenseless against the northerner's charm, should he get Cat alone and put it on full display.

Cat had said she still was innocent, and last night proved he had no reason to doubt her word. Two years ago, they'd come close, Cat and he, to making their marriage inevitable, but had come to their senses in time.

How he regretted their restraint now. He would have had a soft, warm, fiercely loving woman by his side, and perhaps a bairn or two by now. Instead, he'd seen and done things that would weigh on his conscience as long as he lived. He'd betrayed his friend and laird by deserting his kin. And in turn been betrayed by that she-devil, Marilee, who had taught him what it meant to have a broken heart.

He and Cat could have been together these past two years, and he would not have gone to France.

CHAPTER 10

That evening around the campfire, the men began telling tales of Red Harlaw, so called for the amount of blood spilled that day. Lively music drifted over from another campfire beyond the crest of a nearby hill, an odd and unseemly counterpoint to the horror of their tales. "Who is doing that?" Catherine asked.

"Some of the gallowglass," Iain answered, his tone clipped. "They fought for Domnhall. They're close by, headed west like the rest of Domnhall's army."

Kenneth stiffened, but didn't elaborate on Iain's comment. Instead, the men continued with their tales.

Catherine hated hearing the details, but curiosity drove her to listen.

"They killed the camp followers, ye ken? Lasses and bairns, all of 'em," someone said.

Catherine shuddered.

An older voice rose above the general murmur of the others. "In none of our battles have I ever seen so much blood. So many innocents slaughtered..." Someone tossed a stick onto the fire. A shower of sparks drifted up like the souls of the dead.

Shocked, Catherine exchanged a glance with

Kenneth. Thank the saints they'd arrived too late for him to join the fight. He'd been right. She should not have been with him—not for a battle such as that. His stern expression said plainly she should have boarded a ship in the St. Andrews harbor when he told her to. But she hadn't, and she was here. They were lucky the worst of the fighting was over.

After listening to the stories, Catherine was certain she'd never get to sleep tonight. Cam bedded down away from the campfire, claiming with his northern blood he would rest better away from its heat. Kenneth made his bed next to hers. "I'll no abandon ye, lass," he told her. "No' in the midst of all these men. Brodies are one thing, but men of other clans—and lands—are nearby. I willna leave ye alone."

His nearness was a great comfort, as well as a great temptation. But what could they do in the midst of an armed camp?

Rolled up in her blankets, she watched the stars move across the sky. Sleep eluded her. She'd seen and heard too much this day. It was more than she knew how to handle. Suddenly, she wanted to go home. Despite how much she wanted to be with Kenneth, and as much as she dreaded facing her father's wrath, she was tired of all of this. She needed to be safe behind Rose's walls.

Her thoughts took a darker turn. She feared how her father would punish her for running away. She'd left him a note berating him for his attempts to marry her off. Once he got her back, he'd force her into a marriage she didn't want and lock her in her chamber until it was done. And once he found out how she'd gotten away, he'd know Mary had to be involved and he'd punish her, too. Catherine deeply regretted involving her eldest sister, but she never would have succeeded without her help. Now Mary would pay for her kindness. He'd kill Kenneth if he assumed she'd been ruined on the trip home—if not before then. And if Cam was still with them, he would see it all, which would embarrass her father before Sutherland when Cam returned home to tell the tale.

She should have obeyed her father. She should have…nay, she mustn't think this way. Mary would be there, and once Da settled down, everything would work out. Kenneth would speak with him and ask again for her hand. She and Mary would make sure their father agreed this time, and her future—their future, hers and Kenneth's—would unfold as she imagined it. As she had spent the last two years longing for it. But first, they had to survive this trip.

Drunken laughter and singing from a campfire beyond the next hillside added to her discomfort. Despite Kenneth's clansmen around her, she did not truly feel safe.

THE NEXT MORNING, KENNETH WOKE HER BEFORE sunup. He held a bundle in his hands. "Take this with ye when ye go…to be private…and put these clothes on."

"What…why?" Catherine sat up, still sleep-fuddled from lying awake long into the night before finally dropping off. She pushed aside the plaid that had kept her warm during the night. It wasn't Kenneth, but it had served, since he would not hold her in his arms in the midst of these Brodies as he had often done to keep her warm since they'd left St. Andrews. It was his way of keeping Cam at bay. But the reason wasn't as important as having Kenneth's arms around her, his body stretched out behind hers, his heat and hunger for her making her feel safe and loved…and full of hope he would fall in love with her again.

They both knew Iain would be furious if she behaved with anything less than complete respectability. She could understand why. As his wife's sister, her actions would reflect on him. But having Kenneth so near and yet untouchable rankled.

Now, Kenneth's words made no sense. The clothes she wore sufficed these past days while they'd traveled. She could see no reason for him to give her new ones.

"They're a lad's clothes, Cat." He spoke quickly, his tone impatient. "We're in the midst of Domnhall's army, so 'tis too dangerous for ye to be seen as ye are— for ye and for Brodie."

She lifted a hand to her throat. "What do ye mean?"

"There are no' so many Brodie men here. We canna protect ye from all the others."

"My being here puts Brodie at risk?" Catherine's belly clenched. "Iain, too? I never meant…"

"I ken, lass. Iain does, too. He wants ye safe, but no more than I do."

The urgency in his voice had been replaced by yearning. Reassured, she took the bundle and tucked it under one arm.

Kenneth took her other hand and helped her up. "Go on and change before it gets too light. I'll stay nearby. Do ye need help with yer dress?" His expression went from earnest concern to a quick grin he knew she couldn't resist. He must be thinking about the night in the inn.

She slapped at his hand and stepped away. "I can dress myself, thank ye." Then she gave him an answering smile. She hadn't needed his help that night. She'd wanted it. His teasing lightened the fear and dismay the bundle of clothes had made her feel. "As a lad, what will my position be in this army?"

Kenneth's eyebrows lifted. "Position?" He shrugged. "The idea is to make ye invisible, Cat, 'tis all."

"I'll be yer groom, then, so I can stay with ye," she announced with a saucy toss of her head.

Kenneth swallowed. He lifted a hand, then shook his head. "I've a bonnet for ye, as well, to hide yer hair."

Had he been about to tangle his fingers in her hair?

"As for the other," Kenneth continued, his tone serious, "I dinna ken whether Iain will approve..."

She straightened, determined. "Iain will no' have a choice. If I canna stay by ye, I'll...I'll go back to St. Andrews." The thought of the return trip, and of what they'd seen on the way here, daunted her, but, she continued, "Cam will escort me, I'm sure."

"Dinna be daft, lass." He rolled his eyes. "Ye canna go back there. And certainly no' with Sutherland. I dinna trust him with ye." He crossed his arms over his chest. "Very well, ye'll stay by me. I'd rather ye did, anyway." He grinned again, longer this time, and for a moment seemed more like the younger Kenneth she'd fallen in love with. Then he brushed her cheek with the back of his fingers and he was the Kenneth of today, older, perhaps wiser, more certain of himself.

Catherine gave him a triumphant smile and headed for the nearest patch of bracken and shrubs. He cared. She hadn't realized how much she needed reassurance until he gave it to her.

Kenneth followed, then took up a position with his back to her as she waded into the brush. She needn't have threatened him with Cam. He'd never meant to let her leave him. Her plan was working. By the time they got to Rose, he'd be ready to demand her hand and give her da no chance to deny him. Perhaps Iain might even back him in refusing to take no for an answer. Or she might even be able to convince him to handfast before they reached Rose.

Heartened, she pulled and tugged as her dress caught on branches, and fought her way through the undergrowth to a clearing large enough to move about as much as she needed to undress. It would give her enough cover to complete her transformation from a lass to a lad. Whether the illusion would hold once the sun came up, well, she'd know soon enough.

WHEN IAIN FIRST SPOTTED KENNETH'S NEW GROOM, HIS double-take told Kenneth the disguise would serve, at least from a distance. Iain hadn't recognized Cat right away, and if Iain didn't know her for a lass in the first moment, no one else would either. The challenge would be to prevent men from other clans from coming too close. Kenneth would keep her riding at his side, or have her mount up behind him where she could duck behind his shoulder. For the first time since they'd left St. Andrews, Kenneth felt like he could truly keep Cat safe.

Iain seemed content to ignore their arrangement. While Kenneth had expected an argument, apparently Iain had decided their ruse would add another layer of protection for his wife's sister and went on about his business without comment.

Cam's approach leading his horse and a roan mare put Kenneth on guard all over again. The northerner's expression didn't change until he got within speaking distance, then he winked at Cat, then turned to Kenneth. "Since ye allowed yer laird Iain to give two of our mounts to some of his wounded men, I find it exceedingly kind of Mar to lose so many mounted men, leaving their horses roaming the hills, available for our use. Perhaps yer...groom...could take charge of this one as well as the one ye do have? So ye willna have to ride double..."

Cat snorted a laugh as she took the reins he offered. "Saw right through me, did ye?"

Cam shook his head. "Honestly? Nay, no' until I got closer. I wondered at first where Brodie had found a young lad for a companion and what he'd done with ye. That gave me a moment of contentment, thinking ye might have to turn to me for yer care."

"Over my dead body," Kenneth growled.

Cam's eyebrows lifted and he glanced around. "That would be all too easy to arrange, Brodie. I dinna suggest ye repeat those words too often or too loudly... for yer own good, aye?" He gave Kenneth a stare suddenly and completely lacking in humor.

Kenneth laid a hand on the hilt of the claymore slung over his mount's withers. "Keep yer distance, Sutherland. I'm warning ye—"

"Both of ye stop it right now!" Cat broke in. "I'm no' horseflesh for ye to argue over, much less come to blows. I'll do as I see fit..." she skewered first one man, then the other, with her narrowed gaze, "whether either of ye like it or nay."

Kenneth wanted to applaud, but Cat was still spitting mad and Sutherland looked like he couldn't decide whether to burst out laughing or pull her into his arms and kiss her senseless. Kenneth narrowed his eyes at the other man. "Ye heard me, Sutherland. Back off."

Sutherland nodded and took a step back, then put one foot in the stirrup and mounted. "Ye can be sure, Brodie, I'll be nearby."

"That is good enough," Cat broke in again. "Now get out of my sight, Cameron Sutherland, before I take a claymore to ye myself." She lifted her chin. "And thank ye for the horse."

Sutherland threw back his head and laughed, then

jerked the reins to turn his horse around and rode off, still laughing.

The corner of Kenneth's mouth lifted as he stared at his back.

"And what do ye think is so funny?" Cat demanded as Kenneth made a stirrup of his hands and helped her mount. "I'm mad at ye, too, ye ken."

He nodded, but couldn't seem to wipe the grin from his face as he stared up at her. "I ken it. But ye stayed *with me*." He shouldn't, but he felt lighter than he had in days.

Cat sat up straighter in the saddle and cocked her head to the side. "Ye like that?"

"Aye."

"Good," she said on a smirk and dug her heels into her mount's side. "Now let's go. The sooner I get ye to myself, the better."

Kenneth took off after her, his heart pounding a beat wilder than the sound of his horses' hooves. When it came to a head, Cat had chosen him over Sutherland. And wanted to get him alone? What had she done with the shy and proper lass? Put her away along with the lass's clothing? Was it the breeks he'd made her don? Suddenly, he had a saucy tease on his hands—one dressed as a lad, aye, but he didn't care one whit. Not that she behaved as a wanton. But this boldness was beyond anything he'd ever seen in her—except for the day in the library when she'd challenged him to *teach her*. Aye, he'd teach her. How could he resist her when she challenged him again and again? Naked under the sheets in the inn? God's bones. He was going to succumb if he couldn't make her behave. The problem was, he didn't want her to stop. He wanted his Cat. *His Cat*. But her da had denied them once. Even after Kenneth escorted her safely across half of Scotland, he feared the Rose would still refuse to let them wed.

Then again, what if she didn't remain safe—from him? Was that what she had in mind? His Cat was a devious lass, no doubt. As devious as her older sisters, and then some, if she'd learned from them as well as he suspected she had. Suddenly, despite the army around them and the gallowglass mercenaries that worried him the most, he looked forward to the rest of the trip. Consequences be damned.

CHAPTER 11

atherine stuck close by Kenneth the rest of the day. He kept them in the middle of the thickest group of Brodies, the better to shield her from others' eyes, she knew. She also knew he chafed to ride point with Iain by the way his gaze followed Iain's every move, only darting away to check the hillsides they passed between.

"He'll be fine," Catherine told Kenneth after another hour.

"I dinna like the way he keeps getting out ahead," Kenneth admitted. "If Iain gets in trouble up there, I dinna ken if I can get to him fast enough."

"Ye are no' his only warrior here," she reminded him. His curt nod had to satisfy her, because he lapsed back into watchful silence. His anxiety for his friend made her stomach sour with guilt. If not for feeling responsible for keeping her safe, he'd be beside his laird, in his rightful place.

Then she noticed his jaw clench and glanced ahead. *Ach, nay.* Also mounted, Cam had joined Iain at the head of their column, in what Kenneth regarded as his place. This could only lead to trouble.

She offered the only solution she could think of.

"Go on up to Iain. Send Cam back to me," she suggested, knowing she was wasting her breath, but tired of the sullen silence Kenneth had fallen into as they rode. What had happened to his lighter mood? Ah, of course. Kenneth could not be in two places at one time. If he could, which would he choose—her or Iain? Right now, he didn't look as though he felt free to make a choice, he just hated seeing Cam at Iain's side. She pressed her lips together. If he wanted to ride with Iain, he should go on ahead. Even if she was on foot, she'd be safe in the midst of all these Brodies.

"Damn him."

She gave Kenneth a side-eye glare. After days—and nights—on the road, he still didn't trust Cam Sutherland. Or perhaps… "All that snarling back there between ye two—will ye never give over? If Cam has no' harmed me before now, he willna harm me in the midst of yer clansmen, nor let me come to harm, yet ye still dinna trust him around me, do ye?" The thought irritated her, as did the frown that flitted across Kenneth's face before he turned to look at her.

"Ye are my responsibility. I'll no risk ye with anyone else."

She nodded. "I thought so. Ye dinna trust him around me." Or around Iain, apparently.

Kenneth snorted.

"Ye needna fash," she assured him. "Cam is merely the friend of a friend, naught more."

Kenneth's expression remained stony.

She decided it was time to poke the badger with a stick. "Aye, he's charming. Ye canna deny it. And he's full of flattery, which pleases me…"

He sneered. "So the lads yer da tried to wed ye to didna flatter ye enough to win ye, aye?"

Her mouth fell open. Yet, what did she expect? Badgers fought back—ferociously—when attacked.

Kenneth's gaze stayed to the front, searching their route for hidden dangers while his words stabbed her through the heart. "Ye canna be serious," she gasped. "What a horrible thing to say."

"Was it? Ye light up when Sutherland speaks to ye. Perhaps ye should turn your attention to him."

Instead of me. She heard the words Kenneth didn't say as loudly and clearly as the ones he actually uttered. After a week of traveling with Cam Sutherland, what had made Kenneth suddenly—finally—admit to his jealousy of the older northerner? Did seeing Cam ride beside Iain really make Kenneth angry enough to finally loosen his hold on his temper and lash out at her?

Was it truly jealousy? Or was this another attempt to distance himself from her? To make her rethink what he claimed to be her infatuation and childish hero-worship of the friend he had been years ago? She knew he had not been that lad for two years. He'd seen war. And other women. None of it should matter, but she couldn't escape the heavy sense of dread every time the subject of his past came up.

She had to set all of those feelings aside. Today, now, Kenneth was here. She needed to know—did he really resent her being here so much?

"Cameron Sutherland will never be the man ye are," she ground out. "The man for me."

"I think ye are wrong, " Kenneth responded evenly, not looking at her. "Ye should give him a chance."

"And I think ye are trying to make me angry. So I think I'll go check on the wounded men and let ye sulk by yerself for a while."

"Sulk!"

Kenneth's outraged objection echoed off the nearby hillside as she turned her mount around and rode to the cluster of men near the end of their column. She would have laughed, but she was too annoyed. So it took accusing him of childish behavior to get through his indifference? To the devil with him.

The army's pace was slowed by the men on foot and by the wagon carrying the most badly hurt remaining with them. The worst of the injured had already been sent ahead. Catherine was not naive enough to think all of those men would make it to Brodie, but she wished them well, knowing Iain would worry, and would carry every death on his conscience. Nor did she expect their conveyance, like the horses she and others now rode, would ever be returned to its original owner. Since the horses and wagons were taken from the battlefield, she doubted their owners still lived.

When she reached the wagon, she gave her mount to a man limping alongside it and climbed in. Two of the men it carried were mercifully asleep—or passed out. One of those tossed his head and moaned when Catherine laid her palm on his forehead. Too warm. He was developing a fever. He needed a healer's potions, and soon. The other two in the wagon were awake and watched her through pain-filled eyes as she checked their wounds. She'd just finished when Iain rode by, headed, she presumed, for the men guarding their back trail. She called out to him.

He approached and nodded. "Had enough of Kenneth today, eh?"

She ignored his comment. "These men should also be sent on ahead," she told him, kneeling in their midst. She pointed. "That one has a fever, and these two may soon, as well. They need a healer's care."

"They have ye."

"And I have naught but a kind word to offer. They need more than I can do for them."

Iain's lips compressed into a thin line. "These men

ken I canna split my forces any further without putting everyone at risk, including ye."

She straightened on her knees and grasped the wagon's top rail to steady herself as she squared off with Iain. He wouldn't take her seriously if she fell onto the men. She held on tight as the jostling of narrow wheels across rough ground nearly pitched her out. "Dinna stint their care because of me," she said when she steadied. "Kenneth, Cam and I can go on as we arrived, alone."

"Some of the clans returning home along the same route are no' friendly" Iain reminded her.

"And then there are the gallowglass men," one of the lucid wounded men added. "They fought with us, but they can, for enough coin, or enough whisky, as easily fight against us."

Iain nodded, his expression bleak. "I can only promise we'll be home in a few days."

Catherine dropped her gaze to her hands, conceding defeat. She was worried about these few wounded men, a heavy enough burden. But Iain carried the fates of all of his men—and her safety as well—on his shoulders. She nodded, so he turned his mount away. God willing, the wounded men would survive the trip.

Before Iain could continue toward the rear, Kenneth rode up and gave him a nod. Then, without warning, he wrapped an arm around Catherine's waist and pulled her across his lap. In the midst of her spluttered protest, he nodded again to Iain and rode forward. Iain's laughter curled around them like smoke on a breezy day.

Despite their earlier argument, Catherine leaned back in Kenneth's arms, surprised but pleased. Did this mean he was changing his mind about her? She soon dozed, lulled by the rocking rhythm of the horse's gait, safe and cared for as she'd never dreamed she'd be. Later, they dismounted to let an injured man ride, but Kenneth always insisted on getting Catherine off her feet after a few hours and traded places with a healthy rider. She appreciated his concern, but wondered how many young grooms rode while their masters walked alongside his horse, or rode held secure in their masters' arms.

As eager as she was to reach home, she'd prefer to walk than to be seen as getting special favors. Men who needed care still kept pace on foot with their fellow Brodie warriors. When they stopped for the night, Catherine made a point of visiting each of the walking wounded to check their bandages, care for their wounds as best she was able, and speak with them. She was not trained as a healer, but it took little sense to know wounds should be kept clean, bandages changed, and notice taken if a fever developed. Not that she could do anything about their care except offer cool water to drink, and bathe a sick man's face with more cool water, but the men seemed to appreciate her efforts. For their sake, the sooner they reached Brodie, the better.

THE NEXT DAY, SUTHERLAND RODE BACK TO THEIR CAMP just before sunset. Kenneth had seen Iain send him off at dawn and suspected he knew the reason why. But his pride was pricked by Iain using this northerner rather than asking him to scout. He'd been at Iain's side since they were lads. Before he'd run to France, and before Iain sent him to Sterling, he'd been Iain's second-in-command. He didn't know what he was to Iain now, and it rankled.

Truth be told, he knew why Iain didn't send him on

whatever errand he'd sent Sutherland. Iain intended for Kenneth to remain with Cat. To keep her safe. Kenneth was certain Iain believed his arrival with Cat brought more trouble to the army than good. And perhaps he'd picked up on the tension between Kenneth and Sutherland over her. So Iain made a choice—one Kenneth could hardly fault. Cat was his responsibility, and if anything happened to her, neither he nor Iain would be welcome at Brodie upon their return. Iain's wife Annie, Cat's middle sister, would see to that. She'd make Iain's life hell, and Kenneth's even worse. He didn't know what would be worse than hell, but Annie would contrive to create it.

Aye, he'd been a fool. Cat was in danger here, yet she would have been no safer, had he left her behind without a host of Brodie warriors to protect her, without even him. At best she would have found herself a guest of the bishop, trapped inside the castle. At worst? Kenneth didn't want to consider the worst. Death would have come to her as a blessing.

He hated to admit Sutherland had been right about finding a ship. If only they'd been able to sail for home and avoid all this. He hated that Cat had seen the destruction wrought by Mar's *caterans* and heard the men's tales of Red Harlaw. No lass should be exposed to such brutality. Thank the saints she was made of stern stuff. Any other lass would have swooned or dissolved into tears and hysterics. Not his Cat. Kenneth's gaze slipped to the side to take in the Brodie encampment and the smoke signaling other camps beyond the hills. But, she was a lass surrounded by men and...

Sutherland.

Kenneth watched him report to Iain, then dismount and hobble his horse with the others. He narrowed his eyes at the man's long-strided approach. Cat hadn't seen Sutherland yet. Her back was to him. She faced the small cooking fire Kenneth had built for her to make broth for the man with the fever and venison stew for the rest of the injured men. She maintained those two things would do the men more good than water, ale or whisky, and who was he to argue?

Kenneth, however, sat at an angle to Cat and the fire and so had a clear view. As Sutherland came closer, his gaze never left Cat. Kenneth's jaw clenched, recalling how Cat had defended Sutherland and claimed Kenneth was jealous. And how he'd told her perhaps she'd be better off with Sutherland than continuing to pine after him. What a fool he was.

"Ah, Lady Catherine, is the mouth-watering scent coming from yer cook pot for me?"

Cat started at the sound of Sutherland's voice behind her and turned to regard him as he joined them at the fire.

He took a seat on her opposite side and gave Kenneth a nod.

"Nay, 'tis for the sick and injured," Cat informed him, then raised a brow. "Ye are neither."

"No' for lack of trying, but thank the saints, ye speak true. Ye are an angel of mercy, lovely Catherine. If ye were no' already spoken for, I'd be tempted to offer for ye, myself."

Kenneth surged to his feet at Sutherland's ill-considered words. "She is—"

"I am no' spoken for," Cat interrupted, giving Kenneth a slant-eyed glance, then returning her gaze to Sutherland.

Kenneth's heart fell to his feet at Sutherland's immediate grin.

"Indeed?" Sutherland's gaze slid from Cat to Kenneth and his brow arched. "Ye led me to believe ye were married. How convenient, aye Brodie?"

"I am, however," Cat continued with a glare at Sutherland that did Kenneth's heart good, "no' interested in being any man's property, so ye can get any such idea right out of yer head."

Well, he liked that she'd put Sutherland down, but not the way she'd done it. Not interested, was she? Kenneth would have sworn she'd spent the entire trip trying to convince him to renew his offer to her father. To make her his. She'd tried everything but standing before him, nude, and tearing his clothes away. The closer they got to Rose, the more likely she'd turn to something like that as her last resort. Kenneth was looking forward to seeing what she'd try—until he recalled her challenge for him to teach her the skills used by the French mademoiselles. He ran a hand through his hair, imagining Cat on her knees before him, or draped over the side of a bed, her skirts tossed up over her back. Dear God, if he wasn't careful, Sutherland would see on his face what he was thinking...and so would Cat. He forced his gaze from her to Sutherland.

"Where did Iain send ye?" It pained him to ask, but he had to change the subject.

"To catch up with Domnhall or one of his lieutenants. To see where they are headed—back to Dingwall or on to Islay. They're going to Dingwall to consolidate Domnhall's hold on Ross. I told the Brodie. He seemed pleased at the news."

He would. Domnhall's attention would stay well to the west of Brodie—and, he hoped, Rose—territory. Kenneth nodded and caught Cat's eye. "Given that news, it might be best if we ride north to the firth, then west along the coast past Brodie to Rose, well away from what remains of Domnhall's army. I dinna ken how well yer...disguise...will hold up if any of his men get too close."

"And the sooner we go, the better," Sutherland added, standing.

"No' now." Cat looked up at him and raised a hand. "'Tis time I see to the men."

Sutherland took her hand and helped her to her feet with a smile that made Kenneth's jaw clench. He didn't like to see the other man's hands on her, even for something so innocent. Somehow, with Sutherland, nothing seemed innocent.

Cat nodded her thanks, then bent and pulled the cook pot from the fire. She ladled rich broth from the top of the pot into one cup, then dug deeper and filled other cups with the heartier stew of meat and barley. "If we go, who will care for the injured until they reach Brodie?" She spoke without looking up from her task.

She had a point, but... "Surely for the next few days someone else can do what ye have been doing." Kenneth gained his feet, conscience pricked by her concern for his clansmen. He reached for a cup. "I'll help ye with these." Kenneth couldn't help but be impressed by Cat's devotion to the Brodie wounded. She was more than the spirited daughter of a difficult laird. She cared what happened to these men.

Sutherland frowned. "Who will care for them if ye are taken by another clan and more Brodies are hurt or killed attempting to defend ye?"

"'Twill no' come to that," Kenneth objected. "But I agree remaining with the army is dangerous. We can travel faster on our own. We'll leave tonight."

"Nay!" Cat surged to her feet, ladle dripping broth in one hand.

"We must, Cat, and well ye ken it. The men will survive until a Brodie healer can care for them." Or they wouldn't. He would spare her the reminder. Mentioning the possible outcomes would only hurt her. They had to go. The risk to Cat of remaining in the midst of Domnhall's men was too great.

"What if some of the army has gone the way ye plan to go?"

Kenneth shook his head. "They willna—they'll follow Domnhall."

With a frown, she returned the ladle to the pot, gestured for the men to carry the other cups, and headed for the wagon with the cup of broth for the man with the fever. Kenneth exchanged a shrug with Sutherland and they followed.

CATHERINE KNELT OVER HER PATIENT, LIFTED HIS HEAD and dribbled broth between his lips, grateful when he swallowed it. She knew she was running out of time. If they left tonight and traveled without stumbling into any remnants of Domnhall's army, they could reach Rose in two or three more days—or nights. If her idea to seduce Kenneth was going to work, she needed time alone with him. Could she convince Cam to stay with Iain? Or to go on ahead on his own, to make for the nearest port and sail north to Sutherland? Left to their own devices, she and Kenneth would be fine. Better than fine, if she got her way. But everything hinged on convincing Cam to leave them.

Should she just tell him what she meant to do? He behaved as though he had designs on her. But she didn't return his interest, and, despite his teasing, which she sensed was aimed at Kenneth more than her, he knew that, too. Would he cooperate, or would he tell Kenneth what she intended?

She clenched her fist, which made her grip the cup of broth even more tightly. It was hot, but thankfully, not enough to burn her skin—or her patient. She couldn't risk scalding the fevered man she was trying to save. She sighed and forced herself to relax. But her patient started tossing his head. He felt nearly as hot as the cup in her other hand, and she feared he was becoming delirious. If so, he wouldn't live much longer, no matter what she did. But before she could move away from him, Kenneth joined her on his other side, squeezing with care between the fevered man and the man next to him. Kenneth took his head in both hands and stroked carefully while speaking softly. In moments, the man calmed. Kenneth lifted his gaze and nodded for Catherine to try again to get the man to drink. She did and he took a few sips, but then sighed and went boneless.

Kenneth lowered the man's head and shrugged. "Passed out again. Yer broth may have helped him some."

"I fear 'twas no' enough to do him much good," she replied. "But I thank ye for calming him. We'll try again when he next wakes."

Kenneth took her free hand and stroked his thumb over the back. "If we are still here."

What should she do? As much as she needed Kenneth, these men needed her more. "How can I leave…?"

"Ye ken ye must. This man would no' want ye to come to harm caring for him."

"He speaks the truth," a man with a broken leg interjected. "We all are grateful for yer care, but ye must go. What happened to those camp followers should never be spoken of. Ye have been kind to us. We dinna wish to see ye meet the same fate. Go, lass."

She lifted her gaze to Kenneth's. He met and held hers, concern written in the crease between his dark brows. Since the moment she'd first seen him in St. Andrews, though his words painted a different picture, he'd done his best to protect her. To care for her. Surely his actions meant he still loved her, even if he had not said those precise words. They were still meant to be together. The nod she gave him barely dipped her chin. But he saw it. And saw in it her capitulation. Aye, she would go with him. What he didn't see—couldn't see—was the determination behind her reluctant agreement. The next few days—and nights—would make all the difference.

As soon as darkness fell, she, Kenneth and Cam bid Iain farewell and rode north, cutting away from the main body—and the path—of Domnhall's army. By the time they left the hills behind and the scent of saltwater freshened the air, Catherine was nodding over her horse's mane. Even in the darkness, Kenneth must have seen.

He called a halt.

"We should keep going," Cam argued.

"Cat needs sleep. We've come far enough to let her rest," Kenneth responded.

"We've come far enough, Cam," Catherine interjected, "for ye to make the coast by sunup and find a ship across the firth." She yawned, then continued. "Kenneth and I can turn west and be on familiar ground soon enough."

"I dinna like to leave ye..."

"Ye must." Catherine shrugged. "Earl Sutherland needs to ken what happened at Harlaw and what Domnhall is likely to do."

"A day or two will hardly matter." Cam pulled his mount's reins through a loose fist. "But having two of us to protect ye until ye are safe behind Rose's walls may make all the difference."

Catherine knew Kenneth, as much as he would like to see the last of Cameron Sutherland, would agree with his point, but he was keeping silent to avoid irritating Cam into staying. Cam would accept comments from her that would start an argument with Kenneth. "Chances are we'll soon run into a Brodie patrol from the keep," she offered. We canna be far from the border of yer lands," she added after a glance at Kenneth. "Another day will see me home. Really, Cam, ye can tend to yer own concerns. I'll be safe with Kenneth." *As I always have been, damn it.*

Cam shook his head. "Brodie can ride onward to his clan, and I'll see ye to Rose. From there, I've nay doubt I'll find transport."

Nay. Letting Kenneth leave her was not at all what Cat had in mind. Alone with Cam? *Ach,* and would her father think the worst and force her into marriage with Cam? He would tempt her father—Sutherland was a powerful clan. Nay. Not only would Kenneth never agree to it, nor could she.

Indeed, Cam's offer finally swayed Kenneth to speak. "Go on, Sutherland. I can see Cat home from here."

Catherine found she wanted to kiss Cameron Sutherland after all.

He looked from Kenneth to her. Catherine held her breath until he finally nodded.

"Very well. I'll be on my way."

Catherine nodded. "Thank ye, Cam, for yer care. I wish ye safe to yer home."

"And ye to yers." He glanced at Kenneth and spared him a, "Brodie."

Kenneth nodded. "Sutherland. Safe travels."

In another moment, Cam disappeared into the darkness, the only evidence of his passing the soft and fading rumble of his horse's hoof beats.

"Let's make camp," she suggested after a moment. Kenneth's gaze was still on the forest where Cam had disappeared. He nodded and dismounted.

"Should we build a fire?" Knowing Kenneth's contrarian mood, whatever she suggested, he'd do the opposite.

"'Twill be too dangerous," he told her.

Just as she'd hoped. To stay warm, they'd have to put their blankets together.

He looped his mount's reins around a convenient branch, then helped her from hers.

As soon as his hands went around her waist, Cat leaned into him, bracing her hands on his shoulders as he lifted her down, then slid her arms around his neck and let her body slip down the length of his. The catch in his breathing told her the sensation of her body against his had the desired effect.

"Cat..." he warned, his voice a low rumble against her chest.

"Aye?" she replied lightly, running the fingers of one hand through his hair.

"Did ye and Sutherland...Did ye get him to agree to leave us alone?"

"What? Never!" She leaned away from him, but kept her lower body pressed firmly against his.

"Nay? Ye are making me think that's exactly what ye had in mind."

"What are ye accusing me of, Kenneth Brodie?" She leaned into him and wrapped her hands around the back of his neck, then brushed them up into his thick hair. She shifted her weight from one foot to the other, making her hips rock against his thighs. The growing evidence of his desire against her belly made her bold. "Of wanting to be alone with ye?"

"Aye. Ye dinna ken where that might lead."

"Then show me." She pulled his head down and traced her tongue along his neck and jaw.

"Cat, nay."

Then she brushed her lips across his mouth.

Kenneth stood still for a moment.

Cat held her breath. He could still push her away, but then he groaned and answered her kiss with a deeper one.

Exultation sent hot shivers through her core. They spread and heated as Kenneth's kiss became more demanding, more urgent. He pulled her tightly against him, and she instinctively wrapped one leg around his hip, opening her center. If only all the layers of clothing between them would magically disappear, if she still wore a skirt instead of these breeks, she could make him hers, and she his, in moments.

Instead, Kenneth pulled away, then set her away from him and went to the horses. When he pulled blanket rolls from behind the saddles, her heart leapt. Would he...?

Aye! He unrolled one and spread it on the ground, then the other, next to it. "My lady..." he murmured, waving a hand at their impromptu bed.

"My laird," she responded, grabbed his hand and pulled him along with her, down onto the wool. At first, they sat facing each other, their gazes locked, studying every nuance of expression made visible by shafts of moonlight penetrating the tree canopy. Catherine was afraid to move, even to breathe, for fear, like a startled deer, Kenneth would back off and flee. He'd kept her safe, even from himself, for weeks. She'd had enough of his reserve. But then his hand cupped her cheek, and his finger traced her temple, her cheekbone, her jaw, then brushed across her lower lip. She opened her mouth and sucked it in, swirling her tongue around it and using her teeth only when Kenneth threatened to pull it from the warm, moist confines of her mouth. She didn't release his finger until he groaned and lifted his other hand to pull her onto his lap and into his embrace.

This must be heaven, a place where Kenneth's heated kisses trailed fire over her lips, her face, her neck. She could hardly credit the sensations rushing through her body. They got even more intense when he pulled the neckline of her borrowed shirt aside and trailed fire down her chest. He bared one breast and licked her nipple to a hard bud. She cried out his name and he laid her back on the blanket. Pulling the shirt from the waist of her borrowed breeks and over her head, he left her bare from the waist up. Her first instinct was to cross her arms over her breasts, but when she saw the hunger in Kenneth's gaze, she dropped her hands and let him look his fill.

He bowed over her and took one nipple in his mouth, sucking and tonguing it until she arched off the blanket, unable to contain the fierce longing his mouth drew from her. Then he kissed his way across to the other breast and did the same. Catherine moaned and reached for him, needing... Something to fill the sudden emptiness between her legs. Her core clenched painfully, aching for something only Kenneth could give her.

Her heart pounded as if she'd run all the way from the Brodie camp to this secluded spot. Her body melted and liquefied so completely she feared sinking into the forest floor, never to be found again.

His hand traced down her belly and inside the breeks.

She should have protested, but the magic he worked with his touch kept her mute and panting. She arched up to meet him as his fingers tangled between her legs, slippery with her own moisture, and delved between her folds into her hidden places. He groaned in answer to her little cries of pleasure, but she wanted more. More of his voice vibrating in his chest and against her ribs, more of his touch, deep inside her body, more of his mouth claiming hers. She clutched his shoulders, then reached down to untie her breeks and give him better access.

She stilled when his mouth left hers, but instead of withdrawing from her completely, he began slowly trace a trail of hot, wet kisses down her belly. He pulled her breeks down her legs and pushed her knees apart, then kissed the inside of each knee and trailed his tongue up the inside of one thigh. At first the path heated, then cooled as the night air chilled the moisture he left behind.

Cat didn't think she could take any more of the pleasure until his tongue found her center. He stroked her there, hot and wet, moaning her name between licks and gentle sucking, until she came apart, gasping out his name and writhing beneath his mouth until she was utterly spent. Only when she stilled in exhaustion did he lift his head.

She wanted more. She wanted him. The deep aching emptiness inside her was back, clenching, more demanding than before Kenneth had taken her to the heights. So she reached for him, running her hands down his chest, but instead of stopping at his waist, she kept going, covering and exploring the hard length she found beneath his breeks. Hungry for him, she untied them before he could stop her and pulled his length free of the cloth, stroking and squeezing him until he groaned her name and rose to arch over her.

"Are ye sure, Cat?"

"Ye ken I am. I want only ye, Kenneth. I always have."

"But the others I.."

"They dinna matter. Ye are mine, and I am yers. I always have been. Make me yers, Kenneth. Take me here. Now. I canna wait any longer."

"Nor can I, Cat."

His body pressed into hers, hot and strange, slowly stretching a part of her she never knew capable of such a thing.

"Ye will stop me if it hurts," he murmured as he pushed forward.

Cat wrapped her legs around his back, despite the tightness wanting more, wanting all of him. She gasped when he breached her barrier. "That hurt."

"It will be better soon," he soothed.

"I ken it." And it was. The pain subsided almost as quickly as it came. She tightened the hold her legs had on his hips and nodded. "'Tis time"

"Ach, my darling Cat, 'tis past time. Once I took yer maidenhead, ye were mine. The pain was the old Cat dying away. Ye are a new Catherine now. My woman, forever."

Tears filled her eyes. "Truly?"

"Aye. And now, my love, I have to move."

"Nay! Dinna leave me." He filled a void in her she'd only guessed existed.

"No' yet, Cat," he said as he withdrew a bit, then pushed into her again.

He didn't leave her body completely before he filled her yet again, building a rhythm she quickly learned and rose to meet his thrusts. "I canna wait any longer, Cat. I've wanted ye for too long…"

"Then take me," she cried as he thrust into her, hard, and stilled there, shuddering as his hot seed spilled and filled her. He withdrew a little, then thrust into her again, moaning her name. "Catherine, my love, my life."

Catherine's tears fell freely. His words touched her soul. "My love," she answered. "Forever."

CHAPTER 12

They stayed locked together for minutes longer, then Kenneth withdrew and rolled to his side, pulling Catherine against him and pulling the second blanket over them. "Sleep, my love. I will keep ye safe," he promised as she drowsed and fell into slumber.

Kenneth kept watch, dozing with one eye open as he'd learned to do in the army in France, resting but aware of his surroundings, the quality of the light, the constancy of predawn birdsong above them.

While Cat slept, he marveled at their joining. All these years, all those mademoiselles, and he'd never known what it could truly be. What it could truly mean. Cat was his, had fought to be his, risked her life and her virtue to be his. He was unsure how to accept such a gift. He only knew he must, because he swore to himself, he would not hurt her ever again.

Deep in his memories, it took a moment for him to realize the birds had gone silent. He opened his eyes a slit and studied what he could see. Cat's shoulder and hair just in front of him, his arm over her side and his hand cupping her breasts under the blanket, her backside pressed gloriously against his erection. Trees and undergrowth, moving slightly in the wind off the nearby coastline. Nothing else. Yet something had silenced the birds.

"I see her ploy worked."

Sutherland! Kenneth started to rise, then recalled he was naked—and so was Cat. "What the hell are ye doing back here?" Hoping not to wake Cat, he kept his voice low as he sat up and reached for his breeks, but let his irritation show in his tone. Ploy? What ploy? What had Cat confided to the northerner?

Sutherland leaned against a tree and crossed his arms, his gaze on Cat's sleeping form under the blanket.

Kenneth's movement had exposed her back. He reached over and pulled the blanket over her shoulder, covering all of her but her hair.

Sutherland grinned, then answered softly. "I ran into a pair of gallowglass men a few miles up the coast. For the sake of the lass, I thought it best to warn ye. Yer way home is no' as safe as ye'd hoped."

"Only two?" Kenneth stood and pulled on his breeks. The hell with what Sutherland saw.

Sutherland lifted his gaze to the trees while Kenneth righted his clothing. "Only two. That doesna mean they dinna have friends. Likely they plan to steal a boat to sail home rather than walking to Dingle with the Lord of the Isles."

"Speaking of walking, where's yer horse?"

Sutherland gestured over his shoulder. "Tied up back there. Since I meant to bring ye news, I didna want to ride up and startle ye into hiding."

Kenneth nodded. He would have sent Cat into cover at the first sound, naked and wrapped in a blanket, but safe. Instead, Sutherland had been canny enough to let the lack of sound—the forest's sudden silence—announce his arrival to Kenneth's discerning ear.

"Ye have told me. Now what do ye plan to do?"

"Ride with ye, of course. She's safer with two of us than just one." He glanced at Cat's shapely form and twisted his lips. "Obviously."

"What's between Cat and me is none of yer business —or anyone else's."

"I dinna expect her father will agree with that sentiment."

"My father will have naught to say about this."

Kenneth whirled to face Cat as she sat up, pulling the blanket away from her face and securing it under her arms. "We gave him the chance to approve our marriage and he failed to do so. Instead, he tried to give me away to three other men. Three other clans. Now, my virgin's blood will see the matter settled the way I've always wished it to be."

She gave Kenneth a shy glance and he nodded. He'd known when he took her this would be the outcome. Somehow, the prospect pleased him, no matter how it had come about. They'd only to find a priest to make it official. Too bad they were no longer in St. Andrews.

"Unless we run afoul of those gallowglasses. Then Kenneth's blood may put an end to yer plans." Sutherland shrugged. "In that case, I'll be pleased to step in to salvage yer virtue. The Sutherland despairs of ever seeing me wed, but Lady Catherine has made the idea seem somehow…attractive." He shook his head. "Something I never expected to happen."

"Yer sacrifice willna be necessary," Kenneth growled, reaching down to help Cat to her feet and ensure she stayed covered.

"I'm *pleased* to be of service in awakening ye to the idea of wedded bliss," Cat added with a haughty lift to her chin as she echoed Sutherland's choice of term, "but as ye see, I'm no' available to ye or any other man." She glanced proudly at Kenneth. "Only this man."

Kenneth squeezed her hand and was rewarded with her smile.

Sutherland bowed. "I wish ye happy, then, milady," he intoned as he straightened. "Brodie," he added with a nod to Kenneth. "Now, shall we carry on? The sooner ye see the coast and determine how far ye are from yer clan, the more pleased I'll be."

"Aye," Kenneth answered. "Those two gallowglasses may no' be the only ones who've tired of marching with Domnhall and prefer sailing home in a Highland *birlinn*. If we're to run a gauntlet, let's learn what sort of gauntlet it will be."

CATHERINE DRESSED QUICKLY AFTER CAM LEFT THEM TO retrieve his horse. She didn't think he'd be gone long. Kenneth watched her with a gaze so hungry, it pained her. She wanted to go to him, wanted to kiss him, to let him hold her and do what they'd done before she fell asleep, but suddenly, there was no time. The bond they'd established would have to stand without more time alone together—for now at least.

Dressed, she carefully folded the blanket stained with her virgin's blood. If her father required proof, it would have to serve. The blood on her thighs would wash away too easily, as would any remaining on Kenneth's body. Sudden shyness kept her from asking him if he bore the proof. He might show her, but show her da? Nay.

It seemed they were doomed to travel with Cam. There would be no more privacy for them until they reached Rose and declared their union. She had only the unaccustomed soreness between her legs and the memory of melting into Kenneth's embrace to sustain her. She had no idea how to go forward; how to prepare for the battles she knew would come. The gallowglasses might be the least of their problems. Her father could still deny them. She would not let that stop them. She loved Kenneth. Had always and only loved Kenneth. Without him, she felt like a specter, a fraction of herself. Only Kenneth could keep her solid. Only by touching her, holding her, and joining his body with hers would she remain whole.

She wanted to reach for him. Instead, she clutched the blanket to her middle and answered his hungry gaze with one of her own.

As quickly as she'd feared, Cam returned, leading his horse. She should be grateful he'd walked back instead of riding and given her more time to ready herself.

Kenneth helped her mount, his hand lingering on her waist longer than necessary to steady her seat. "Are ye well?"

She appreciated his concern, since he was responsible for the strange soreness between her legs. But the discomfort was nothing she couldn't bear. "I'm well."

Almost before she could catch her breath, they were on their way.

They reached the coastline as the sun's disk began to clear the tops of the trees behind them. The Moray firth spread out before them, down a bluff and much wider than it appeared at Rose.

"Do ye recognize the coastline?" Cam asked, his gaze on the water instead of one of them.

Catherine shook her head. "I've never been this far east."

"I have," Kenneth responded. "We've another long day of riding. Barring…interruptions…we could reach Brodie after sunset, then go on to Rose the following day. 'Tis nearer to cut inland a small distance and go across country than to follow the coastline."

Catherine's heart leapt at that news. If they went to Brodie, Annie would help her. She and Kenneth could handfast or even wed there if they had a priest in residence, and she could send word to her father to say she was well...and wed...without having to face his wrath. Could Annie send for Mary so both her sisters could be with her without their father finding out and putting a stop to her plans?

She ignored the discussion Kenneth and Cam were having, preferring to lose herself in her dream of making Kenneth unassailably hers...forever. Aye, going to Brodie would solve several problems.

❦

Hours later, they left the concealment they'd found when they spotted a group of riders between them and the sea, and Kenneth identified them as more gallowglass men.

"How many of those bastards did Domnhall bring with him?" Cam groused. "It seems like all of Ireland is wandering about the Highlands."

"Iain might ken, but we didna think to ask him. In any event, we willna make Brodie this day." Kenneth hated to see the disappointed expression on Cat's lovely face, but he would not risk her. They would continue to go slowly and carefully until he could get her behind Rose's walls.

Kenneth sent Sutherland to scout ahead while he stayed with Cat. They rode side-by-side, in careful silence. She had been overjoyed at the news they would go to Brodie first. He'd had to remind her about the danger posed by the remnants of Domnhall's army in the area. Since then, she'd opened her mouth to speak several times, thought better of it, and closed it again, slanting an annoyed glance in his direction. Surely she didn't blame him for the chaos the Lord of the Isles caused?

She must be eager to see her sister, Annie, probably to enlist her aid with their father.

While Kenneth expected the man to be relieved Cat was alive, he would surely still be furious she'd run to St. Andrews. And once there, failed to let anyone know where she was. Despite his rancor over James Rose's refusal to let him wed Cat two years ago, he felt some sympathy for the man. If she'd done the same to him, he would have been furious, but also terrified she'd come to harm. Kenneth winced again. She had. With him. She was safe, but no longer untouched.

He glanced aside and caught her smiling at him. He couldn't help himself—he smiled back. Then he turned his gaze back to their surroundings. No question about it—his Cat was scheming.

Since Kenneth had saved and protected her, Cat believed this time her father would agree. Her purity— or lack of it—need not become part of the discussion.

Kenneth couldn't muster the same sense of certainty. The honorable thing to do would be to seek her father's approval and marry her right away. If the Rose refused yet again, Kenneth would have to tell him Cat was at risk of carrying his child. The rush of feeling that thought caused nearly bent him double in his saddle. Joy. Warmth. Pride. His heartbeat raced until the consequences occurred to him, then his blood turned to ice in his veins. Those consequences could be dire for Cat. If she survived bringing his babe into the world. If the babe survived. Carrying his bastard, unless they wed, would prevent her from marrying anyone else. Would leave her a virtual prisoner in her father's house, dependent on James Rose and whomever followed him as the Rose laird.

Rose had tried to give her away elsewhere—several times. After Harlaw, clan and crown disagreements were sure to worsen. The number of alliances a clan could claim would be even more important. Cat dismissed its significance, but one fact remained crystal clear to Kenneth. Annie Rose had married Iain Brodie. The Rose sisters might not agree, but to him it was plain—the Rose did not need another daughter to marry into clan Brodie.

CHAPTER 13

*W*hen Kenneth finally called a halt, they made camp in a small clearing surrounded by low trees and bracken. Once again, they dared not risk a fire. Catherine resigned herself to another night sleeping on the cold, hard ground and set about laying out blankets and their dwindling provisions while Kenneth took care of the horses. She spread hers and Kenneth's together, as was their habit, and left it to Cam to choose where he preferred to sleep when he returned from scouting ahead. Often, he went away from them. Giving them privacy, she supposed, or simply not wishing to overhear a repeat of what had led to him finding them naked together.

In any case, his absence at night suited her. It also suited Kenneth, though he professed not for quite the same reason. Aye, well, that reason, too, but having a scout away from camp meant someone might hear trouble coming before they did, or be able to come in behind an attacker. Or at worst, though Kenneth never said this and would not admit it, could carry news of their fate to their clans.

Kenneth returned and settled next to her on the blankets. "Sutherland has wandered off again," he reported just before he bit into the oatcake she'd handed him. He chewed thoughtfully, then studied the food she'd set between them. "We'll make Brodie tomorrow, so *dinna fash*," he added, with a nod at the meager fare on the blanket. "We willna starve before then."

Catherine nodded. "'Twill be good to have a hot meal—and to sleep indoors." She'd hesitated to bring up the subject of sleeping arrangements—and all it implied—but they needed to have this conversation before they reached Brodie and her sister.

Kenneth's lips pressed into a thin line. "About that—"

"Aye?" Catherine's heart raced. If he was going to deny her, he'd tell her now, before Cam returned, and before he had to justify himself to Iain or Annie.

"Iain has seen us together, but Annie will be taken unawares."

"I dinna wish to be kept from ye…"

"Yer sister will do what she thinks yer da would want for ye."

"Annie? Ye have met my sister, aye?"

Kenneth's serious expression slipped, and he chuckled for a moment.

"That I have."

"She will be on my…on our side." His sigh made her heart plummet to her belly.

"If ye are with child, I will care for ye and the bairn, ye ken I will, aye?"

Catherine didn't like the sound of this at all. "And if I am no'?"

He looked away and ran a hand through his hair. "Ye can do better than to wed me, Cat. After what I did in France…"

"None of that matters to me," Catherine interrupted

him, grabbing his arm and pulling his gaze back to her. "Ye should be certain of me by now."

"Ye'll make an enemy of yer father. After all I've done, I am no' good enough for ye."

"Do ye love me?" Ice filled her veins and her belly as she waited for him to speak. She thought she knew the answer, but he could destroy her dreams with one word.

"I...ye ken I do."

Tears formed behind Catherine's eyes and she took a deep breath, trying to force them back. Before she could speak, Kenneth continued.

"I care about ye. I want to see ye safe. I want ye... even more now that we..."

"Just no' enough to wed me? What are ye trying to say?"

"Cat..."

"After all we've been through. All we've—done...we said *forever*."

"Ye said that. And I'm sorry—for everything."

"Sorry!" Catherine dropped her head into her hands, unwilling to believe any of this.

"I'll see ye home safe. Once ye are there, ye will see I'm right."

She shook her head as she turned away from him. "Never." She wanted to reach for him, wanted his arms around her, his lips on hers. But she couldn't bear to let him see her tears. "Once I am home, my da will lock me away until he can marry me off. I'll...I'll never see ye again. Is that what ye want?"

He remained silent for so long, Catherine turned her head so she could see his face. His expression surprised her. He appeared to be in pain, features drawn down, arms crossed over his belly, and the hand she could see clenched into a fist. She spun to face him and rose up on her knees, too fast for him to hide what he was feeling. "Ye do want me. Ye do care. Ye canna convince me otherwise."

Something in him gave way, and he reached for her. She fell into his arms, blissfully aware of every touch, every hungry kiss as he claimed her. Arguing with Kenneth made her blood heat and added fire to their joining. He might use words to tell a tale, but his body could not lie. He needed her, and even more, he wanted her.

She arched into him as they tumbled onto their sides, hands searching for ways inside clothing. His kiss burned a path down her throat. His hands fumbled at her waist and her borrowed breeks suddenly slid down her hips. His mouth followed, nibbling, licking and kissing a scorching path down her belly and between her thighs. In moments, she was flying, free as a bird from the constraints of her earthly body, drenched in pleasure so fierce she forgot to breathe.

Then he pulled away and turned from her, shoulders heaving as if he fought for control.

Catherine kicked aside the corner of the blanket twisted over her lower legs and reached around him to grasp his fists. When he refused to turn to her, she swiveled around his body and straddled his legs. Before he could react, she pushed him onto his back. She left a hand on his chest in mute command to stay there as she worked loose the ties of his breeks and spread the fabric, freeing his shaft to stand tall and proud before her. Kenneth groaned and turned his head aside. "Dinna do it, lass. Ye'll make a babe for certain."

She had no intention of mounting him. Not yet. Instead, she leaned down and sucked his tip into her mouth, then curled her tongue around it.

Kenneth arched up and cried out, whether in pain or pleasure, Catherine didn't know and cared even less. She meant to explore him and to do to him what he'd done to her—use her mouth to bring him pleasure. His hands pushed at her shoulders, but she kept him in her mouth, using her tongue to lick along his length and raking him gently with her teeth. When he grew even longer and thicker, she knew she was pleasuring him. When his fists dropped to his side, she raised her head. "Is this what the mademoiselles did for ye?" she asked.

"God, aye. How can ye ken that?"

"Because ye like it so," she responded and took him in her mouth again, sucking until he bucked and pulled her off.

He rolled away from her, thrusting into his hand, then gave a long groan and froze, his body arched and stiff for moments.

Catherine watched, fascinated, until he relaxed and started breathing again, then gripped his shoulder and pulled him back to her. His staff, still in his hand, had shrunk and softened, but as she studied it, it firmed and lengthened again. "Do ye want more?"

In response, Kenneth pulled his breeks closed over it and shook his head. "Go to sleep, Cat."

THEY WERE SO GOOD TOGETHER, KENNETH COULDN'T imagine losing her. He wanted her too much. But he had to control himself or risk a babe neither one of them was ready for.

"I'm no' done." Cat reached for his breeks, but he pushed her hand away.

"Nay, lass. I'll no' take ye again." He'd already put her at risk.

Cat draped herself over him and laid her head on his chest. "Nay? Very well. Perhaps ye need to rest."

"That is no' the reason, and well ye ken it." He kept his arms at his sides. She expected him to hold her. He knew where touching her again would lead. Having her draped across his torso was sweet torture. He wanted her so badly, he was already rising again. He had to keep her attention away from his lower half. "And throwing yerself at a man is no' seemly."

She bolted upright on a gasp.

That did it. He rolled away from her and retied his clothing as he muttered, "Now go to sleep." He dared not comfort her.

Thank the saints they would reach Brodie on the morrow. The sooner he got Cat to safety and away from him, the better. Her sister could take charge of her, behind Brodie's walls, until Iain returned.

Yet, he'd promised to take her home. Brodie was his home, not hers. Hers lay most of another day's ride to the west, bordering Brodie's territory closer to Inverness. Did he really want to return her to her father, only to have him give her to some other man?

She thought her sister would side with her if he would only offer for her. He cared for her. He even loved her. But she couldn't assume he wanted to wed her. He'd warned her he was not worthy of her, and he meant those words with all his heart. Though he'd done nothing in France that every other able-bodied man he knew hadn't also done, his actions now shamed him. And what Cat had just done for him—God's bones! From whom had she gotten such an intimate idea? From her cousin in St. Andrews or her sister, Annie? And how had she made the connection to mademoiselles he had encountered? Cat was too clever, too perceptive. Or too much in love with him.

Of course, he knew the difference between the actions of a French doxy and his Cat's desperate attempt to pleasure him in order to bind him to her. Yet, if she did the same as his wife, would he feel the same guilt—the same sense of responsibility for corrupting her? Or would he be grateful for having such an adventurous woman to love?

He needed to talk to Iain. Before his friend met and married Cat's sister, Annie Rose, Iain had bedded more than his share of lasses.

Only how could Kenneth explain to Iain what so disturbed him now? About Annie's sister? Nay. He could not. The only solution he could see was to handfast. If her father respected it, that bond would protect her from him and give them a year and a day to be certain they wanted to wed in the kirk. Sutherland could witness when he got back from hunting, once the sun came up.

Her father could still try to wed her elsewhere, but Kenneth thought he'd give them the year and a day rather than try to make a different match for a daughter who had run away rather than wed another, and who was no longer untouched.

Decided, he listened to hear if Cat had gone to sleep or was still upset and, perhaps, crying. But instead of her soft breathing, he heard men approaching.

CAT THOUGHT SHE'D JUST DOZED OFF WHEN KENNETH touched her shoulder, then whispered near her ear, "Be silent. I hear something." Heart pounding, she nodded as his hand left her shoulder and he rolled carefully to his knees. Low pitched voices reached her ears, sending a cold shiver down her spine. In the predawn glow she could see Kenneth turn his head, first one way, then the other, trying to locate where the men's voices came from.

Were these the gallowglass men they'd thought would stick to the coast? Or were these different soldiers from Domnhall's army? Kenneth was armed and alert to the danger. But where was Cam? Was he alive or had someone found and killed him?

Kenneth suddenly stilled. "Dinna move from here, lass," he whispered. "Unless they're friends of ours, I dinna want them any closer to ye. I'll draw them away." Then he crept off into the darkness. A few moments later, she heard horses moving away, then running hard, followed by the sound of something crashing through the brush. He'd left her! Had he ridden away or whipped the horses into running and made more noise to confuse the invaders? She didn't know!

She rolled slowly to her knees and waited, listening hard for any hint of sound telling her there were others around, or that Kenneth—or even Cam—had returned for her.

Nothing.

She sat back on her heels and tucked her hair up into the bonnet Kenneth gave her with the rest of her disguise. Should she stay? Or go? If she followed the coastline she would come to the Brodie keep eventually. Kenneth would find her, either on the way or once she reached it. Cam too. Even on foot, she might get there late today. Or meet a Brodie patrol.

But nay, Kenneth had made a lot of noise to draw away the men he'd heard. If she moved, she might draw them back. And with the sun coming up, any move she made might be seen. She eased down slowly to a more comfortable position and settled in to wait. Cam would make his way here eventually, even if Kenneth kept going to lead trouble away from her.

Then she heard Kenneth's voice—and others. He'd led them away, but not far. And he was outnumbered. She stood.

CHAPTER 14

enneth didn't wait to watch Cat's horse run away. Instead, he broke for the undergrowth, running with his mount in a different direction, then he swatted his and sent it running ahead while he changed directions again, making as much noise as he was able to in the process. He might be caught. The gallowglass might get his horse, or they might chase Cat's and round hers up. But in none of those scenarios would they find Cat and harm her. He would see to that if it cost him a wound, his life, or both.

He made it farther than he thought he might before they caught up with him. Three of the Irish warriors faced him, grinning. Right now, he couldn't think about Cat. He had to survive.

"Well, then, laddie," the dark-haired one taunted. "Ya gave us a merry chase, but your fate was never in doubt, was it lads?" He glanced at his two red-headed companions as they moved in on Kenneth. He must be the leader of this merry little band. The other two looked enough alike to be brothers.

"How did ye ken to chase me instead of rounding up the mounts?" Kenneth asked, backing away to give himself plenty of room to fight. The nearest red-headed man carried a halberd, which had probably been quite useful against Mar's mounted cavalry at Harlaw. It gave him a longer reach than Kenneth could claim, but it was awkward to use in close quarters. Kenneth was confident of his abilities with a claymore and dirk. The attacker would try to use the reach of his weapon, but they would quickly come to close-quarters fighting, where Kenneth would get inside his defenses.

The first man feinted, thrusting the halberd toward Kenneth.

Kenneth leapt back and warned him off with a swing of his claymore, two-handed, that connected with the halberd's steel with a clang. The shock ran up both his arms, but he didn't care. As long as the men thought he needed both hands for his weapon, they'd underestimate his fighting ability.

The second red-haired man moved in from the side with a dirk. That told Kenneth they were used to fighting paired—the man with the halberd to pull a knight from his mount, then the man with a sword or dirk to finish him off if the first man couldn't get close enough to gut or behead his victim. They wanted to kill him, but he was not going to let them. Cat depended on him, and Sutherland, wherever he was, would not end up with her if Kenneth could help it.

The dark-haired leader stood aside, watching, as the two moved in a macabre dance around Kenneth.

He let it go on for a while, careful with these two and conscious the leader could ambush him at any moment. Their tactics never changed, only the direction they came from and the sequence of who attacked first. The halberd's long pole soon sported deep cuts from Kenneth's blade, which, though it looked undamaged, must have been dulled at Harlaw. It should have cut completely through the oak the first time Kenneth attacked. But if the man swung the halberd too hard, the pole might break apart in his hands, leaving him with nothing more than a wooden spear. If he moved quickly, he might mange to retrieve the battle axe with a long point on top before Kenneth gutted him. But he'd have to be quick.

When the pair realized the battle wouldn't immediately go their way, they backed off, but kept circling Kenneth. Tired of their hesitation, when the man with the dirk next moved closer, Kenneth finished him off, cutting his head cleanly from his shoulders, despite the dull edge to his claymore. The other redhead shrieked and charged. Kenneth spun to meet him and knocked the halberd from his hands. It tumbled a short distance and the pole broke when it slammed into a nearby tree.

His opponent eyed it, but must have decided it was too much trouble to retrieve. He backed away. His gaze darted to the leader and back to Kenneth too quickly for Kenneth to move in on him. Then he pulled a dirk.

"You could join us," the leader taunted, drawing Kenneth's attention. He pulled a short sword and brandished it.

"There willna be an *us* to join," Kenneth boasted as the other man's gaze strayed again to the leader. Kenneth slashed his shoulder, taking him out the fight without sending him to hell the same way he'd send his partner. The man fell and lay moaning, gripping his wound as blood seeped through his fingers, then he passed out. Kenneth spared a moment's thought that he should have killed him outright, but likely he'd bleed to death soon enough.

The leader moved in for the kill, but too slowly. His skill was little better than his followers.

Kenneth faced him. He had seen better tactics from the gallowglass men in France. "How did the three of ye survive Harlaw?" Kenneth asked, genuinely perplexed. "Did ye avoid the battle altogether? Did ye stay at the rear with the camp followers?" His taunts must have hit home.

The leader growled and charged with a battle cry that did little to impress Kenneth, and did nothing to save the Irishman.

Kenneth sidestepped and knocked the blade from his hand. It landed with a dull thud in the loam just out of the man's reach. "If ye are wise, ye'll take yer life and yer other man and go home," Kenneth warned him. "For yer support of Domnhall, I'll give ye that chance. Ye dinna need to end up like yer friend."

Instead, the man pulled a throwing knife and cocked back his arm.

Kenneth flexed his knees, prepared to dodge the blade.

Before the gallowglass could release it, Cat came out of the woods behind him and struck him over the head with a stout branch. He went down like a stone dropped from a tower.

"Well done," Kenneth congratulated her tightly as he moved to the man and checked to see if he still lived. He did, but he'd be out for a long time, judging by the blood streaming from the back of his head. He stepped clear and turned back to Cat. "But I told ye to stay put." Now his battle lust was fading, anger replaced it. "Instead, ye disobeyed me and put yerself in danger."

Cat's hands landed on her hips, a familiar gesture that boded ill. "So ye canna thank me for saving yer life?"

"I wouldha finished him soon enough." Kenneth had fought too many battles to cede this one to a lass.

"Ye might have," Cat allowed. "Or ye might have had his dirk stuck in yer throat."

"No' likely."

She huffed out a breath. "Ye have saved me enough times. It was my turn to return the favor."

He raised an eyebrow. "So we are keeping score, aye?"

Cat crossed her arms and sniffed.

"No matter. We have to find the horses and go. This man will wake up sooner than we like and be after us again."

"The solution to that problem is easy enough," Sutherland announced, leading their three horses into the clearing. He put a hand on the hilt of his dirk. "Cut his throat."

"Nay! He's unarmed and unable to defend himself," Cat objected.

Sutherland handed her the reins and leaned over the man. "Still breathing." He pulled his dirk and glanced at Kenneth. "Are ye certain ye dinna want me to finish him?"

Kenneth approached and crouched down. "If we had some rope, I'd tie him up and leave him for his friends to find. It appears they've spread out through these hills, rather than following meekly behind Domnhall as we'd hoped." He twisted around to find Cat. "Can ye manage without those laces at the top of yer dress?"

Sutherland grinned and Cat blushed. "If I must. The dress is in the pack on my horse..." she waved a hand toward their mounts.

Kenneth nodded then stood. "As ye said, he's unarmed and unable to defend himself. I'll fetch it," he announced, then turned to Sutherland, "if ye can keep him quiet without cutting his throat."

Suddenly, their prisoner bolted upright and pulled a dirk from his boot. It caught the light and silvered as he drew it back to throw it. Not at Kenneth. At Cat. Kenneth dove for her and knocked her out of the way as Sutherland tackled their prisoner and pulled his own blade.

The scuffle lasted mere moments and was over before Kenneth could be sure Cat was all right and join Sutherland in subduing the man.

Sutherland pushed himself up with a groan. Sutherland's dirk was buried in the man's chest. He looked up at Kenneth, who was helping Cat to her feet, and shrugged. "Well, I didna cut his throat." Then he sank to his knees, suddenly pale and grasping his side.

The prisoner stirred and pawed at the blade in his chest.

Kenneth saw his arm shift and ran from Cat toward their prisoner. How could he be alive?

Kenneth reached him as the gallowglass pulled the dirk from his own chest. Blood welled as he rolled to his side. He should be dead, yet he still fought. Somehow he found the strength to swing the steel toward Sutherland. Kenneth kicked it out of his hand before Sutherland had time to react and dodge the blade. He buried his own dirk in the man's throat.

"I did cut his throat," Kenneth said, answering Sutherland's comment before the attack. He straightened, eyeing the man as his blood seeped into the forest loam around him. "He's dead this time."

Sutherland nodded weakly, a line of red quickly spreading to darken his shirt. "Thanks for that. Now, if ye would be so kind as to bind my wound with something, I'll do my best no' to bleed to death along with him."

Cat rushed forward and tugged his shirt free to check his wound. "Not too bad," she informed him, bunching the cloth and pressing it against his side. "But it needs tending. Hold this." She ran for their supplies and returned with a spare shirt.

Kenneth didn't want to watch Cat touching

Sutherland so familiarly. His heart still pounded from the fight and the surprise attempt on Cat's life. Even though she was only tending Sutherland's wound, their nearness made his jaw clench. Sutherland had flirted with Cat the entire trip. Yet she had chosen him, not Sutherland. He took a deep breath and told himself to grow up and do something useful, as Cat was, until his blood cooled.

Instead of watching Cat minister to Sutherland, he rolled the gallowglass man over with his boot, having learned from Sutherland's mistake not to bend too close until he was certain his quarry was dead. There could be no doubt the man was dead. Kenneth bent and retrieved his dirk, then stabbed it into the dirt to clean off the Irishman's blood. "We need to go. These three may have friends in the area."

"The news is no' bad, no' good," Sutherland announced, then hissed when Cat padded the gash in his side with cloth she tore from the spare shirt.

She grabbed his hand and pushed it in place over the padding. "Hold it tight," she ordered, then tore a long strip of cloth and reached around Sutherland's body.

Kenneth's eyes narrowed at her nearness to the northerner's bare torso.

Sutherland saw and tensed, looking like a cornered animal watching the approach of a wolf. His gaze flicked between her hair just below his chin and Kenneth.

Kenneth presumed Sutherland saw the muscle jumping in his jaw. Good. If Sutherland dared even one sharp inhale of her scent, Kenneth might give into the temptation to tear Cat away from him and finish the job the gallowglass had started. Her body aligned entirely too closely with Sutherland's for Kenneth's comfort. Then Cat got the makeshift bandage where she wanted it, pulled Sutherland's hand free, and tightened the bandage in place. When she nodded and moved away from Sutherland to rinse his blood from her hands, Kenneth took a breath.

Sutherland did, too. Cat's nearness might have aroused him, but bleeding and pain had made him pale. As he leaned to the side to tuck his shirt into his breeks, he lost even more color.

Kenneth had to be satisfied with that.

"'Tis what I returned to tell ye before we were so rudely interrupted." Sutherland said after a moment in which he regained some color. He gestured at the bodies on the ground around them. "I presume those are why I found yer mounts running loose nearby. Ye set them free as a distraction? Good thing I was able to round them up. We canna get to Brodie—there are more men like these in the way."

Kenneth nodded. "Then we must ride for Rose. If more in Domnhall's army are pillaging the countryside, the safest place for Cat is behind her father's walls."

"Unless Rose is in danger, too," she interjected. "Brodie is closer."

Sutherland shook his head. "We willna get near the keep. I fear yer men coming behind may no', either. But there are more of them, so perhaps they'll prevail over what we must avoid."

"I should ride back and warn Iain, but I canna leave Cat with ye, wounded. Ye canna defend her."

"Sadly, ye speak truth." Sutherland glanced at Cat, then dropped his gaze.

Cat spoke up then. "But Iain, and the wounded he brings…we could wait for them, go to Brodie with them."

Kenneth took Cat's hand. "'Tis no' up for argument. I ken ye are reluctant to face yer da, but I am reluctant to see ye harmed—or killed. We'll go to Rose."

"And..."

"And we'll deal with the rest when ye are safe."

❧

NIGHT HAD LONG SINCE FALLEN BY THE TIME THEY arrived at Rose. From their vantage point in the trees, the closed gates loomed massive and forbidding in the deep darkness. They did not appear to be damaged, so despite the lack of torches to light the battlements, Sutherland agreed with Kenneth's assessment. Domnhall's army must not have had the chance—yet—to molest the keep. The two men rode forward, leaving Cat in concealment for the moment.

"Ho there," Kenneth called, then added his name. "Open the gate."

"Brodie, ye said?" The gate guard's voice rang out firmly in the night. A torch suddenly flamed over the top of the wall and a man peered down at them.

"Aye," Kenneth answered. "With a Sutherland, and one other."

"I see only two of ye."

"God's bones, Fergus, it's me, Catherine," Cat called as she broke from the cover of the woods and rode up to join Kenneth and Sutherland.

Kenneth gave her a fierce frown and hissed, "Have ye nay sense?"

Sutherland merely raised an eyebrow.

"That's Fergus," Cat replied, unimpressed. "I've heard his voice every day since I was in swaddling."

"Lady Cat...Catherine!"

Cat waved.

A grin split the man's bearded face. Then he looked aside and waved his hand, palm up, gesturing for someone to raise the portcullis. "Someone fetch the Rose and Lady Mary. Lady Catherine is back."

With that, the gates opened and Cat rode forward, not giving her escort a chance to make sure the keep was truly in Rose hands before she raced inside its walls.

Kenneth traded a disgusted glance with Sutherland and took off after her, Sutherland bringing up the rear.

Inside the bailey, only the night watchmen on the walls were visible. Fergus slid down a ladder's rails, the fastest way off the wall, as Kenneth helped Cat dismount. In seconds, he'd stepped between them and gave her a hearty hug.

"Where have ye been, ye wicked lass? And what are ye wearing?"

James Rose rushed out of the keep's heavy doorway as they dismounted. He paused on the steps, hands on hips, his head turning to survey the bailey. "Mary Catherine, where are ye? Who said she is here?"

Kenneth realized Fergus and her horse hid Cat from her father. "Cat!" he hissed. "Yer da."

Cat peered around her horse's head, then patted Fergus on the shoulder and ran to her father. "Da! I'm sorry."

The Rose's expression changed in an instant, from annoyed to smiling, to frowning.

Kenneth dropped the reins he'd been about to hand to a stable boy. He didn't think the Rose would harm his daughter, but he would do anything necessary to protect her, including fighting her father. Much to his relief, Rose enveloped his daughter in his arms and hugged her tightly. "Ye daft lass. Ye've given us weeks of worry."

Cat nodded. "I ken it. But I dared no' write. I needed time..."

Rose set her away from him with a grunt. "Let's no' discuss this out here. Who brought ye..." He trailed off as Kenneth stepped forward, Sutherland a pace behind, at his shoulder. "Brodie," Rose said, his tone suddenly cold and flat.

"Aye, Laird Rose, with Cameron Sutherland. I...we rescued Cat...Catherine from St. Andrews when news reached us..."

"Rescued? St. Andrews?" Rose tugged Catherine's arm. "Come inside." He glanced at the men. "Ye two as well. This bodes to be too long a tale to be heard while standing in the night air."

Kenneth nodded but didn't move as Rose led his daughter inside the heavy door. Nerves suddenly held him in thrall. The reality of where they were—and what he'd done—consumed him. Would Cat confess she'd lain with him? If she did, what would Rose do? Suddenly Kenneth doubted even that would convince the Rose to allow the wedding Cat wanted. Now he'd brought her safely home, he was suddenly unsure what he wanted, as well. "I'm a dishonorable cur," he muttered.

"Mayhap." Sutherland nudged his shoulder. "'Tis time to face what ye have done. If his daughter still wants ye, will the laird agree?"

Kenneth shook his head. "He refused me two years ago. Why would he agree now?"

"Perhaps because ye have now bedded the lass, aye?"

"That's what Cat is counting on." He forced his feet to move. "The bottle dungeon at St. Andrews might have been a better fate than what the Rose will do when he finds out."

Sutherland paused on the steps, breathing harder than he should have to. "She loves ye. Ye ken it, aye? She'll convince her da. She's no' the same lass she was two years ago."

Kenneth looked over his shoulder and met Sutherland's gaze. "And how would ye ken that?"

Sutherland quirked an eyebrow. A corner of his

mouth lifted in a pale reflection of his usual grin. "She told me so. Ye had to leave us alone every now and again. The lass needed to unburden herself."

Kenneth clenched his fists. "To ye? I wasna aware ye are a priest."

Regret shone briefly in Sutherland's eyes, surprising Kenneth.

"Nay, I am no'." He held up a hand. "And I never touched yer lass. She merely told me about losing ye the first time. She seemed quite determined no' to allow ye to slip away again."

Kenneth ignored Sutherland's pallor. "So ye two plotted…"

"Nay. I merely stood aside to give the two of ye the time ye needed—alone—together. Time Cat was certain ye would never have once ye got her home."

Kenneth frowned. "I dinna ken whether I owe ye my thanks or should gut ye where ye stand." And how ironic—now they were out of danger from the army they'd sought to avoid, he suddenly found comfort having Sutherland at his back.

"I'll be content with yer thanks. Now we'd best go inside, aye? Laird Rose is waiting."

Kenneth heaved a breath and turned to the doorway with a nod. Sutherland's wound needed attention. And the next few minutes would decide Kenneth's future, one way or another. Honor demanded he admit ruining Rose's daughter and accepting whatever punishment Rose cared to inflict. Honor be damned. She wasn't ruined to him. He'd marry Cat because she wanted it, even if her father tried to exile the both of them as a result. They'd make their home in France if that was what it took to make Cat happy—and to keep Iain from skewering him for destroying his alliance with Rose. He didn't care where they lived. But he'd prefer to stay at Brodie. Cat would prefer to be near her sisters, no doubt. He hoped Iain would agree, even if it strained his relations with James Rose.

Inside, the entryway was empty. Kenneth had expected a crowd of Roses to gather near the door at the news of Cat's return. Then he heard the rumble of voices from the great hall. Quick footsteps betrayed the arrival of a latecomer hurrying their way, then a swirl of skirts preceded a lass through an archway into the hall where they waited.

"Mary!" he greeted the late arrival—Cat's eldest sister.

"Kenneth Brodie!" Mary came to him with her hands out. "I heard someone brought Catherine back to us—it was ye?"

Kenneth took her hands, then turned her to regard Sutherland. "We did. Mary Elizabeth Rose, this is Cameron Sutherland."

For once, Sutherland's usual charm with the lasses seemed to fail him. He stood, silent, his gaze fixed on Mary Rose. When she smiled quizzically, he shook himself and bowed slightly, then winced. "At yer service, milady."

"Where did Cat and yer da go?" Kenneth asked, attempting to cover Sutherland's sudden awkwardness.

"His solar, I imagine," Mary replied, her gaze shifting from Sutherland back to him. She cocked her head. "But based on the noise coming from the great hall, perhaps not until after she greets everyone gathered in there. Let's go there first."

Mary led the way and paused just inside the door, allowing Kenneth and Sutherland to arrange themselves beside her. No one paid them any attention. All the focus in the room was on Cat, who was being passed from hug to hug as she greeted everyone. Kenneth had no doubt she was also delaying the confrontation with her father for as long as she could.

Finally, when Cat seemed to run out of clan members to greet, Mary stepped forward. Cat saw her and ran to her eldest sister. "*Ach*, Mary, thank ye. I wish I'd been able to write to ye..." she apologized as she fell into Mary's arms.

"Now, now," Mary soothed, patting Cat on the back as Cat's tears finally spilled. "All will be well. Ye will see." Over Cat's shoulder, Mary frowned at Kenneth.

He shrugged and turned his gaze back to Cat, wishing she felt she could run to him for comfort the way she did old Fergus and her sister. Instead, she'd unburdened herself to Sutherland? What was he doing wrong?

Cat nodded and pulled back to meet Mary's gaze, wiping tears from her cheeks. After a sniffle, she glanced at Kenneth, then added, "We may need to gang up on Da again."

Mary nodded and gave Kenneth a knowing smile before turning back to her sister. "*Dinna fash.*"

"Did ye meet Cam?" Cat asked, sniffed again, and reached for Sutherland's hand.

Kenneth tensed at the familiarity. One more sign she had bonded with Sutherland when he wasn't looking. He didn't like it.

Mary blushed and nodded. "I did."

Sutherland bowed again. "My very great pleasure, milady."

Kenneth wasn't certain which sister he addressed, but he was certain only he saw Sutherland grimace as he straightened up. His wound had worsened while riding here. Cat had not been able to give it the care it needed. But with their father approaching, the sisters had turned to face him. Everything else would have to wait.

"My solar, if ye please," Rose said and waved a hand in that direction.

His tone of command told Kenneth he had spoken as Laird Rose rather than simply as Cat's father. His daughters traded an undecipherable look, then obeyed. Kenneth stiffened his shoulders, nodded and followed the lasses. A glance aside revealed Sutherland at his back.

NEEDING HER SISTER'S SUPPORT TO FACE HER FATHER, Catherine chose a chair next to Mary. The round table in the laird's solar was a recent addition, one she was certain Kenneth had never seen. Instead of being seated with the others, he would be expecting to stand before her father's desk. She hid a grin as Kenneth entered and took in the new arrangement. He hesitated, then stepped aside to allow Cam and Da to enter. Contrary to what she expected, her father didn't join her and Mary at the round table, but took his accustomed seat behind his desk, leaving Kenneth and Cam standing. "Da, Cam needs the healer. He was wounded..."

"I'm well enough," Cam interrupted.

Her father waved their comments away. "Explain yerself, daughter. Where have ye been and why are ye in a lad's breeks instead of dressed as a lady?"

"'Tis no' Cat's fault..." Kenneth said, but her father waved him to silence as well.

"I'll no' hear from ye until I wish to," he warned. "Until then, dinna interrupt."

Catherine bristled but Mary's hand on her arm kept her in her seat. "Tell us," Mary prompted softly.

Catherine wondered where she should start. Since confronting her father over his attempts to wed her to someone other than Kenneth seemed sure to bring a hasty end to any hope of reconciliation, she chose a different beginning. "I've been staying with *maman's*

Duncan cousins in St. Andrews. Abi and her stepfather were kind to me. But when word came about Domnhall's army and his threats against Aberdeen, Kenneth and Cam, separately, decided it was no longer safe for Highlanders in St. Andrews. Kenneth helped me leave, and we met Cam on the road. He's a friend of cousin Abi's."

Her father's face had reddened with each word she uttered. Catherine couldn't see how this was going to turn out in any way good for her and Kenneth. But before the explosion she expected took place, help came from an unexpected source.

"Catherine is right," Cam said. "I received information that a Highland-sympathizer priest had been captured. Soon after meeting up with Kenneth and Lady Catherine at a mutual friend's outside St. Andrews, we were told the priest had been hanged."

Mary covered a cry with one hand and gripped Catherine's arm with the other. Catherine laid her hand over Mary's. "We left just in time."

"Remaining in town would have been dangerous for all of us," Kenneth added. "We travelled mostly at night and avoided settlements."

"Ye couldha sailed and arrived sooner without dragging my daughter all over the Highlands..." her father objected. crossing his arms.

"Harbors were full of royalist troops, so we were forced across country," Cam explained.

"We met up with a group of Brodies—Iain included —two days after the battle at Harlaw," Kenneth added. "We spent a night and a day with them. Iain had sent the worst wounded ahead. Cat...Catherine's nursing the rest may have saved Brodie lives."

Relief at her father's approving nod made Cat's muscles weaken. She hadn't realized how she'd tensed until then.

"But Domnhall's army, gallowglass men included, was breaking up and spreading out over the countryside," Kenneth added. "It was nay safe place for a lass. In borrowed clothes, Cat appeared as a lad, but her disguise wouldna stand up to close scrutiny. We resumed traveling as we had been, avoiding settlements. Yesterday, we ran afoul of three gallowglass men. That's when Cam was wounded."

When her father rose to his feet, Catherine tensed again.

"It seems a miracle ye arrived safe and whole, daughter."

All the blood seemed to drain from Catherine's body to her belly, then rise in a heated torrent to her face. Aye, she was safe, but far from whole. She fought to keep her gaze from Kenneth as she nodded. "I had excellent protectors in Cameron Sutherland and Kenneth Brodie."

"Indeed." Her father's flat tone left no doubt he'd seen her blush and suspected the reason for it. When he cut his gaze to Kenneth, she rose.

"Ye have no' asked why I left," she bit out.

"I ken why ye left. I read yer note. What I dinna ken is how ye have come back. Are ye wed? And if so, to which of these…" he inclined his head at Kenneth and Cam, "…protectors?"

Mary gasped, but Catherine stiffened her spine and faced her father. "Kenneth is the only man I have ever wanted as my husband." She turned to him and nearly swooned when he moved around the table, stood at her side and took her hand.

"We are…married in the old way," he admitted, smiling at her, then turned back to her father, his expression grim. "With yer blessing, we'd like to be married in the kirk."

"Ye expect me to condone yer disobedience?"

Her father hadn't shouted, which frightened her more than if he had.

"I can only assume ye planned this…this tryst…and arranged to meet in St. Andrews," he growled.

She and Kenneth cried, "Nay!" at the same moment.

Kenneth squeezed her hand. "Iain sent me as hostage for Brodie to Sterling. From there, I was moved to St. Andrews, probably at Albany's orders to move all the Highland hostages from where their clans might expect to find them after Domnhall took Dingle. I didna ken Catherine was also there until I saw her walking with some friends."

"He avoided me for days…weeks," Catherine added. "Even then, he sought to keep me safe. I pursued him, Da." She couldn't help the small smile curving her lips. "And I caught him." Then she risked showing her father the anger that had driven her to run away and glared at him. "It just took more than two years longer than I'd hoped."

"So ye have dishonored yerself and this clan, and ye come before yer laird boasting of yer actions?"

Mary stood at the rising cadence and volume of their father's words. "Da, ye ken fine she is no'—"

"Silence, daughter. Ye and yer sisters worked yer…*will*…on me once before. Ye willna do so again. Mary Catherine, ye are confined to yer chamber. Kenneth Brodie and Cameron Sutherland, I will grant ye hospitality only so far as to spend the night in the stable. Ye will be gone at first light."

"Da! Cameron Sutherland needs a healer's care," Mary objected before Catherine could refuse. She pointed at the red staining the side of his shirt.

"He can be tended in the stable. Now all of ye get out. I have much to think upon, no' the least of which is the future of the alliance between Rose and Brodie."

Kenneth's eyes widened at the implied threat, but he

took Catherine's elbow and helped her from her father's solar.

She welcomed his assistance, unsure she could stay on her feet without his strong arm supporting her. Her father had just compounded the misery they shared by threatening the alliance with Kenneth's clan. Even though Annie was married to its laird. She could only imagine what Kenneth must be thinking, and how furious Iain would be if her father made good on his threat.

Cam followed them, his expression grim.

She stopped in the hallway and put a hand on his arm. "Ye willna go to the stable. Ye need care." When Kenneth frowned at her hand on Cam's arm, she withdrew it and turned to her sister. "Mary, please. Ye ken I am right. Will ye take charge of Cam and see him cared for?"

"Of course." Mary took Cam's arm, ignoring his raised eyebrow. "'Tis a shame ye could no' stop at Brodie. Yer wound would have received care sooner and be better than it is now." She paused and tugged on his arm to get him moving toward the stairs. "Come with me. I'll see ye settled in a chamber where the healer can attend ye."

"Yer father—"

"Need no' be told. Now come."

Catherine grinned at Cam's bemused expression as they ascended the stairs. He might not be accustomed to being ordered around by a woman, but Mary was impossible to ignore when she was in this mood. Besides, Cam was hurt, and probably too weak to resist.

"What about me?" Kenneth asked.

Catherine grimaced. "'Tis best ye keep out of his sight for a while."

"I think the same applies to ye."

Catherine nodded and pointed up the stairs. "Let's find ye a place, then."

"Yer chamber, perhaps?"

"Only if ye want Da to throw ye in the dungeon when he finds out. The stables would seem sumptuous from there."

CHAPTER 15

$\mathcal{C}$atherine flung herself across Mary's bed. Mary's chamber was not where her father had ordered her to go, but she would defy him at least this far—if she could not be with the man she loved, she would be with the sister who loved her. She needed the comfort being here provided. The same comfort she'd sought here since their *maman*'s passing all those years ago. How many times had she lain like this while Mary stroked her hair from her face or dried her tears or just talked, then crooned a lullaby, Mary's soothing tones lulling her to sleep? As a child, she'd loved waking with Mary's body curled protectively around her, telling her without words everything would be all right.

Not this time.

This time, Da was on guard against all the ways they might manipulate him. Over two years ago, they'd made it impossible for him to refuse Annie's wishes when she'd decided to marry Iain Brodie. He knew their tricks.

Catherine feared her love for Kenneth was hopeless—doomed never to result in the marriage and family with him she longed for.

"*Dinna fash*, Catherine," Mary told her for the

hundredth time since they left the laird's solar. "Kenneth will think of something. Or we will."

"Da kens us too well. We willna succeed again."

"Do ye have so little faith in Kenneth? After ye found him again, after ye traveled all this way with him, have ye no' seen how he cares for ye? How he looks at ye? Like he did when he first saw ye. 'Tis as if the last two years never happened at all."

"What good does that do if he willna ask for me, or steal me away to Brodie." Catherine paused and swallowed a sob. "We became so...close...on the way here." She looked up and met Mary's concerned gaze. "We slept together." She gave a choked laugh. "We did more than sleep." Then she wrapped her arms around her middle. "I could be carrying his babe, even now."

Mary pulled her arms away from her middle and took her hands in a warm, sure grip. "If ye are, Da will have to agree to let ye wed. But even if ye are no', he can be persuaded."

Catherine shook her head. "We've tried. I fled to St. Andrews to keep him from marrying me off to someone else. I didna wish to return—ever. I missed ye. And Annie. But I couldna risk what Da might do." She pulled her hands from Mary's and dropped her head into them. "Then the troubles started and Kenneth feared I would be taken prisoner or worse. He made me go with him. I hoped we'd stop at Brodie, wed there, before ever having to confront Da. But the gallowglass men..."

"So ye came here because Kenneth was determined to see ye safe before aught else."

Catherine nodded. "I ken he cares about me. But bringing me home might also be a way for him to get rid of me."

"Nay, Catherine, I dinna believe that. He will do what is right, especially if ye are with child."

"I dinna want him to wed me because of a babe! I want him to love me. To be unable to live his life without me. I want him to long for me as I long for him. On the way here, I thought he might feel all of that…but if he obeys Da, he'll leave at sunup and leave me behind. Maybe forever!"

"After all he has shared with ye since St. Andrews?"

"I dinna care where he's been or what he's done. I love him still."

"Has he said he loves ye?"

Suddenly Catherine wasn't sure. Had he ever actually said the words? Cat shook her head. "Ye would think I'd recall something so important. But I dinna ken if I recall my own longing to hear the words, or if he really said them."

"Then chances are, he has no' admitted his love for ye yet—no' in words."

"Yet we talked about handfasting, about betrothal. Would he even say those words if he did no' love me?"

Mary nodded sadly. "Even the best men will sometimes say whatever will get them what they want at the moment…"

"Nay! Kenneth wouldna!"

"Ye told me he spent two years in France. What do ye think he did there?"

Catherine slumped. She knew what he'd done. Fallen in love. Then out of it again. "He nearly married."

Mary covered a gasp with her hand. "Why nearly?"

"I dinna ken. He told me he thought he was in love, but he was wrong. He didna tell me the rest. Ach, Mary, I dinna ken what to do!"

The next morning, Kenneth prepared to leave for Brodie, donning his travel clothes, perhaps for the last time. He should reach Brodie tonight.

He didn't want to go, to leave Cat, but counted on obeying the Rose gaining him some favor he—to all appearances—still lacked.

Traveling alone, he'd be vulnerable to any band of marauders he had the bad luck to encounter. But he'd take the risk.

He couldn't ask Sutherland to make the trip. His home lay in a different direction. And he was wounded. He should stay at Rose for a few days to heal, then find a ship headed north. And that would be that—likely he'd never see the man again.

Despite their initial animosity, Kenneth had come to respect the northerner, at least when he wasn't flirting with Cat. It had taken most of the trip for Kenneth to understand the teasing talk was just Sutherland's way. Cat had been correct—he really meant nothing by it. Unless he was prodding Kenneth every now and again, to make him jealous—or at least to make him pay attention to the lass right in front of him. Not once—that Kenneth knew about—had Sutherland tried to poach Catherine away from him. Instead, he'd given them time and space and privacy, though Kenneth now regretted the latter.

He'd ruined Cat and made their joining a matter of urgency. So why was he preparing to ride to Brodie? Because he felt the Rose gave him no choice.

He should have waited. If Sutherland had stayed close, he would have been forced to wait. But none of this was Sutherland's fault. Kenneth should have respected Cat—and her father—enough to leave her untouched until he returned her home. Then asked, honorably, for her hand. Again. Two years ago, the Rose had thought his daughter too young—both of them, really—and refused. They weren't too young now. They'd both seen and done too much to claim innocence as a reason to prevent their marriage.

And if she carried his child?

Kenneth hung his head. If she did, she would find a way to let him know. This time, he would stay close. Even if Iain tried to send him away again, he'd refuse. He'd speak to Annie and confess what he'd done. She would help him. Once the Rose sisters worked their magic on their father, he would come back and claim Cat for his own. For his bride. As he should have done more than two years ago, instead of tucking his tail between his legs and running to France.

He'd been a fool. Many times a fool. Leaving Cat. Getting involved with Marilee and the others. Getting involved with Phillippe and the French wars, which had nearly cost both of them their lives…and their eternal souls. He'd known where sleeping with Cat would lead. *He'd known.*

He was dressed. He couldn't delay any longer. A glance out his chamber's window revealed Cat, sitting on a bench in the Rose's summer garden. He owed it to her not to sneak away.

He'd say goodbye before he left. Then he'd go.

The heady scent of so many blooming roses nearly choked Kenneth when he entered the garden and closed the gate behind him. Cat stood and smoothed her skirts, a sign of nerves he'd come to know well.

"I'm doing as the Rose demanded," Kenneth told her when he got close enough to speak without being overheard. "But I dinna want to leave ye. I wanted ye to ken at least that, before I go." He wanted to take her in his arms, but they might be seen. He couldn't afford to anger her father any more than he already had.

"Is that all ye want to tell me?"

Her voice was so low and subdued, if he hadn't been

looking right at her, he would not have believed his Cat had spoken.

"I dinna ken what to say, Cat. If I'm ever to gain favor with yer da, I must obey him now. Can ye no' understand?"

"I dinna care if ye gain his favor. Or if I do. I canna bear to see ye leave me behind again. Take me with ye. You said we are married. I am yer wife. A wife belongs with her husband."

"Ye want me to steal ye? From yer da's own keep? Are ye daft? He'll have me killed on sight. The alliance between Brodie and Rose will be over. Annie will never be able to come home. Mary will never see either of her sisters again. Is that what ye want?"

She shook her head, but dropped her gaze to the ground between them. "We've spent too long apart already. Why must we give up each other for the sake of an alliance? We've already sacrificed to keep my father happy. When do we get to be happy?"

"No' today, my love. Ye must trust we will be together. Just no' today."

❧

CAT KNEW DA WOULD BE ANGRY IF SHE RAN AWAY AGAIN, but she did not want to leave a future with Kenneth to chance. She might be the youngest of his daughters, but being last didn't mean she couldn't be the strongest. She wanted to prove it to him, to Kenneth—but most of all, to herself.

"I understand ye feel ye need to leave without me. If ye think that is the way to preserve the alliance between our clans, then aye, ye must do as ye think best. But so must I. So, I will leave Rose, too. If no' with ye, then later today. Or tomorrow. Sometime soon, ye will find me at the Brodie gate. I hope when that happens, ye will be glad to see me."

"Ye will no' leave these walls alone, Cat. No' even to walk to the firth. Promise me."

His expression was so fierce, she knew what was coming and didn't flinch when he grasped her shoulders and gave her a little shake.

"Promise me," he demanded and shook her again, harder this time. "Ye ken what's going on outside these walls. 'Tis too dangerous for a lass to be about, especially a lass alone! Ye canna imagine what those men could do to ye."

Cat took pity on him and nodded, recalling how Cam had been injured. "I promise. I willna leave these walls today."

"No' until I return for ye, Cat. I mean it. There are too many gallowglass headed for Inverness." He released her shoulders and traced her cheek with his fingertips. "Now I've found ye again, now that we've..." He stopped and cleared his throat, pressed his lips together until they turned white, then spoke. "I willna lose ye to marauders."

Though he'd all but promised he'd return for her, he had walked away from her before. And betrayed her trust, though to be fair, he'd thought she was married to another man. Still, she couldn't resist one last turn of the knife. "Nay, but ye have always been willing to lose me to my father's dictates."

Kenneth's expression went cold and hard.

The gate creaked and Catherine suddenly wished she'd never even thought about her father, much less mentioned him.

He stood glaring at them with the open garden gate in one hand, the other clenched at his side.

"I told ye to stay in yer chamber," he barked at Catherine. Then he turned his ire on Kenneth and growled. "'Tis past time for you to get on the road, aye? Yet I find ye here with my daughter. Again."

"He was just saying goodbye," Catherine told him, keeping her chin up and turning so her shoulder shielded Kenneth's body from her father's furious gaze in the small measure her slighter form could provide. Fury and frustration made her reckless. "He is my hus..."

"I'll leave ye now," Kenneth interrupted and stepped around her. He turned to her father with a nod. "Laird Rose."

Her father allowed Kenneth to pass. Catherine nearly swooned in relief. Let Da be angry with her. She didn't care. He would not harm her, not really.

But he could kill Kenneth, and nothing she could do or say would stop him.

The door to the kitchen swung open with an ear-splitting squeal of rusty hinges behind her. Catherine flinched but welcomed the distraction, hoping it would break the tension as she and her father watched Kenneth walk toward the stable.

"Wait!" Mary called.

Catherine spun to face her sister. "Mary? What's amiss?"

"Kenneth," Mary called more loudly as she stepped out into the garden and hurried forward. "Da, Cameron Sutherland has developed a fever. He canna travel until he is well. And given what he and Kenneth have told us about the dangers roaming the Highlands at this time, ye canna send Kenneth on his way alone."

Catherine wanted to hug her sister, but to do so in front of their father would make it look as though they had conspired to keep Cam—and Kenneth—here. They had not.

Cam was sick? "How bad is he?" She glanced around, trying to see her father and Kenneth at the same time, to judge their reactions to Mary's news. Was this the reprieve from her father's demands she and Kenneth needed?

Kenneth had paused and stood in the bailey, his upper body turned back toward them, as though uncertain whether to keep going or obey Mary's summons.

Da approached his daughters, his expression severe. "This had better no' be another of yer attempts to…"

"Ye are welcome to visit my patient and see for yerself," Mary sniffed, planting her hands on her hips. "He's ill, Da. The wound he suffered from the gallowglass, despite Catherine's best efforts to care for it while they traveled, has festered. He hid his discomfort last night, but there is no denying the state he is in this morning. Go on." She waved a hand toward the kitchen door. "See for yerself if ye dinna believe me." She turned to Kenneth, who had slowly approached the garden gate, now her father had left it. "He's asking for ye," Mary told him.

Catherine crossed her arms and fought to look concerned. Not to smile, not to look at Mary. She regretted Cam's pain and illness, but if it kept Kenneth near, she could be a little glad of it, couldn't she?

Her father growled and gestured for Kenneth to precede him back into the keep.

Kenneth frowned but came forward, treating Mary to a quizzical frown as he passed.

Catherine exchanged a glance with Mary behind their backs. Mary smiled and nodded. Was Cam really sick or had Mary—nay, she couldn't. Could she?

CHAPTER 16

Kenneth couldn't believe the change in Sutherland since last evening. Mary had spoken the truth. His wound had worsened, and the fever he'd developed left him dry in the mouth but sweating, then chilled. The Rose had taken one look, shook his head and left the room. Kenneth took that to mean Sutherland's—and his—banishment was officially postponed. He knew better than to think it was cancelled.

He called the northerner's name softly as he approached the bed. Sutherland opened reddened eyes and frowned from beneath heavy eyelids.

"Brodie."

"Mary said ye asked for me."

"I did?"

"Do ye no' recall it?" Or did Mary say something in front of her father to get Kenneth back within the keep instead of headed for the stable?

"I dinna ken…" He dragged a hand from beneath the covers and wiped his face. "Is it hot in here?"

"Ye're feverish, man. Yer wound is worse. Mary has gone for a healer, I think."

"Nay, she cleaned the wound and put some foul-smelling poultice on it before binding it up again." He grimaced. "Hurt like the fires of hell. I recall that much." Then his eyes closed. "She does have nice hands. Better than auld Agatha at home."

"Auld Agatha?" Kenneth prompted, though he should leave and let Sutherland rest. But Mary had sent him in here for a reason, so he'd stay and talk as long as Sutherland wanted to.

Sutherland's eyes opened and tracked to Kenneth's face. "Our healer. My father's. Hell, my grandfather's, too, no doubt. Hands of cold chapped leather." He turned his head and lay silent for a moment, staring at the ceiling. "No' warm and soft like Mary's. Lovely Mary. Kind..."

Sutherland's eyes drifted closed, and Kenneth supposed his last comment had been made by a man half asleep, or half out of his head. Aye, Cat's eldest sister was kind enough, but she could never be as beautiful or kind or smart as her youngest sister. Then again, Cat had told him she thought Sutherland more Mary's age or a year or two older, rather than close to theirs. Perhaps that gave Sutherland a different perspective on the sisters.

"How is he?"

Cat's soft voice startled him into turning, then he relaxed and shrugged. "Complaining of the fever and the Sutherland healer. Apparently, he prefers Mary's care."

Cat's eyebrows arced as she joined him at Sutherland's bedside, then she smiled. "Really?" She looked back at Sutherland, planted her hands on her hips and cocked her head. "That could be very good news."

"What do ye mean?"

"Never mind. I want to think on it."

Kenneth shook his head and crossed his arms. "I ken

what ye have in mind. But if Sutherland is interested in Mary, I wish him luck. Yer da will never marry her away. I've heard Annie complain to Iain often enough that she wishes he knew some likely suitors yer da would accept so she could do something for Mary."

"Perhaps Annie willna need to." Cat smiled and leaned forward to pluck a rag from a bowl of water. She wrung it out and placed the cloth on Sutherland's forehead, then stroked his cheek.

At the intimate gesture, jealousy burned from Kenneth's belly up to his throat, but he swallowed it down when Cat stepped back and took his hand. "Let's go. He's still too hot. He needs to rest."

Kenneth pointed with his free hand. "What about that cloth?"

"It will help keep him a little cooler. I'll tell Mary we've been here, and she'll come sit with him."

"He'll feel better soon, then."

"Not too soon, I hope," Cat replied and pulled him from the room.

CATHERINE INTENDED TO KEEP KENNETH OUT OF HER father's sight for the rest of the day. He agreed to go as far as the beach below the Rose keep, but only if several men went with them.

"We dinna need an escort in sight of the Rose keep," she argued as they walked toward the stables. She wanted to get him alone and knew if she tried to take him to her chamber, someone would tell her father and Kenneth would find himself confined to a dank dungeon cell, Catherine in the cell next to him. Nay, somewhere away from the keep, out in the open, was a much better idea. But not with a dozen Rose warriors following everywhere they went.

"Then we shallna go anywhere," Kenneth informed her and turned back toward the keep.

"Allo!" A man's voice called from outside the Rose walls. Catherine spun to ensure the gates were closed. They were. Kenneth had fixed his gaze on them as well, which pleased her. Her family's safety was important to her. She was glad Kenneth cared, as well.

"Who goes there?" The guard on the battlements nearest the gate peered down.

"We've two wounded and we're hoping you'll be of a mind to help," the man outside answered with an Irish lilt to his voice.

Kenneth shifted beside her, then ran for the ladder propped against the wall. "Wait!" he shouted and clambered up quickly.

Catherine clenched her hands over her waist. More gallowglass men? This could not be good.

Kenneth peered over the wall, then went to the guard and conferred in low voices.

Catherine couldn't hear what they said, but neither looked pleased.

Both wore frowns and fingered the dirks thrust through their belts while they talked. In moments, the guard turned away from Kenneth and spotted her in the bailey. "Get yer da, aye?"

Catherine nodded and ran for her father. Something was wrong. She found him in his solar and filled him in as they hurried back outside.

"Wait inside," he told her and headed for the ladder.

She watched him climb and confer with Kenneth and the guard. They moved away from the gate, and while they kept their voices down, Catherine could still hear them.

"Dinna trust them," Kenneth warned her father. "We had trouble with three gallowglass men on the way here."

"Ye told me. I havena forgotten. Are ye certain ye left none of those men alive?"

"Nay, I'm no certain." Then Kenneth shook his head. "The one I wounded may have been found soon enough to have survived. Cam said there were more gallowglass in the area—more of their group may have found them and will seek to avenge them. It was very early—still mostly dark."

"I canna refuse Highland hospitality. They claim to have wounded with them."

Kenneth turned to the guard. "How many are there?"

"At least six."

"So, more than the band we encountered. But if they are at all like the ones we encountered, and if the man I wounded is with them, there will be trouble."

"Then we'll have to keep them under close watch, aye? Ye'll stay away from the wounded, in case the one ye left alive had the sense to mark yer faces and can recognize ye." Her father crossed his arms and nodded to the guard.

As the gates swung open, Kenneth frowned. "I'll stay to help protect Rose."

Her father shrugged. "Ye are needed more at Brodie."

Catherine's heart stuttered. Would Kenneth let her father talk him into leaving? He met her gaze and pursed his lips just as the strangers came through the gate into the bailey. She ran for the door to the keep and slipped inside.

&

SUPPER WAS A TENSE AFFAIR. EVEN KENNETH COULD feel it. The Rose serving lasses moved quickly around the Irishmen, dodging grasping hands and sloppy kisses. Rose kept Cat at the high table with him. Mary was tending Sutherland. The visitors had not seen her and did not know she was in the keep. Kenneth hoped she stayed out of sight. Kenneth had the honor of Cat's other side. The gallowglass leader sat on her father's opposite side.

Every time one of his men would grab or pinch a serving lass, Cat would stiffen as if the man's hands were on her. "Da, do something," she whispered to her father, but he just shrugged.

Kenneth understood not wanting to rile the visitors. The Rose had been free with his ale and whisky. If he expected them to pass out from all they'd eaten and drunk before they got entirely out of hand, Kenneth knew he'd be disappointed. The gallowglass men he'd fought with in France had a prodigious tolerance for spirits. And an equal capacity to cause trouble. He stayed alert. The sooner he got Cat out of the great hall and behind her chamber's heavy oaken—barred—door, the happier he'd be. Even if he was not in there with her.

Finally, the meal ended and the Rose nodded, signaling to all they were free to leave the hall. Some did, but some stayed, keeping an eye on the visitors as the lasses cleared the tables.

A gallowglass man pulled one of the lasses onto his lap and clasped his hands on her breasts with a roar of satisfaction. "I've got ya, ya darlin' lovely!"

The lass shrieked and shrugged to get free, but the man kept pawing at her.

Two nearby Rose men came to her aid and pulled her out of the Irishman's grip.

The Rose stood. "That will be enough!"

"What's the harm?" The Irish lilt came from the gallowglass leader sitting next to him. "The lads are only doin' what lads will do."

Rose turned to him and snarled. "Keep yer men in control, or ye willna stay till morning. Ye will leave Rose now."

In answer, the man stood and drew his sword. "Ye owe me and mine. The men who killed two of my men had a lass with them and talked of coming to Rose." At Cat's gasp, he nodded. "That very lass, perhaps? Now that we are here, I think you'll find tossin' us out a might harder than ye wish it to be."

Kenneth rose and made sure Cat stayed behind him as her father also brandished his blade.

The gallowglass men in the hall joined the fight and in moments, they'd overturned tables and arranged themselves back to back, blades drawn. The serving lasses fled while the men fought. Kenneth stayed out of it, protecting Cat and letting her father fight his own battle until he and his opponent's struggle carried them to the great hall floor. When Kenneth saw another gallowglass swing a blade at the Rose and miss, Kenneth jumped down. The man moved toward the Rose again, forcing Kenneth to intervene. He stabbed the man in the chest, protecting the Rose from being stabbed in the back.

A shriek filled his belly with icy dread and he turned on suddenly shaky legs, consumed with regret he hadn't let the Rose take his chances.

The last Irishman standing had grabbed Cat. His blade lay against her throat.

CHAPTER 17

Catherine held herself still, furious at allowing herself to be grabbed. The man hadn't hurt her, and likely wouldn't, given that his other hand was busy fondling her arse. As long as that's all he did, she'd tolerate his assault to keep Kenneth and her father from rushing forward and making the man cut her throat. He probably imagined he could force her from the hall and have his way with her somewhere private. If he tried to take her in front of them, all hell would break loose again. She had no doubt one of them would kill her attacker, but whether she'd survive was somewhat in doubt.

On the other hand, she still had her eating knife in her pocket. If she could stab her assailant before he cut her throat, she'd be fine. She had taken a man down armed with nothing more than a tree branch. She could handle this.

"Let the lass go," her father demanded.

The man at her back laughed and thrust a hand between her legs.

"I'll kill ye if ye harm her."

Catherine hated the note of desperation in her father's voice.

Kenneth started forward, but she gave her head a slight shake, careful of the blade at her throat, trying to tell him she was unharmed, for now. Thank the saints for all the layers a woman wore.

"If ye harm her, he willna have to kill ye," Kenneth spat, venom in every syllable. "I'll do it for him."

She'd never seen him look so fierce. But then, he'd never seen her in the hands of a man bent on molesting her or killing her right in front of him.

"If ye want the lass to live," the man snarled and moved his hand from between her legs to her hip, then slid it up to grab one breast, "ye'll let me take her from here."

"Let her go—now," her father shouted.

Catherine knew she would be embarrassed later that her father saw her being assaulted this way, once she'd had time to think about it and recall his expression. But at the moment, she was more concerned about Kenneth's reaction. His eyes were narrowed to mere slits and the muscles in his jaw bunched tightly enough to crack teeth.

"Ye can leave," Kenneth ground out, without a glance at her father. "Only if ye let the lass go."

The man behind her laughed again, close enough to her ear to cause pain. "We'll go. 'Tis up to ye whether the lass lives when I'm done wit' her or whether I use her up, then do to her what ye did to my lads, and let the fairies take her."

The man pulled her back to the wall and made for the door to the bailey, sliding sideways so no one could get behind them.

Kenneth, her father, and several other Rose warriors followed, but backed off a pace every time the man twisted the blade he held against her neck.

His laugher made fury climb like a firestorm from her belly and she stopped, forcing him to stumble against her. Then she felt a warm, wet trickle down her neck, and realized she'd only made things worse. Once Kenneth or her da saw blood, they'd attack.

"Let's go," Catherine hissed and they moved on, out the door and into the bailey.

The man turned her to face the men following them from the hall. He kept her stumbling backwards, toward the stable. The few people in the bailey moved quickly out of the way. "Get us a horse," the man called as they reached the stable wall. He put his back against it, Catherine shielding his body in the front. "Or I'll ride this piece right here."

"Ye'll die trying," Kenneth taunted.

Catherine turned her head away from the blade at her throat, trying to see what was around her that might help her get away. For once, she cursed Mary's insistence that the lads keep the area around the stable clear of pitch forks and other implements. From the corner of her eye, she saw a stable boy stick his head out of the door and look wide-eyed at her and her captor. His gaze shifted to Kenneth, who nodded. He disappeared back inside for long minutes while Catherine fought for calm and endured her captor's grip on her breast. Then the lad led out a saddled horse.

Too quickly for anyone to reach them, the gallowglass swung up and dragged Cat up behind him.

Cat knew once out of the keep, she'd be in worse trouble.

❦

KENNETH HAD NEVER KNOWN ANGUISH LIKE THIS. ALL the other mounts, his included, were in the stable. He couldn't outrun a horse, even one carrying two people. Archers on the walls couldn't shoot as they rode out of the keep—they'd hit Cat. He ran forward anyway, hoping to grab Cat and pull her off the horse, but the man kicked the horse into motion, outrunning Kenneth's attempt.

Suddenly, before they reached the gate, Cat hit the man in the neck and the horse reared as he jerked the reins. Cat tumbled off the back, landing hard, a bloody eating knife still clutched in one hand.

Kenneth scooped her up, heedless of the bucking, rearing horse only a few feet away and dragged her clear. A shout warned him as the man turned the horse and swung his blade, aiming for Cat.

Kenneth pushed her aside, then blocked the man's arm. He got enough of a grip to pull him from the horse. Kenneth gutted him as he fell. He landed heavily, air whooshing out of lungs that no longer needed it, his blade lying useless a few feet away from his outstretched hand.

Someone stepped forward to control the horse, but Kenneth barely noticed as Cat ran to him and clung to his body, burying her head against his chest. "Are ye harmed, Cat? Did ye fall on yer blade?" Kenneth held her away from him and looked her over. "There's blood on yer arm."

"His," she replied and leaned into him again. "I'm unhurt."

Kenneth pulled her to him and hugged her, hard. "Thank all the saints," he whispered into her hair. Then he looked up. The Rose stood a few paces away, watching them, but saying nothing. He pursed his lips and turned away. Gesturing at the body on the ground, he ordered two of his men, "Get that offal out of my keep. All the rest of 'em, too."

"Da, the wounded..."

"Can stay where they are as long as they cause no more trouble," Rose answered her. Then his gaze lifted to Kenneth's. "Let's get her inside. We all could use a wee dram."

"Or two," Cat answered from within the circle of Kenneth's arms.

IN THE LAIRD'S SOLAR, OVER WHISKY, ROSE ADMITTED HE should have listened. Kenneth couldn't believe what he was hearing. The Rose laird, admitting to a mistake? From Cat's expression, raised eyebrows and parted lips, she was equally surprised.

"Just because the Irish fought for Domnhall doesna mean they are on the Highlanders' side," Rose concluded. "Sassenachs would have been better partners, had Domnhall been able to convince the English king to send troops. Too bad he had to rely on those gallowglass men."

Kenneth could only nod, though he couldn't give his wholehearted agreement. The English had done more than their share of damage on Scottish soil. Inviting them in would be like inviting the wolf inside your gates. He couldn't think of a thing to say that wouldn't sound disagreeable, so he kept his mouth shut.

Mary arrived in time to save him from continuing the conversation. "*Ach*, I heard what happened." She went straight to Cat, took the whisky glass from her hand and pulled her to her feet. "Come with ye. Ye look half asleep and should be resting after such an ordeal."

"Kenneth..." Cat started, then yawned and covered her mouth with a hand.

"Will be here in the morning," Mary interrupted, giving her father a narrow-eyed glare. "Let's get ye to yer chamber."

Cat nodded and went with Mary, but she trailed a hand across Kenneth's shoulder as she passed. Kenneth reached up and squeezed her hand, but let her go. Her father's steely glare prevented anything more affectionate than the brief touch.

The two men sipped their whisky in silence for a few tense moments. Then Kenneth set aside his glass and broached the subject that had been on his mind all the way from St. Andrews. "I asked ye before, more than two years ago. I'm asking ye again. I want to marry Cat—Catherine in the kirk. Two years ago ye thought her too young. She's grown up now."

"Aye, demonstrated by running to St. Andrews without telling a soul, with nary a thought for what might have happened to her on the way, or the worry she caused. If ye think her behavior was mature, ye're no' better than she is. Perhaps ye deserve each other." He gulped the rest of his whisky, set the glass down and refilled it. "Then she runs away from kin in St. Andrews with ye to go halfway across Scotland, meet up with an army, and finally get home." He sighed and set his glass aside. "Only to nearly be stolen away and have to stab a man to save herself. Inside her own keep. My bairn."

The Rose was working himself into a fine temper. Kenneth had a bad feeling about anything he might say next.

"Ye claim ye saved her from trouble in St. Andrews, and from ruffians on the road. I saw ye save her from that gallowglass bastard. I suppose ye think that entitles ye to my daughter, aye? That I'll respect this marriage in the 'old way' ye claim to have undertaken."

"We could have handfasted already, if ye feel that is more binding, but yer approval is important to us both," Kenneth said, softly, and lying through his teeth. Cat was ready to go ahead, with or without her father's approval. Kenneth was the one who wanted it. For

Iain's sake and the sake of the alliance between Rose and Brodie.

"I ken what ye're thinking," Rose told him. "Rose doesn't need another alliance with Brodie. Ye are right. I'd be better off marrying her to one of Domnhall's allies—even to an Irish noble."

Kenneth surged to his feet, furious, and stalked out of the solar while Rose laughed. He stormed through the hall and outside, where servants were cleaning up the blood he'd spilled there in defense of Rose's youngest daughter.

Rose had been playing with him this whole time. He'd never approve their marriage.

Catherine revived a bit as she and Mary crossed the great hall. The walk with her sister did her some good. "How is Cam?"

"Better, I think."

"Can we stop by to see him? I haven't spoken to him in days."

"Of course."

Cam turned his charm on Mary as soon as the sisters entered his chamber. "*Ach*, my angel of mercy, and lovely Catherine, come to see if I yet live?" He waved a hand. "I'm harder to kill than that."

Catherine smiled. "I'm glad ye are better. I wanted to see for myself. Mary has been monopolizing yer time."

"Now wait a minute..."

"Mary, my love, ye ken I live for every moment ye are with me."

Catherine grinned as Mary blushed.

"Ye are full of nonsense, Cameron Sutherland," she objected.

"I have heard the same said a time or two," Cam replied and winked at Catherine, then turned serious. "But ye, lass, had quite a scare today. Are ye well?"

Catherine nodded. "Of course, I am. Kenneth took care of the gallowglass."

"After ye had to stab him in the neck," Mary added, incensed.

"Oh ho!" Cam cried, then began coughing. Mary rushed to his side and placed a hand on his chest. In moments, the fit subsided. "I'd have a care around yer sister if she has a blade in her hand," he gasped, then grinned. "She can take care of herself, she can."

Mary snorted. "I hope she'll no' need to be using one too often."

Cam took Mary's hand and kissed her knuckles. "She's got the healing touch, like ye do. She'll get more use from that."

Catherine backed up to the door. "I'll leave ye to rest. Be well, Cam." After a few steps down the corridor toward her chamber, Mary joined her. "I thought ye would stay with Cam a while longer."

"Nay. He needs to rest. And ye need me more than he does tonight."

"Are ye certain? He seems quite taken with ye."

"He has charm, that one. More than any man needs."

Catherine laughed softly. "He does."

"But I think he's merely grateful for his care."

"I dinna ken," Catherine answered. "But I can tell ye this: I met Cam in St. Andrews and spoke with him several times there before he joined us on the journey here. He flirts, aye, but he has a big heart in him, too. I've seen evidence of it many times. He warned me of danger before we left town, and he helped Kenneth keep me safe, though he had no obligation to either of us. We didna always trust him. He has secrets, but he proved himself, over and over again. He lies here, wounded and ill because even after we sent him away, he returned and did what he could to keep all of us safe.

He may be a youngest son, but he is a worthy man, if ye decide to give him a chance."

Mary nodded. "I'll keep what ye have said in mind."

She and Mary settled in her room. Mary helped her undress and sat her in front of the small hearth, picked up a comb and ran it through her hair. Tension she didn't realize she'd been carrying since being stolen by the gallowglass man slipped little by little off her shoulders with each stroke of the comb. "That feels good."

"Tell me about the trip here."

Some of the tension came back. "Ye have heard most of it already."

"Trouble seems to follow you both," Mary chided. "Are you sure marrying Kenneth is a good idea?"

"Aye." Catherine had never been more sure of anything. "It's taking us longer than it should—thanks to Da—but Kenneth is the man I want to spend my life with. If only Da doesna get in the way."

"We convinced him once," Mary reminded her as she continued to comb Catherine's hair. "Annie is very happy with Iain at Brodie."

"She is. But that's the problem. Da kens what we might do."

"I still hope to marry away from Rose, so if ye marry Kenneth, and Da doesna wed Mhairi Grant, since her clan supports Albany, Kenneth could be the next laird. Is he capable of taking on so much responsibility?"

"Of course. He's brave and smart, and he fought in France. Besides, none of that matters. It won't happen for years. Da is hale and could still find a lass young enough to give him sons."

"He could."

Frustrated at being kept from Cat, Kenneth tossed and turned without getting any rest. Up early, he paced in his chamber until daylight showed through the narrow slit of a window, then he went down to the great hall to break his fast. Afterward, he checked on his mount in the stable and watched Rose lads practice at arms until the midday meal. Cat never appeared, so after he'd eaten, knowing he dared not approach her chamber, he sought her in the garden, where she often went no matter the time of day. As he'd hoped, she was there, sitting on a stone bench among the roses. He paused at the gate and just looked, drinking in the sight of her, then pushed open the gate and went to her.

"I feared ye had already gone," she said, beaming at him. Then her mouth flattened. "Ye are no' here to tell me ye leaving, are ye?" Cat asked, dismay in her tone.

"No' yet. But I think ye should ken what yer da said last night after Mary took ye away." He related her father's objections to their marriage. "In his mind, nothing has changed. He still doesna want to *waste* ye on Brodie."

"He doesna have any choice. We are wed in the old way. We'll formalize it in the kirk if we can. I care no'."

"But ye ken I do. Iain needs the alliance with Rose."

"And if, some day, ye are laird Rose, the alliance will be in safe hands." She told him about the conversation she and Mary had. "If Da doesna marry again and have a son, and if Mary leaves, my husband will become laird."

Kenneth's gut suddenly filled with ice. "I canna be Iain's designated heir and Rose's, too."

"Iain's?"

Kenneth nodded. "I already am."

Cat's hands flew to cover her face. "Ach, nay."

"I'm sorry I didna tell ye, lass. It didna seem

important at the time. Iain and Annie have a daughter and will have another bairn soon. A lad, I'm sure."

"But ye will still be his heir until they do, even warden and guardian until any heir they have grows up."

"Or someone else could take on that responsibility." Not that he'd want to relinquish it—except to wed Cat. "At any rate, I didna tell ye because we were intent on returning ye home…"

Cat shook her head. "Before I convince my father to let us wed in the kirk, ye must decide which is more important. Brodie? Or me?"

ANOTHER HAIL FROM OUTSIDE THE WALLS DREW THEM from the garden. After a split second wondering if more trouble had arrived, Kenneth knew it had—he knew that voice. As if conjured by Cat's last comment, Iain had arrived, and with a small party of Brodie warriors.

The Rose met them as they rode through the gates, but Kenneth stood with Cat, off to the side. It was not his keep and not his place to welcome guests, even Iain. He was happy to see them, but Cat appeared worried.

Iain dismounted and went straight to Cat. "Greetings, sister. Thank the saints ye are here and well. Annie would have my head if ye were no'." Then he turned to her father. "Annie would give me nay peace until I made certain Kenneth got Catherine home safely. I hope ye will forgive me greeting her first. Given the number of ruffians roaming the countryside, I am much relieved to see her."

Kenneth cleared his throat.

Iain grinned. "Aye, and Kenneth, too."

"Understandable," the Rose agreed. "Come inside. We have much to discuss."

He cut an unmistakable look at Kenneth. In his opinion, Cat was home, yes. He looked as if he intended to extract a penalty from Iain for Kenneth taking her, son-in-law be damned. Kenneth bristled at the implication he'd ruined Cat.

Iain must have seen Kenneth tense. "Brodie men are honorable," he stated as he joined Cat's father in crossing the bailey to the keep. "Yer daughter has been well cared for."

"I'm aware of how she's been cared for," her father answered dryly.

Iain having to defend him made Kenneth squirm. Iain had suspected where things had gone between him and Cat, but as Kenneth's friend, had not made an issue of it when they met on the way from St. Andrews. Now he would have to negotiate with a lass's father as Kenneth's laird. Kenneth hoped he was up to the challenge.

Cat was glaring at her father's back hard enough, he was relieved for her father's sake she no longer had a blade in her hand. If the situation weren't so serious, Kenneth would be amused. Though it was not her fight, her fierce determination made him proud.

"Easy, lass," he whispered as the Rose and the Brodie went through the door into the keep. "Iain has learned a lot from Annie in the past two years about dealing with yer father."

"He'd better, or Mary and I will take him on."

"I dinna think that will be necessary," he soothed. "We've only to wait a wee to see what Iain can do."

Iain leaned out of the doorway and beckoned. "Kenneth, with me, please."

Surprise at being included sent a chill of anticipation racing through Kenneth's chest. He might have a lot to answer for but he might also be able to help Iain persuade the Rose, even though he had been unable to on his own. He squeezed Cat's hand. "*Dinna fash*, lass." If only someone would tell him the same thing.

CHAPTER 19

Kenneth could barely contain his anger at the Rose laird, but he stayed silent as Iain told Rose what happened at Harlaw. Neither Albany's general, the Earl of Mar, nor the Lord of the Isles could claim victory, though Domnhall might have, had he pressed the advantage he'd gained in the first day's fighting and finished off Mar and the remains of his vastly outnumbered *caterans* the next day. But he'd chosen to withdraw. No one knew why.

"My men are not back yet," Rose said, his expression bleak.

"I'm sorry to be the bearer of such news, then," Iain added quietly. "But they may only be slowed by traveling with wounded."

The Rose did not look reassured.

"We were lucky enough to find a wagon and sent ours straight to Brodie with an escort," Iain continued.

"So the tug of war between Albany and the Isles will continue," Rose said, turning his cup in both hands, a thoughtful expression on his face. Then he looked at Kenneth. "Good reason to make alliances as broadly as possible."

It was a challenge. Kenneth grimaced but kept his mouth shut. This was Iain's negotiation.

"Alliances don't have to be made through marriage," Iain commented, his gaze on the whisky in his glass. Then he looked up at Rose. "But in any event, ye could make yer own marriage. What about the Grant woman ye spent time with at our wedding? Or a younger lass. Ye're no' too old to sire a son."

Rose colored and for a moment, Kenneth feared he'd reach for his dirk. But Iain's words were spoken lightly, without rancor.

"That is my business, and none of yers," Rose finally said, with a great deal less heat than Kenneth first expected. "As for him," he added with a lift of his chin toward Kenneth, "and my youngest daughter, I had good reasons to turn him down once before."

"Things were different then," Iain said, speaking aloud what was on the tip of Kenneth's tongue. "And ye canna deny the bond between the two of them."

"It seems they've denied themselves little, that's what I can say. I didna like it then, and I like it even less now."

"Yet ye wish to see Catherine happy, do ye no'? Certainly, her sisters do." Iain let the comment hang in the silence while the Rose stared at him with narrowed gaze.

The Rose didn't rise to Iain's bait. "Ye'll stay the night, and in the morning, ye will take that one back to Brodie with ye."

Iain stood. "As ye wish." He gathered Kenneth to his side with a tilt of his head. "We'll see ye at supper, then?"

"Nay."

"We'll leave ye with Brodie's formal offer in the morning," Iain responded calmly to Rose's churlish rudeness.

Kenneth moved toward the door. The man had to be seething. He'd just seen his daughter attacked within his own walls. Save by her actions and the actions of the one man he did not want to have her.

The Rose waved a disinterested hand. Kenneth sent a dismayed glance to Iain, who frowned and left the laird's solar. Kenneth took one last glance at James Rose, his head bent over some document and seemingly unaware that Kenneth was still there. Kenneth followed Iain.

❧

"YER DA HATES ME," KENNETH TOLD CAT LATER. THEY joined Iain and the other Brodies at table, where Mary presided in their father's absence.

"Ye are just now figuring that out?" Iain replied with a grin.

Kenneth shrugged. "I dinna ken why, but it seems he always has and always will."

"Ye once thought he hated ye, too," Cat told Iain.

"I'm still no' sure he doesna." Iain took a drink and set his cup aside. "Though now Annie is about to make him a grandfather again, ye think he'd warm to me a little. Do ye ken, he's yet to ask me how she is, or how soon the bairn is due." He elbowed Kenneth. "Which is another reason, beside yer da's animosity, for me to haste back to Brodie," he added with a nod to Cat. "She's getting close to her time, we think. We're no entirely certain..." Pink tinged his cheeks and the bridge of his nose.

Cat laughed. "Whenever it happens, I canna believe I'll soon be an auntie for the second time," Cat told him, grinning.

"Me, too," Mary added. "As soon as the bairn comes, ye must let us know, so we can come help Annie."

"Have nay doubt—ye'll be the first to hear. I'll send my fastest ghillie."

"I'm a ghillie now, am I?" Kenneth complained.

"Nay, and I wouldna send ye in any case. No' with the Rose still out of sorts with ye."

"Well, that's a relief. I feared I was about to be demoted for angering another laird."

"Ye have angered another one?" Iain's expression was all innocence at the quip.

Mary laughed. "We still have a Sutherland here. He's no' entirely fond of Kenneth, either, though they do seem to respect one another."

Kenneth rolled his eyes at her. "Dinna remind me."

"The same Sutherland?"

"Aye, the one traveling with us. Cameron, a younger son of the laird's," Kenneth supplied. "He was wounded by a gallowglass after we left ye."

"I'll be sure to tell him you appreciate him saving our lives," Cat promised.

"We saved his, too."

"Aye, if his fever breaks and his wound heals."

"He's better," Mary reminded her, "Else I wouldna be sitting here with ye."

Cat nodded. "Ye are good to him," she told her sister. Then grinned and added, "And for him?"

Mary held up hand. "Dinna say such things."

"Ye could help take the heat off of me if ye and Cam…"

Mary shook her head. "Dinna get your hopes up, little sister."

Cat turned her gaze to Kenneth. "Why no'? It seems to work."

Happy warmth bloomed in Kenneth's chest. "It appears so."

Mary snorted and stood. "Since ye have reminded me I'm neglecting my patient, I'll take my leave. Iain, give my love to Annie. I look forward to seeing her and the new babe."

Iain stood, too. "Why no' come with us, to help her through the birth?"

Mary froze, then shook her head. "I canna. No' until I'm sure Cameron—Sutherland—is out of danger."

"May that be soon, then," Iain told her.

Iain and the other Brodies left for their beds soon thereafter.

Cat watched them go, then turned back to Kenneth. "Ye have no' said much about the meeting with my father."

"The Rose has as much as said he will not agree to our marriage, though he did no' outright forbid it. He did order all Brodies, including me, to leave at first light."

"Ach, no' happy then, was he?"

"Ye could say that. In fairness, I think he's still worried about the Rose warriors who have no' yet returned from Harlaw."

"It may be, or it may be when he looks at ye and Iain, he sees a time when he is no longer laird. When ye, or a man Mary weds, becomes the Rose. He sees his own mortality."

"No wonder he hates me."

"Annie's babe, when it comes, should improve his mood. If it's a lad, he'll have a legacy, even if it's a Brodie legacy, too."

"Iain did suggest he could wed again and sire sons of his own."

Cat gasped. "He didna!"

"Yer da didna take it well."

"I expect no'." She drummed her fingertips on the oak table. "Clearly, he will decide naught before ye and Iain leave. 'Tis time to take matters into our own hands.

If we handfast, he'll no' be able to betroth me again—at least for a year and a day."

"I—aye. I thought about that on the road here, but then we met the gallowglasses and…"

She jumped up. "I'll go talk to Mary. Should Cam do it?"

"What will happen to him if yer father finds out he did?"

"Likely he'll toss him out. And he's still too ill to travel."

"Even to Brodie, aye. So, nay, Sutherland canna do it."

"Mary can. Da willna do anything to her. He needs her too much. She can do it like she did for Iain and Annie. Unless ye'd rather Iain?"

Kenneth pondered long enough Cat started to look nervous. "I think 'tis better for the alliance if Iain does no' ken," he finally said. "I dinna want yer da to blame him."

"He will, anyway." Cat's shoulders came down from around her ears. "Ye took so long to answer, I thought ye were going to refuse."

"Refuse ye? How could I?"

&a.

AFTER CATHERINE TOLD MARY WHAT SHE AND KENNETH wanted to do, and that they needed Mary's help, Mary surprised her.

"Are ye daft? Ye already married Kenneth in the old way."

Catherine's stomach sank and she shook her head. "Which Da refuses to recognize. He canna refuse to accept Kenneth if we handfast. We thought about having Cam…"

Mary crossed her arms over her chest. "He canna do

it. He's too ill for Da to toss him out of the keep into the barn, or out of Rose altogether."

Catherine could see her sister's concern for her patient written in her eyes, and the tension in her shoulders. "We ken that. So ye must do it."

Mary straightened. "I must, eh?"

"Mary, please. As ye did for Annie. Da will do nothing to harm ye. He never has."

"Save keep me here." Her fists clenched in her lap.

"Ach, Mary, I'm sorry." Catherine put an arm around her sister. How many times had Mary soothed her hurts? And she'd just ripped away a very old scab.

Then Mary straightened her shoulders. "What's one more transgression among my many? Very well. I'll do it."

CHAPTER 20

Catherine, with Kenneth by her side, followed Mary to Cam's chamber. "Should ye be sitting up?" she asked, surprised to see him dressed and in a chair by the hearth.

He nodded. "I'm none too steady on my feet as yet, but I couldna give yer ceremony the proper respect from the bed. This seemed the best compromise."

Mary shook her finger at him. "I told ye nay, Cameron Sutherland. Ye have to be the most stubborn man alive."

Catherine laughed at that. "Kenneth and he are in a tie for that honor."

Mary sniffed and cut a glance to her patient, who grinned at her, looking anything but repentant. Then she turned to her youngest sister and Kenneth. "I am the Rose heir." She held up the length of Brodie plaid Kenneth had supplied, gripping it in both hands. "'Tis my right and my responsibility to do this." She glanced at Catherine and softened her tone. "And my honor." She turned the strip of Brodie plaid over in her hands before she turned back to Cam. "Yer job is to be the witness." Then she grinned. "And perhaps to kiss the bride, if her new husband will allow it."

Kenneth gave Cam a sardonic shrug. "I shouldna, but 'tis said to be good luck for all concerned, so I must. All of us could use some good luck."

Cam nodded. "Aye, me especially. I seem to have used more than my fair share of late, to still be here and breathing. But Mary, when yer da hears of this, he'll be furious with ye. He'll no' molest a wounded and sick man, will he?"

Catherine and Mary shook their heads. Catherine hoped not. Cam was merely an observer. Nothing more.

"Well, then, 'tis better for the lovely Mary if I do the deed, ye must agree."

Mary held up the plaid and let it dangle from her fingers. "'Tis no' better for ye. I dinna wish to have to tend ye in the barn. Or on the ground outside Rose's gates. So, nay, I dinna agree." She turned to her youngest sister and Kenneth. "Are ye ready?"

"Aye," Catherine answered.

"More than ye ken," Kenneth added, with a wink at Catherine.

"Very well, then. Hold out yer hands."

As she watched Mary wrap first Kenneth's wrist, then hers, in a strip of Brodie plaid, all softly focused as though she looked through Highland mist, Catherine's heart swelled. Mary did this for her and Kenneth gladly, though she shed tears the entire time.

Her support meant everything to Catherine, who could not stop shedding tears of her own. This simple ceremony made it official—Mary would be the last to marry—if she ever did. Their da had lost two disobedient daughters to weddings he didn't approve, or approved only reluctantly, in Annie's case, into clan Brodie. Catherine feared he'd keep Mary even closer at hand, but held out hope for Cameron Sutherland to change that. Mary did seem interested in him. If anyone could wrest Mary away from Rose, it would be a powerful Sutherland. But then again, Cam was a practiced charmer. A romance between them might come to nothing.

Still, she should not be thinking about them on this night of all nights.

Kenneth looked a little pale, but he repeated his vows in the strong, clear voice Catherine so loved.

Then it was her turn.

"I loved ye when we met, I love ye still—and I always will," she told him. "I would do anything, give anything, to be by yer side for the rest of our lives. I pray we have the chance."

"As do I," Kenneth responded. "I love ye more than I have words to say. And I marry ye gladly."

"'Tis done," Mary announced and leaned in to kiss her sister on the cheek, then do the same to Kenneth. "Ye need to untie that, and leave Cameron alone now to rest. *Ach*, and ye may be past bloody sheets, but if so, I'd suggest a wee prick of the knife—on a finger will do. That *proof* will give Da some measure of comfort."

Catherine nodded, understanding. If he could believe she went to her marriage bed untouched, he might accept they were truly wed all the sooner.

"I dinna wish to lie to yer da," Kenneth told the sisters, frowning. "He kens we wed in the old way. Will he believe we never consummated our union?"

"He might because he'll wish to. 'Twill no' be a lie—exactly," Catherine told him. I still have the plaid we traveled with, if ye think we must use it, but seeing it will anger him more than seeing this. Either way, 'tis done."

"Catherine is right," Mary told him. "Ye willna besmirch yer honor with this small kindness."

Kenneth studied them both for a moment, then

glanced at Cam, who nodded. Kenneth sighed and nodded his agreement.

Catherine breathed out a sigh of relief.

Mary smiled. "I'll leave ye now," she said and slipped out the door. Kenneth closed it softly behind her.

"Iain willna seek ye out during the night?" Cam asked as he forced himself to his feet and claimed the kiss the bride owed him. Kenneth went to him, took his arm and escorted him back to the bed. The man had lost a stone of muscle since they'd gotten him here, perhaps two. He settled on the mattress with a relieved sigh, more pale than when they'd entered his chamber.

"Nay," Kenneth told him while he settled. "I told him I might be restless, so he might no' find me in my cot."

"But will he think to find ye in mine?" Cat teased as she wrapped the length of Brodie plaid around her shoulders.

Cam waved them out and closed his eyes. "Be gone. Ye have worn me out."

Out in the hallway, Kenneth laughed and pulled Cat to him. "Let's find out, shall we?"

❧

KENNETH TOOK CAT'S HAND AND LED HER BACK TO HER chamber, the enormity of what they'd done leaving him warm and contented—and a little worried. He'd feel better when they left Rose tomorrow for Brodie. He opened the door, then scooped his bride up into his arms. She stifled her giggles against his chest as he carried her across the threshold and set her down inside. She reached behind him and pushed the door closed. Kenneth grabbed the handle at the last second to keep it from slamming, then locked it, earning another giggle from Cat. "Let's no' wake the keep, lass.

Yer da may have no compunction about throwing me out into the night but I dinna want that for ye."

Cat nodded. "Ye are right. I dinna wish anything to disturb us this night."

"And nothing shall."

She reached up and kissed him. "What if I scream?"

He laughed. "What if I do?"

"Ach, nay, milord. Ye are no' the screaming type. But depending on what ye do to me, I may develop the habit."

"Let's find out, shall we?"

They stood for a moment, just looking at each other. "Ye are so beautiful, my love," he told her, then cupped her face in both hands and leaned in to kiss her.

When they came up for air, she laid her head against his shoulder. "I canna believe we finally have what I've longed for these past two years." She grasped the edge of the Brodie plaid on her shoulders and wrapped it around his, too, binding them in a woolen cocoon.

"Hush, lass. We willna speak of that."

She looked up at him with luminous eyes. "I dinna wish to, except to say those years do no' matter. We start anew today. Now. We will make our own future, together." She nodded at the plaid.

The warmth that suffused Kenneth nearly brought him to tears. "I'm sorry for every moment of worry, of loneliness, of feeling betrayed that I ever caused ye. I didna mean to. When I heard your da had betrothed ye, I snapped. I shouldna have done that. I should have trusted ye would find a way to wait for me. I should have tried again and again, until he said *aye*. I'm more sorry that I can ever say for what I put ye through."

"It doesna matter anymore, Kenneth. We are together. And we will stay together. We start anew, now."

Kenneth pulled her more tightly into his arms,

then kissed her, again and again, leaving her breathless. In moments, they both panted with need for each other. He gently untied her laces and pulled her dress over her head. Her slippers came next, and her shift, until she stood before him clad only in her stockings.

"Beyond beautiful ye are. The way the firelight dances over yer skin is breathtaking."

She reached for his shirt and pulled it from his breeks. "Then let me see how it dances over yers, my love." With another tug, she freed his shirt and he stripped it off. "Ah, my brave warrior," she murmured, tracing scars he'd long forgotten he carried, from battles he'd sooner forget. "Ye have fought valiantly and wisely, for ye are still here, and ye are with me." She looked up into his eyes. "Firelight doesna lie."

Her gaze caught Kenneth's in a way that he could not escape—and did not wish to escape.

She untied his breeks while she held him entranced, then pushed them down his hips, freeing his straining member. "I think 'tis time to consummate our handfasting, my husband. I see ye do, too."

Kenneth stepped out of the puddle of cloth at his feet and kicked off his boots, leaving him completely naked before her. "Yer husband agrees." He backed her up to her bed, then helped her lie down on it. He gently rolled her stockings down her legs and set them aside, then bent over her and dropped kisses down her belly. "Open for me, lass," he commanded.

She spread her legs, giving him access to her moist center.

Kenneth kissed her there, then traced his tongue around the nub, while Cat moaned and bucked her hips. "This is the first time we've been able to do this in a bed," he told her as he kissed his way up to her breasts, took one rosy nipple in his mouth and suckled it. "If there is anything ye want, anything I can do, ye will tell me, aye?"

Cat nodded, her eyes closed, lost in the sensations he was creating with his tongue and lips. "I want ye inside me, husband. I need ye there."

"All in good time." He shifted to the other breast. "All in good time."

She reached for his stiff member and wrapped her hand around it. "The time is now."

Kenneth grinned and moved over her as she continued to stroke him. Much more of her touch and he would not be able to contain himself. "Leave off, lass. I'll do as ye bid." He settled between her thighs with a satisfied groan, the head of his cock already coated with her dewy moisture. "Are ye sure ye are ready, love?"

In answer, she lifted her hips, pulling him into her silky opening. "What do ye think?"

"Aye, ye are ready." He thrust into her fully, then had to stop for a moment and just feel. Appreciate the sensation of her body, heated and wet, enveloping him. Enjoy the fire in her gaze as she smiled at him. "Ye're a wonder, lass."

"Am I?"

"Nothing compares to being right here, right now, with ye."

"Then take me, husband. Make me yers again."

"How can I refuse an offer such as that?" he replied and started thrusting into her tight core with joy in every movement. Cat must be feeling the same. She started chuckling, then smiled as he took her to the heights.

"Aye, Kenneth, just like that."

In moments, her climax hit her and she cried out, "Ah!" while her body pulsed around him. He held her until she stilled, then moved again until he rode his own climax. With Cat. With the woman he loved and always had. And always would.

&

THE NIGHT PASSED TOO QUICKLY FOR CATHERINE. SHE loved lying in Kenneth's arms. They'd made love several times, then while he dozed, she'd slipped out of bed and packed what she'd need to take with her.

The morning gloaming was upon them when Catherine woke Kenneth with a kiss. "'Tis nearly time. We must dress. Mary will meet us in the great hall."

She was glad to see Kenneth come immediately and alertly awake. He nodded and sat up, then reached for her and traced a finger down her cheek. "Ye are certain this is what ye want?"

She glanced at the bloodstain they'd left on the sheets. "I want only to be yer wife and live with ye, whether at Brodie or in France or anywhere else. Da will do as Da must do. As will I."

Kenneth pulled her between his legs and kissed her soundly, then set her back, stood and stretched his arms over his head. "Very well. Dressed it is. He glanced at the window. "Though I could wish ye had woken me earlier."

Catherine smiled and looked him up and down, admiring the strongly muscled body that he'd used to love her so well, and the proud erection that told her why he'd wished for an earlier start to this morning. "We'll have tonight and many more days and nights before us. 'Tis time to take our leave of Rose."

"If ye are certain…"

"I am." But she let her disappointment show as clothes hid his body from her sight.

Mary met them in the great hall as she'd promised.

Iain arrived at the same time, looking bemused.

"Are we ready for this?" he asked, addressing no one in particular.

Mary roused him, too? Catherine nodded. Good thinking. Iain's surprise and support might help calm their father.

"I told Da," Mary announced.

"What?" Catherine couldn't believe her ears.

"I told him. When I left ye last night. I told him what I'd done. What we'd done. I told Iain, first, in case of trouble."

"And he let ye be," Iain added. "He's resigned to it—at least for now. Give him time."

Their father came out of his solar then.

Catherine tensed, but Kenneth did not. Was he so sure her father would let them leave?

He pinned Kenneth with a glare. "Mary advised me ye have taken the decision out of my hands—for now—and confessed her role in it. Ye Brodie men seem adept at seducing my daughters into doing yer will. Very well. I'll give ye yer year and a day." He turned his gaze on Catherine. "But if ye are no' with child by then, ye'll marry as I see fit."

Catherine lifted her chin and smiled at her father. "Ye ken I like a challenge, Da. Thank ye for that."

He rolled his eyes at Iain, then at Kenneth. "She's yer problem now. So go. Be off with ye." Then he turned to Mary. "As for ye, lass..." He growled and shook his head, then turned and stalked back into his solar, slamming the door behind him.

Kenneth took Catherine's hand. She gave a parting hug and smile to Mary, then walked out of the Rose keep with her beloved husband at her side.

EPILOGUE

atherine needed to find her husband. She didn't want to go outdoors. The weather had suddenly turned chilly, and she was warm and content in the hall, but Annie agreed. Kenneth would want to know her news immediately. "He's out there, practicing with Iain, aye?"

Annie nodded and set aside the letter she was writing to Mary. "Aye. And Euan and the others. Since the two of ye got here, they've been hard at it. I think Iain expects Domnhall to stir up more trouble with Albany. He's determined to be ready. For all of Brodie to be ready." She sighed and laid her hand on her hugely rounded belly. "I hope it doesna come to that. Our losses were light at Harlaw, but any loss is one too many. And the injured Iain sent home, some are still being treated for their wounds."

Cat crossed her arms. "I wish I could have done more to help them."

Annie shook her head. "*Dinna fash.* Ye saved several, I think, who would no' have survived the trip home without the care ye gave them. Ye can rest easy on that."

Catherine nodded, tears filling her eyes. "Thank ye."

"Now dinna get all emotional on me. Go find yer

husband. Drag him away from Iain and back inside. Ye dinna need to be out in the *dreich* for very long."

"What if he willna come?"

"One look at yer sweet face, sister mine, and he'll stop what he's doing. Just stand on the side where he can see ye. Dinna venture into the midst of the men and their blades. And *dinna fash*. They concentrate so fiercely, it may take a moment for him to see ye."

"I ken it. I've practiced at archery with yer lasses. All ye see is the target."

"Aye. And all they see is the blade—or blades—coming at them. 'Tis a good skill to have."

Catherine gave Annie a grateful smile for helping her settle down. She shouldn't be so emotional about such a tiny thing, but it wasn't really a tiny thing. It meant the world to her, and to Kenneth. She grabbed her cloak from a peg near the door and tossed it around her shoulders. Once she opened the door out into the bailey, she was very glad she had its warmth wrapped around her. Not only had the temperature dropped, the wind had picked up, too.

When she reached the men's practice area, she marveled at their display of strength and skill. Their shirts were dark with sweat, yet they didn't seem to notice the cold, wet fabric against their skin. Muscles flexed and blades flashed and clanged. Catherine covered her ears as she searched for Kenneth. He stood on the far side of the practice area—of course—and squared off against two assailants. Catherine waited for a pause in their battle to move into his line of sight.

He saw her immediately, as if some connection between them alerted him to her presence. He muttered something to his antagonists, and propped his weapons against the castle's outer wall. Then he turned back to her and a smile lit his expression, making her heart clench. Would he truly be glad of her news?

When he reached her, his scent hit her nose, strong and fully Kenneth. She loved the way he smelled, even when he'd been working hard.

"What is it, lass?" He cupped her cheek and bent to kiss her, but didn't embrace her.

"Can we go inside? 'Tis miserable out here. I canna believe ye are no' freezing. Yer shirt is drenched." Just looking at him made her shiver.

"Aye, let's do that." He glanced over at Iain and waved toward the great hall's door. Iain nodded and went back to knocking his opponent to the ground.

Once inside, he took her cloak and hung it on a peg, then they walked to a bench by the hearth. Annie had gone, though Catherine suspected she watched from somewhere nearby. She would want to see this news delivered.

"What is it, Cat?" Kenneth said as he saw her seated, then settled beside her. He took her hand. "Is something wrong? Are ye ill?"

"Ill? Nay…quite the opposite." She drew in a breath, then met his gaze and smiled, "The healer confirmed it this morning. I am with child. Ye are going to be a father, Kenneth. And my father can never barter me away again."

Kenneth jumped to his feet, elation written in every line of his body, his arms lifted toward the rafters. Then he clenched his fists and sat down again, glanced down at his sweat-soaked garment and shrugged. "I'm going to hug ye lass, and kiss ye senseless, right here in the hall."

She grinned at his shirt, made nearly transparent in the firelight, every muscle outlined and defined. She traced over his heart, then she wrapped her arms around his steaming neck. "I dinna mind, my love. Do yer worst. Ye have already done yer best."

He kissed her until she could barely breathe, but she clung to him. "We are free," she told him when she could speak. "Truly free."

"And we'll marry in the kirk before ye get too far along, aye? Yer father canna touch ye after that. Iain willna allow it. Nor will I."

"Aye, we will. Annie is already planning it. And a celebration after."

"Does Iain ken?"

"Nay. Only Annie and the healer. And ye, my love."

He straightened, and declared, "Then we'll tell the clan at the evening meal, if that's all right with ye."

She nodded. "Ye can be proud, Kenneth. What we have done together gives both of us the future we've always dreamed of."

"I can be no more proud than I am of ye, my amazing wife." He stood and held out his hand. "I'm for our chamber and a bath, and then I wish to make love to ye, if ye will permit it."

"Always, Kenneth. Always and forever."

READ THE NEXT BOOK IN THE SERIES

HIS HIGHLAND BRIDE

A Dutiful Daughter No More

When Mary Elizabeth Rose's father marries a much younger lass in hopes of siring a male heir, Mary sees her chance to escape her role as his chatelaine, but fears his next step will be to betroth her to a stranger. She has a different future in mind—with a sometimes charming, sometimes difficult and arrogant wounded Highlander.

He Owes Her His Life

Cameron Sutherland is not too delirious to recognize Mary Rose is the first woman he could seriously consider taking as his bride. He'd like nothing better than to spend years repaying the debt he owes his angel of mercy for taking him in and saving his life. First, he must convince her to defy her father one last time.

Will They Put Love Before Duty?

For Mary, Cameron has become the man whose

every smile has the power to bring her to her knees. But he is as duty-bound as she is, and responsibility calls him back to Sutherland, where she fears he will stay, forgetting her and all they've shared. With another powerful clan's interests at stake, Cameron's return sets events in motion that will have life-changing consequences for the woman he can't forget.

Keep reading for a sneak peek…

THAT EVENING, Mary asked a serving girl to take Cameron's supper tray to his chamber. She couldn't face him again. Not yet. Not with what, to her, felt like a betrayal hanging between them. The fact that her father was forcing her to do it made little difference. In Mary's heart, she knew the right thing to do was stay with Cameron. But her head argued for the duty she owed her father and laird.

She had just finished her own meal in the great hall with some of the clan, when the serving girl came running back and stopped below where she sat on the raised dais.

"He's acting *tetched* again, milady. I think ye need to come."

Mary stood immediately and joined the girl in hurrying out of the hall. "Fetch the healer," she ordered when they reached the stairs. "Then bring cold water and some cloths. I'll go on up."

"Aye, milady." The lass hurried away and Mary ran up the stairs.

Cameron tossed his head as she entered his chamber.

She rushed to his side and put a hand on his brow.

"Damn it," she muttered under her breath. His fever had increased again. "Cameron, 'tis Mary. It appears ye did a wee too much today. How do ye feel?"

"Like hell. Sorry, lass."

"Apology accepted." She pulled the covers aside and untied his shirt. It was already wet and clammy with his sweat. What had happened between earlier today and now? "Cameron, let me pull up yer shirt. I need to see yer wound."

His eyes remained closed underneath a fierce crease between his brows, but his hands pawed at his waist, trying to help her. At least he wasn't so far gone in fever he couldn't understand what she said to him.

It took effort, but she got his shirt free just as the healer bustled in, followed by the serving lass.

Mary stepped aside to let the healer examine the wound. "I'll take those," Mary told the serving girl, who waited by the door with the water and cloths she'd asked for earlier. "Fetch some watered ale, too," Mary saw the concern written in the girl's wide-eyed expression and cocked her head.

"He'll no' die, will he?" the servant asked softly. "I like him. I wouldna want him to die."

"He willna die, nay. We dinna want him to, either." Mary gave her a reassuring smile and sent her on her way.

The healer stood and moved away from her patient. "I canna understand what set him off again. The wound looks to be healing well."

"So 'tis the blood fever again?"

She shook her head. "I dinna ken. What did he do today?"

"I found him in the garden. We sat and talked, then walked—not far—before I brought him back up here. He claimed he needed some fresh air. He did seem better."

"Well, we'll resume the willow bark tea…"

"Ach, nay," Cam objected. "That bitter stuff."

"Twill save yer life, ye daft man. If ye'd stayed abed as I told ye to, this might no' have happened."

"Ye told him to stay abed? When?"

"Just this morn. I found him in yon chair." The healer gestured at the wooden seat by the fireplace.

"Bored," Cameron complained. "And now Mary will leave me. More bored. Need water."

Mary rolled her eyes and saw the healer smile. "Ye are no' so sick as all that. I'll get ye a book. But for now, we need to cool ye." She dropped the cloths into the pitcher to let them soak, then pulled one out and wrung it out. "This will be cold."

"I ken it. 'Tis no' like ye have no' done this to me before."

In answer, Mary dropped the cold cloth on Cameron's chest.

"*Ach, shite!* Could ye warn me?"

"Ye could open yer eyes." She spread the cloth across his chest, then reached for another. "Does the light hurt them?"

"A little."

Mary took pity on him and used the next to wipe his face, then laid it across his brow and eyes.

"That feels better."

"I'll get the tea and be right back," the healer announced and left Mary to her cranky patient.

"I dinna ken why yer fever came back," Mary soothed, "but we'll make it better."

"I want ye to stay, Mary. No' to go with yer da. No one cares for me as ye do."

"Nonsense. Why, even that serving girl said she likes ye and doesna wish ye to die. Now, stop being a child. Ye're no' three years old. Ye'll get better whether I have the care of ye or nay."

"So ye have made up yer mind to go."

"I dinna have much choice, now do I?" Mary wrung out another cloth and stroked it along Cameron's neck and throat. "Brace yerself. I'm going to put this one on yer belly."

"Ye dinna think yer da can take care of himself without ye?" Cameron challenged as she spread the cold cloth below the one on this chest. His only reaction was to tighten the muscles in his abdomen.

Mary was glad he couldn't see her face. She enjoyed looking at Cameron's muscles, and the trail of hair that disappeared into his trews. She knew where it led, of course, but that didn't make it any less compelling. "I dinna ken what that Grant woman is planning, or expecting to achieve with this visit. So, nay, I dinna think he can. I'm sorry, Cameron. 'Tis my duty to him and to this clan."

The healer came back with a cup of the willow bark tea in her hand. "Ye must drink all of this," she reminded him.

Cameron threw an arm over his eyes. Though she couldn't see the upper part of his face Mary knew his expression had to be one of long suffering.

"Let's sit ye up," she told him and stripped the damp cloths from his body, then tugged the one he'd trapped between his arm and forehead. "So ye can drink it faster."

The serving girl returned then, too, with another pitcher. Mary nodded and gestured for the girl to set it down. "Then ye can have some ale."

Cameron grunted and rolled to his side, swung his legs off the bed and sat up. He wiped his face with the cloth, then handed it to Mary. He accepted the cup from the healer and tossed it back, wincing as he swallowed. "Ale...please."

The serving girl poured some into a clean cup and handed it to Mary. Mary passed it to Cameron.

He tossed it back, then held the cup out. "More. I can still taste that bitter tea."

The healer nodded, so Mary let the girl refill the cup and gave it back to him. "Slower this time, aye?" He surprised her by obeying. When he finished, he held the cup out to her.

"That's enough for now," the healer told him. "I'll check on ye in an hour. I expect to find ye asleep."

Cameron gave her a wry smile. "I'll do my best." Then he turned his gaze to Mary. "Will ye stay?"

"Aye, if only to torture ye some more." She waved the serving girl out and reached into the water pitcher for another wet cloth. "Lie on yer belly if ye wish and I'll try to cool yer back."

Cameron nodded and did as he was told, stretching out on his belly, resting his head on his arms, his face to the side.

Mary wrung out the cloth and laid it over this head, leaving his face uncovered, but trailing a corner of the cloth over as much of his forehead as she could reach.

Cameron sighed.

After warning him, she placed another cloth on the back of his neck and was rewarded with a groan of pleasure.

Then she covered his back, though it took three cloths to span his shoulders and reach down to his waist. She longed to trace the dip in his lower back, but dared not touch him in any way that was not clearly meant to help him heal. When the cloths warmed, she replaced them with cool ones until his breathing slowed and evened out. She placed a hand on his forehead. Cooler. Something had helped.

Buy His Highland Bride

ACKNOWLEDGMENTS

A book is the product of an author's heart and soul. But more than the author's craft is needed to take ideas from rough draft to polished.

My heartfelt thanks go out to my Beta reader, Laura Stephens, and my editor, Maureen Sevilla, for your critique, ideas and encouragement. And to my cover artist, Tamra Westberry, for brilliantly interpreting my stories into beautiful art.

And last but never least, my eternal gratitude to my husband, Laird Peter. You are always my inspiration.

His Highland Heart

His Highland Rose

His Highland Heart

His Highland Love

His Highland Bride

Highland Talents

Heart of Stone

Highland Healer

Highland Seer

Highland Troth

The Healer's Gift

When Highland Lightning Strikes

Sweetie Pie (A Candy Hearts Novella)

Waiting for the Laird

When You Find Love

ABOUT THE AUTHOR

Willa Blair is an award-wining Amazon and Barnes & Noble #1 bestselling author of Scottish historical, light paranormal and contemporary romance filled with men in kilts, psi talents, and plenty of spice. Her books have won numerous accolades, including the Marlene, the Merritt, National Readers' Choice Award Finalist, Reader's Crown finalist, InD'Tale Magazine's RONE Award Honorable Mention, and NightOwl Reviews Top Picks. She loves scouting new settings for books, and thinks being an author is the best job she's ever had.

Willa loves hearing from readers!
Contact her:
www.willablair.com
authorwillablair@gmail.com

Sign up for my Newsletter
Find links to the rest of my books

9 781648 390982